Everything you e[...]
—an[...]
about

WORLD'S MOST ELIGIBLE BACHELOR
Rance Phillips

His Motto: "No one tells me who I'm going to marry!"

His Undeniable Charm: "Charm? Is that what has all those women in a tizzy over me? I suppose I got my so-called charm from my family— five generations of Montana ranchers living and loving under the Big Sky."

His Soft Spot: "I didn't think I had one till I realized I had a son. And then I saw his mother, and all those old feelings came back to me. Now I'd do anything for them both."

Marriage Vow: "Getting hitched isn't as easy as you might think. *Especially* for a wealthy cowboy. First there's all those women your family keeps sending your way. Then there's the matter of my boy's mother. She's got me so fired up, I don't know if I'm coming or going—to the altar, that is...."

Dear Reader,

Thank you for joining us for another WORLD'S MOST ELIGIBLE BACHELORS story. This brand-new series focuses on the twelve sexiest, most-sought-after bachelors in the world, with all the intimate details of their lives written by twelve very talented authors.

The concept: *Prominence Magazine*—a fictitious publication created by our editors—has handpicked twelve confirmed bachelors who would really make excellent husbands…they just need a little nudge. They get that push from some very determined heroines out to win the men of their dreams.

There's a whole busload of women in search of bachelor #12, Rance Phillips. This *Cowboy on the Run,* created by award-winning author Anne McAllister, wants nothing to do with the passel of eligible females interested in catching themselves a husband. So he hightails it out of town to the ranch of his first—and only—love. But she's got a little surprise for Rance, as well, and it just might lead to marriage. This compelling story is also part of Anne McAllister's CODE OF THE WEST miniseries. Look for more stories featuring these Montana cowboys from Silhouette Desire and Special Edition.

And also be sure to look for more stories from all of the wonderful authors who've contributed to the WORLD'S MOST ELIGIBLE BACHELORS series. Silhouette Books is proud to bring you both their continuing miniseries and stellar stand-alone novels—unforgettable romances all.

Wishing you all the romance you deserve,

THE EDITORS

Please address questions and book requests to:
Silhouette Reader Service
U.S.: 3010 Walden Ave., P.O. Box 1325, Buffalo, NY 14269
Canadian: P.O. Box 609, Fort Erie, Ont. L2A 5X3

World's Most
Eligible Bachelors

Anne
McAllister

Cowboy
on the Run

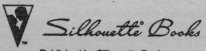

Silhouette Books

Published by Silhouette Books
America's Publisher of Contemporary Romance

For David and Eric,
father and son

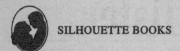

SILHOUETTE BOOKS

ISBN 0-373-65029-9

COWBOY ON THE RUN

Copyright © 1998 by Barbara Schenck

Printed in U.S.A.

A Conversation with...
RITA Award-winning author
ANNE McALLISTER

What hero have you created for WORLD'S MOST ELIGIBLE BACHELORS, and how has he earned the coveted title?

AM: Rance is a reluctant hero. He can't help it that he's a drop-dead-handsome former rodeo bronc rider, a fifth-generation Montanan who runs one of the biggest ranches in the state, and is a practicing attorney, with a Harvard law degree. He thinks it shouldn't be held against him—and it certainly shouldn't be bringing women around in droves!

This original title is part of CODE OF THE WEST, a Silhouette Desire and Special Edition miniseries. What about this series so appeals to you? Do you have future spinoffs planned?

AM: I've always loved cowboys, mythical and real—and I like writing about the values they live by. They are independent and self-reliant on the one hand, and caring and generous on the other. The best of them are tough yet gentle, dependable yet flexible, reliable yet spontaneous. And they are invariably driven by a fierce sense of honor. I find them endlessly fascinating, and I'll probably go on writing about them forever. More CODE OF THE WEST titles will be available throughout 1999 in both Silhouette Desire and Special Edition.

What modern-day personality best epitomizes a WORLD'S MOST ELIGIBLE BACHELOR?

AM: My three sons. They are, of course, all drop-dead-handsome guys who are independent, self-reliant, caring, generous, tough, gentle, dependable, flexible, reliable, spontaneous and honorable. Plus, they do their own laundry. What more can I say?

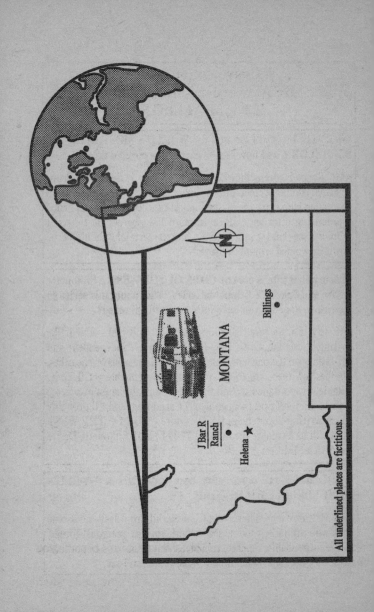

MONTANA

Billings

J Bar R
Ranch

Helena ★

All underlined places are fictitious.

One

It was the tour bus that did it.

One minute Rance Phillips was entirely focused on the dark red Simmental calf he'd roped and thrown to the ground, tying it for branding amid the sound and fury of bawling mother cows, bleating calves and the cussing and whooping of half a dozen cowboys.

And the next moment everything stopped.

The low diesel drone in the background, which had seemed like no more than the result of a shift in the wind bringing the sound of truck engines on the highway a half mile distant, suddenly grew very loud indeed.

"Will you look at that," J.D. Holt, the ranch foreman said.

Instead of branding the calf, Shane Nichols, who was wielding the iron, stood up and did just that.

His brother, Mace, who was supposed to be vaccinating, straightened, too. He took off his hat and said, "Now I've seen everything."

And Cash Callahan, who was turning baby bulls into steers, looked up, dropped the knife and whistled. "Whooo-eeeee."

"What the hell—" Rance demanded. He tightened his hold on the calf. "This isn't a Sunday-school picnic, you know. Pay attention!"

They *were* paying attention. Just not to him. Disgusted,

Rance finally looked up to see for himself what was going on.

A tour bus—a *neon pink* tour bus—was pulling to a stop just beyond the confines of the corral. Before he could say a word, the door to the bus opened and a horde of women spilled out.

"Ho-leee," Shane breathed.

"Maybe I *haven't* seen everything," Mace mumbled.

"Look at those mammas!" J.D. grinned as the women—all of them young, most of them pretty and not one of them dressed appropriately for a branding—advanced toward the corral. They seemed oblivious to the cattle, but they were evidently looking for something—or someone. Their eyes darted from this cowboy to that one.

Then one of them pointed straight at Rance. "There he is!"

Oh, no. He didn't believe it. *Refused* to believe it!

But no sooner had they spotted him than they made a beeline in his direction.

Rance said a very rude word under his breath. He let go of the calf and, as it bolted, he looked around for a bolt-hole of his own. There was none. The women descended en masse.

"Oooh! Rance! My name's Jolie, Rance."

"Ah, Rance. You're even handsomer than your pictures!"

"Rance, baby! You probably don't remember, but my mother and yours—"

The babble of female voices was deafening. The women were getting closer, swarming over the corral fence.

Rance straightened up and took one more desperate glance around, saw the astonished and bemused faces of his friends and knew there was no hope for it. He had to stand his ground.

So he did, but he was furious. For the past few months—ever since that damn article in *Prominence Magazine* had named John Ransome Phillips IV "one of the world's most eligible bachelors"—Rance's life hadn't been the same.

He had always had women batting their lashes at him. A few, here and there, had simpered and cooed. As he'd grown to adulthood, Rance had to admit that he'd become accustomed to seeing heads turn occasionally and hearing muffled female giggles when he looked their way.

But he'd never in his life get accustomed to this!

Everywhere he went now, women ogled him. They turned up in his law office, they followed him down the street. If he went into the grocery store, they trailed him down the aisles. If he ran into town for baling wire, women stampeded into the hardware store. They brushed up against him and wiggled their hips in front of him. They tucked their phone numbers into his pocket and patted his rear end!

The ones enterprising enough to have discovered his phone number, called him at three in the morning to chat. And if that wasn't bad enough, his work was suffering, too. His partner, Lydia Cochrane, who used to look up to him as her ideal of a serious, committed lawyer, now rolled her eyes when they couldn't walk down the hall without Rance having to look around corners and sometimes duck and take cover. His receptionist-cum-secretary, Jodi, couldn't get any work done because she was always making appointments for single women who desperately needed legal advice from John Ransome Phillips IV about cases that didn't exist.

Last month he made her get voice mail. He bought an answering machine for his home. Recently he'd stopped going to the grocery store, the hardware store, anywhere off the ranch at all, except to court or to his office.

It still hadn't been enough.

Lately they'd begun turning up at the ranch. Last Monday evening he'd answered the door, expecting his tax man, and found instead a blonde in a miniskirt whose car "just happened to break down" in his driveway—no matter that his "driveway" was five miles of gravel from the nearest paved road.

On Tuesday after a harrowing day in court, during which most of the onlookers were females more concerned with ogling him than with following the case, he'd come home to find another hopeful female already there sipping a margarita on the porch while she chatted with his father!

"You're encouraging them!" he'd accused John Ransome Phillips III.

"Me?" His father had flattened a hand against his chest and stared in wide-eyed innocence at his son.

On Wednesday morning he discovered a brunette in the barn when he went out to do chores. She'd been there all night, lying in wait.

"Proving I'm devoted," she told him as he hustled her to her car. "The article said you wanted your wife to be 'devoted,'" she quoted the magazine as he shoved her in and slammed the door. He didn't bother telling her that they hadn't even interviewed him. They'd talked to his father.

His father had apparently told them he liked apple pie. So many of those had turned up in the mail over the past four months that the post office was getting a little testy about the smell of rotting apples in their delivery vans.

Rance told them they didn't need to bother delivering the pies, but the postmaster had cited some obscure regulation, assuring Rance that the pies had to keep coming.

Of course, half a dozen enterprising women hadn't bothered with the postal service. They'd shown up with their pies in person.

He felt hunted. Stalked. "I need a restraining order," he told his father.

The older man blinked. "Against half the human race?" Then, at Rance's stony look, his father suggested cheerfully, "You could get married. That would put a stop to it."

Of course his father would say that. The earlier protestations of innocence were protestations and nothing more. It was no secret that John Ransome Phillips III, one of Montana's most prominent ranchers and most gifted lawyers, a man with three more generations of successful ranching, lawyering forebears behind him, was eager for his only son to marry and carry on the line. For the last two years, Trey Phillips, as he was known to friend and foe alike, had been telling the world at large, and his son in particular, that he wasn't getting any younger and he wanted to be assured of the succession before he was gone.

"Like you're some damn king," Rance fumed.

"Something like that," Trey agreed amiably.

"Get married yourself," Rance had suggested. "Get yourself another heir if you don't like this one."

They hadn't discussed the topic again. But Trey had made no move to bring home women of his own, and he continued to watch Rance speculatively.

Rance had taken refuge where he could—on the range. It was the one place he could count on not being followed.

Until now.

Rance reached over and grabbed the branding iron from Shane, then pointed the white-hot end of it at the approaching women. Their eager smiles faded. They looked around nervously, at him, at each other, then back toward the bus.

They slowed momentarily, but then, with foolhardy resolution, they came on.

Rance dug in. He brandished the iron. He narrowed his eyes. "Go away. Go on. Outa here. Now. Git!"

The women halted. They cocked their heads. They wetted their lips. They mustered tremulous, come-hither smiles.

"Don't pay any attention to them, sweetheart," the foremost one crooned, jerking her head at the women behind her. "They don't have what you want."

"You don't want a pushy broad like her," the blonde behind her said, smiling, encouraging him to agree with her. "Do you, Rance, darlin'?"

"I only came on the bus because it seemed less intrusive," another one protested. "An organized event to let you take your pick," she said, sounding as if she was quoting from some brochure!

And damn it, she probably was. Rance goggled at the thought. His mind reeled. *Somebody had organized a tour to bring women to meet him?* Who the hell—!

And then a movement in the doorway of the bus answered his question before he even had a chance to ask it. Trey stood there, one arm braced again the window, smiling at him.

It was the last straw.

Damn the old man and his conniving, manipulating, underhanded ways!

Rance leveled the branding iron at the women and headed straight at them. The women began backing up.

"Hey now, Rance," he heard behind him. "Don't be so damn hasty," J.D. protested.

Rance ignored him. He could find his own women on his own time. Trey had no business providing a harem of them right out in the middle of the branding!

"Now, son," Trey began. He jumped down out of the bus and began to push his way through the gaggle of retreating women.

Rance dropped the branding iron, but still stood his ground. "Don't start," he warned his father. "I don't want to hear it."

"It was a joke," Trey said, spreading his hands.

"I'm not laughing."

"Of course you're not—because you recognize the truth in it. You know damn well it's time. And it's your own fault," his father pointed out, heedless of the fury in Rance's tone. "You're thirty-three years old and you're still playing the field! If you'd get serious about finding a wife yourself, none of this would be happening."

He was serious. Rance could see it in his father's face. In the determined thrust of his jaw. In the steely glint that shone in his version of the Phillipses' blue eyes.

He was serious, and he wasn't going to let up.

The penalty for patricide in Montana was greater than Rance wanted to pay. But not by much.

Rance supposed he was a little old to be running away from home.

But he didn't know what else you'd call it. And he didn't know what else to do.

He needed space. He needed time. He needed room to

breathe. And he wasn't going to get any of them as long as he stayed on the old man's ranch and battled his way through bimbos every day of the week.

So he finished the branding, endured the grins and guffaws of his buddies and gritted his teeth through one more evening of Trey Phillips's heavy-handed hints—"Well, if you don't want any of them, why not marry Lydia?" And when the old man had retired to his bedroom with a Western and a glass of whiskey, Rance left a phone message for his secretary, another for Lydia, threw some clothes into a duffel bag and jumped in his truck and took off without looking back.

He had no goal or destination in mind. Didn't need one. Didn't want one.

He'd had too damn many goals and destinations of late.

"Phillipses have goals," Trey said so often that Rance reckoned it ought to be carved on the family crest. Rance had grown up with a hundred goals all laid out before him. As a youngster he'd been goaled to death.

At eighteen, when he'd seen his life mapped out for him by his father, he'd had enough. He didn't want to grow up, grow old and die without ever making a decision of his own. So he'd turned his back on his old man's goals, rejected his early acceptance at Princeton—his father's alma mater—and had gone off to ride broncs on the rodeo circuit.

"To *live*," he'd told his father defiantly.

"Not on *my* money," Trey had replied at once.

"Not on your money," Rance agreed. He didn't want to be beholden. He'd been determined to make it on his own—or starve to death trying.

In fact he might have if Shane Nichols, with whom he'd gone down the road, hadn't been a better rider than he had. Shane had made enough money to buy gas and groceries on days when Rance had nothing but lint in the pockets of his Wranglers. Without Shane he might have had to pack it in, crawl home and eat humble pie.

But Shane had kept him going, had patched him up, jollied him along, taught him everything he knew. And Shane wasn't the only one. Bronc riders were a small, close-knit group—a family almost. Once it was clear to them that Rance was in it for real, other guys had taken him under their wing, offering him advice, beer, sandwiches, rides. Sometimes Rance thought that the three years he had spent going down the road had been the happiest time of his life.

He'd known, of course, that it wouldn't last forever. Men didn't get old still riding broncs. In fact most barely made it to middle age before they had to find another way to make a living.

Rance knew he would, too. But he hadn't realized it would happen as quickly and irrevocably as it had.

One minute he was getting aboard a snuffy bronc at the Pendleton rodeo, and the next he was on his way to the operating room with a shattered right arm. Three months, two pins and four doctors' opinions later, he was hanging up his spurs and applying to Montana State for school.

"You give it a rest and you'll come back," Shane, ever the optimist, had assured him.

But Rance had seen the worry and urgency written on Shane's normally cheerful face. And the Phillips realism he'd been born with told him he'd seen the end of that dream. Rodeoing had given him a little breathing space. It was wrong to hope for more from it.

So he'd gone to school. He'd wanted the education, even though it hadn't been easy adjusting to the academic

routine. In fact only two things made it palatable at all—
the sweet little rancher's daughter he met in his freshman
English class and the fact that his father was furious that
he still insisted on not going to Princeton.

The rancher's daughter hadn't returned for her soph-
omore year. But the satisfaction of his father's displea-
sure lasted for the next four.

And when Rance finally did graduate, and his father
murmured, "Yale Law" this time, he'd taken further
pleasure in choosing Harvard. He was quite sure Yale,
like Princeton, was everything his father claimed it was.
He'd also been sure it wasn't for him.

Harvard hadn't been his cup of tea, either. But he was
determined, by that point, to show the old man that he
could make something of himself on his own.

He had resolution. He had his own goals. He accom-
plished them.

In the past four years he had developed a thriving law
practice with an office in Helena as well as in his home
town. Three high-profile cases, all of which he'd won,
brought him state accolades and a share of media attention. It got him a share of his father's, too. Trey had been
so impressed that he'd invited Rance to dinner and managed to say he guessed maybe the kid was worth something after all.

"Don't fall all over yourself gushing," Rance had replied, never even looking up from the steak he was cutting.

"Wouldn't think of it," Trey said heartily. "Seein's
how you're an educated feller now, even if you did go
to that Massa-chew-sitts school, I wondered if you might
want to take a look at the land deal Schyler's offering
me."

Schyler was the man whose ranch covered a section

adjacent to the Phillipses' spread. "Schyler's offering to sell?" Rance had asked, his attention caught. From there it had been a small step for Rance to get involved once more in the ranching operation.

He knew that had been his father's intention all along.

Trey added Schyler's ranch to the Phillipses' holdings, and Rance came in to help manage both. But to make sure Trey didn't get everything his own way, Rance had insisted on driving back and forth from Helena where he kept his apartment and office. He'd worn a rut in the highway, he did it so often.

Actually he would have preferred staying at the ranch, but that would have meant coming back under the old man's thumb—and there was no way he was doing that. Or there would have been no way, if last year his father hadn't had a heart attack.

It was minor, Trey assured him. "No big deal," he'd said over and over.

But Rance had been there when his father went ashen, when sweat literally popped out on his brow. He'd seen the pain in his father's eyes and the hold it had on his body. It might not have scared Trey, but J.D., who normally wished the old man to Hades twenty times a day, actually said, "Do you think the old son of a gun will be okay?"

That, as much as anything, frightened Rance enough that he moved back home and commuted the other way for a change.

Since he'd come home, he'd taken over most of the day-to-day running of the cattle operation.

He couldn't believe how much he'd missed it. Rodeo had been a way to stay around horses when he'd left the ranch. But to be honest, ranching had always interested him a lot more than rodeo ever had. It still interested him far more than the law did.

He still had his run-ins with the old man—as stubborn a cuss as ever was born, even after his heart attack. But for the most part Rance had dug in, settled down, enjoyed every moment.

At least he had until that damn article had come out.

Its five full-color pages of photos set Rance's teeth on edge. Its text extolled more virtues than even his doting mother would ever have believed he had.

And if all that wasn't bad enough, it ended by proclaiming:

We'd call John Ransome Phillips IV a golden boy—able to turn his hand successfully to whatever needs to be done—except he's no boy, ladies. Rest assured, the woman who tries to put a brand on the very eligible John Ransome Phillips IV will learn that he's 100% Montana *man*.

Yeah, well, they'd got that right at least, Rance thought as he gripped the steering wheel now and drove into the darkness.

More important, he was a determinedly *unmarried* Montana man.

And at the moment, thanks to them, he was a Montana man on the run.

Rance couldn't remember the last time he had slept in his truck.

Well, actually, if he thought about it very long, he probably could. In the days when he'd been rodeoing, sleeping in his truck was normal. There was no point in renting a place to live; he would never have been there.

But way back then he'd been younger and a damn sight more limber. He woke up this morning with a crick in his neck, a pain in his back and an ache in the arm he'd broken back in Pendleton eleven and a half years before.

But, he noted, pleased as he looked around, there wasn't a single tour bus in sight. No female had written a sexy come-on in lipstick on his windshield. And his pager wasn't beeping with a dozen more messages from contenders determined to be the "woman of his dreams"—only because when he'd left last night he'd made up his mind to leave his pager and cell phone at home.

The only thing he could see in any direction was forest and the remnants of the winter's snowfall in patches here and there on the ground. The only thing he could hear was the drip of melting snow and the call of birds in the trees. He wasn't sure exactly where he was. Somewhere in southern Montana, somewhere deep in the mountains.

Somewhere wonderful, a long way from home.

He sat up and cranked down the window and took a long lungful of cool spring mountain air. It was cool and sharp and refreshing. It made him feel better than he had in months.

His arm still ached and his back and neck were still stiff, but he didn't care. The arm would throb now and then wherever he was. His neck and back would improve once he got moving around. But just knowing that there were no tour buses around the next bend and that, at any given moment, no eligible women were going to jump out at him from behind the nearest lodgepole pine, made him breathe easier and more expansively than he had in months.

He opened the door and climbed out, wincing as he

turned to push the door shut with his aching arm. But as he did so, he realized that the ache in it was more from all the roping and wrestling calves that he'd done yesterday during the branding than from the night in the truck. Oddly, that improved his frame of mind further.

It was as if the reality of the tour bus and the women had less impact here—as if he'd been right to come.

As he stood there looking around, he remembered something that Taggart Jones, one of his rodeo buddies, once said. Taggart had always been the guy Rance had looked to for inspiration. A single dad who'd brought his small daughter down the road with him during most of his rodeo career, he'd always managed to keep his priorities straight and get the job done at the same time.

"Whenever the pressure gets to me," Taggart had explained once, "I take a step back. Or a step up," he amended, "if I'm home."

Rance, mystified, had shaken his head. "Huh?"

"When I'm on the back of a bull," Taggart explained, "it's like that is the only thing that matters. The world shrinks down that far. It isn't true, but it feels like it is— so other times I step back. I go for a drive. A ride. If I'm home, I climb a mountain."

"A mountain?"

Taggart nodded. "I get a new perspective when I do. I see what's important more clearly. And believe me, the biggest, rankest bull around looks pretty damn small from up there."

Rance wondered if a tour bus would, too.

God knew he needed a different perspective. A new focus. A sense of direction.

He started to climb.

He wasn't sure how long he walked up the narrow path toward the summit. Long enough to regret wearing cowboy boots, certainly. Long enough to wish he'd brought Spider, his black gelding, and a bottle of water along. Long enough for some of his cares to recede as he made his way upward through the pine forest toward the rough snow-pack that led to the peak. Long enough for his thoughts to roam, for his attention to wander.

He didn't notice the skunk.

One minute he had nothing more to worry about than plenty of success, far too many women and how best to avoid the matrimonial mousetrap—and the next he was worrying about where his next breath would come from.

"Argh! Damn it!"

Rance put a hand over his face, gagging and stumbling backward away from his black-and-white nemesis. But it was too late. Duty done, the skunk lowered its tail and, with a backward sniff, waddled off up the mountain.

So much for a new perspective.

Rance had started stumbling back toward his truck, when suddenly he heard a crashing through the trees behind him, and a saddled but riderless horse came into view.

Instinctively he started toward it, to try to grab the loose reins. But one whiff of him and the horse turned and bolted away.

"Hey!"

But he wasn't going to catch it by shouting. Chances were he wasn't going to catch it at all. In fact, it was probably the smell of skunk that had spooked it in the first place.

And its rider?

"Oh, hell!"

Somewhere up there, Rance realized, someone had been thrown. Someone could be hurt or unconscious. He started to run.

He'd gone no more than a couple of hundred yards when he spotted a boy limping his way. The boy wore faded jeans, a jacket, cowboy boots and a baseball cap. All of him was dusty, as if he'd just been pummeled into the dirt. He cradled his left arm against his chest.

Rance hurried on. "You all right?" he called.

The boy caught a whiff of him and began backing away. "You seen my horse? I gotta catch my horse." He moved out of Rance's path, presumably to give him—and his smell—wide berth.

"He went that way." Rance jerked his head. But when the boy started in that direction, Rance added, "You can't catch him on foot."

"Got to." The boy kept on going. Then he stumbled over a root and almost fell.

Rance went after him. "Wait up."

But he didn't. He just kept going, still hugging his arm against his chest. If he hadn't stumbled again, and fallen this time, the kid might never have stopped.

He was struggling to get up, his face white with pain, when Rance knelt beside him.

"Hold still. Don't move."

"I'm all right." Once more the kid tried to get up, and Rance, seeing that he was not going to be held down, set him on his feet with the least jolting possible. The movement clearly caused pain. The kid's face was tight-lipped and drawn.

"You're not all right," Rance said. "You've got a broken arm."

"Do not." The boy rubbed his arm, as if that would make it better. "I can't have a broken arm." There was just the smallest waver in his voice.

"Be nice if you didn't," Rance agreed gently. "But I

think the chances are slim. Come on. I'll take you home."

The boy didn't move. "I gotta get the cattle."

"You're not getting any cattle when you've got a broken arm."

"Got to. It's my job. We all gotta do our share."

Rance wondered if the kid had hit his head. Or was he quoting his old man? "No cattle," he said firmly. "No way. Now come on. Somebody else can get your cattle."

"My job," the boy muttered. "I said I'd do it. Cripes, Ma will kill me."

Ma? The old lady was the one who wore the pants in the family? Well, stranger things happened, Rance guessed. Carefully he brushed dirt and twigs off the kid's clothes. "Nobody's going to kill you. It wasn't your fault."

"I shoulda hung on. I shoulda seen—"

"You couldn't see. *I* didn't see," Rance said reasonably. "And I was right on top of him."

The boy didn't look convinced. He just shook his head. "What're we gonna do?" he asked, but the question wasn't directed at Rance. In fact he thought the kid was talking to himself more than anyone else.

"Somebody else'll get 'em," Rance told him.

"Ain't nobody else." The boy sighed. "We got enough problems without this." Then he muttered again, "Ma'll kill me."

"She ought to be glad you're alive."

Why the hell was she sending a boy to do a man's job, anyway? The kid couldn't be more than ten—and a scrawny ten at that. You might send a ten-year-old to bring in cattle where the going was easy. But bringing them down out of these mountains was a job for an experienced hand.

And Rance intended to tell the woman so when he saw her. "Come on," he said again. "Let's go."

But the boy was heading off into the woods again "I gotta catch Sunny."

Rance rolled his eyes. "For crying out loud! Forget it. The damn horse is probably halfway to Helena by now!"

The boy looked back at him, stricken. "He can't be! He isn't gone for good, is he?" There was a note of panic in his voice now.

From what Rance had seen of the shaggy, sway-backed buckskin that had bolted past him, it wouldn't have been a big loss if he was. But he supposed the kid was attached to the animal.

"No," he said placatingly. "I don't reckon he's gone for good. He'll probably just run off his spook, then head for home. Heck," he added in an attempt to cheer the kid up, "he'll likely get there before you do."

The kid really did look panic-stricken now. "He can't! If he comes home without me, Ma will die."

Rance thought the boy's mother must be some piece of work. First she was going to kill the kid herself, then if she thought something had happened to him, she was going to die. She sounded worse than his own old man.

But all he said was, "So you need to get home and prove you're not dead, right? Well, come on. If we hurry, your mom won't worry as long."

The kid didn't hesitate now. Still clutching his arm against his chest, he followed Rance down the mountain toward the truck.

Rance moved carefully, keeping his pace slow and picking the trail with an eye to keeping it as easy as possible. Every few feet he glanced back to see if the boy was doing all right. The kid's lower lip was caught between his teeth, and his upper lip had a thin line of perspiration attesting to his pain, but he never said a word as he followed Rance, uncomplaining.

Stubborn *and* uncomplaining. *And* determined to do a man's job. Rance didn't know a lot about kids—he'd spent his adult life professing no interest in them lest his father get any more dynastic urges—but he was impressed with this one. He thought this one was tougher than the average bear.

He glanced back over his shoulder once more. "What's your name?" he asked the boy.

The kid didn't look up, just kept his eyes on his feet to make sure he didn't slip or fall. "Josh. Josh O'Connor."

"I'm Rance Phillips." For an instant he held his breath for the inevitable wide-eyed, knowing look he got from men and women alike. But Josh O'Connor, bless his heart, didn't seem to read *Prominence Magazine*. At least Rance's name caused no sign of recognition.

Rance grinned his relief. "It's a pleasure to meet you, Josh O'Connor. You just tell me where to go and we'll have you home in no time."

Josh gave him directions, but he wouldn't ride in the cab. "Rather stay in back," he said. "You kinda stink," he added frankly when Rance opened the door for him.

There was no arguing with that. "Fair enough." So he lifted the boy over the side into the back of his truck, ignoring Josh's protest that he could do it himself. "Of course you can," he said. "Just humor me."

The ride to Josh's ranch took them several miles back down the highway, then onto a gravel road that cut to the right and began climbing back into the hills once more. It wasn't far as horses went. It took half an hour by truck.

"Must be hard to get in and out of here in winter," Rance said when he got out to open the gate.

"Sometimes we can't get out to go to school."

"What a shame," Rance said drily.

A flicker of a grin crossed Josh's face, the first one Rance had seen. But then the boy shrugged slightly, "Don't matter. Ma makes us study, anyhow."

Josh's ma, Rance thought, must be one tough bird. He supposed she couldn't be all that old—forty probably or maybe fifty. But he had no doubt she'd be boot-faced and cranky—the flip side of the female coin from the eager air-headed bimbos who had plagued his life the past few months.

He wondered idly if he could charm her. What good was it, after all, to be one of the world's most eligible bachelors if he couldn't sweet-talk one crabby old witch?

It wasn't as if he was interested in enticing her into his bed. He only wanted to disarm her a little bit...make her lighten up a little, go easier on the kid.

He did feel somewhat responsible for Josh's predicament. If he'd been paying attention, he might have avoided the skunk; then the horse might not have spooked; the kid might not have fallen or broken his arm; and his old lady wouldn't be about to kill him—or die herself.

He couldn't fix the broken arm. But maybe he could make life a little easier for the boy. All that world-class charm he was supposed to possess ought to be good for something.

Once they were inside the gate, the road narrowed to a rutted track. As the truck bumped along, every so often Rance caught sight of Josh's white face in the rearview mirror. "Hang in there," he called.

Tight-lipped, Josh nodded his head.

Fortunately they only went another half mile before the road curved and dipped into a small shallow valley where a snug story and a half ranch house sat. Across the yard from it there was a tree house, which made Rance think that at least someone knew that boys shouldn't have to work all day every day. Beyond the tree house was a barn and beyond that, a corral.

In the corral Rance could see three horses watching with interest as two boys even smaller than Josh were trying to put up some new fence rails. Well, maybe not all day, every day—but clearly most of the day. And obviously Josh wasn't the only one she put to tasks beyond him.

"Child labor," Rance muttered under his breath, visions of the old woman in the shoe floating around his head.

Where the heck was her husband?

Had she run him off?

The sight of Rance's truck brought the boys working on the corral to their feet.

"Ma!" one of them yelled.

"Mom!" hollered the other one. "Somebody's comin'!"

There was a movement on the far side of the clothesline, and from behind a line of flapping shirts, a woman came into view.

She was slender and tall, with long, honey-colored hair pulled back from her face. She came toward him as he drove the truck into the yard. And he could see at once that she wasn't at all the boot-faced, humorless hag he'd imagined.

She looked bright and smiling and young. Beautiful, in fact. Very much like a woman he wouldn't mind getting to know.

Very much, in fact, like a woman he once *had* known.

Then she looked at him, and her eyes widened, too. Her smile wavered.

Rance's smile vanished. He brought the truck to a stop, then swallowed hard and stared, disbelieving. *"Ellie?"*

Two

Because it *was* Ellie. No doubt about it.

Ellie Pascoe in the flesh.

At least she'd been Ellie Pascoe when Rance had met her in his English class at Montana State all those years ago.

She'd been the only thing he'd noticed. Her sparkling green eyes, scattering of freckles and long thick braid of honey-colored hair had made Ellie Pascoe the only attraction strong enough to distract him from thoughts of his recently shattered rodeo career.

She was older now. There was obvious maturity in her body, in her face. But in essence she was the same. Nothing had changed much, Rance decided. Except her name.

Now she was Ellie O'Connor.

His jaw tightened at the thought.

Of course, she'd talked to him about marriage that year. She'd been in love with him. It hadn't been a secret. And in his way Rance had loved her.

But to him marriage meant perpetuating "the dynasty." It meant giving in to all those things his father wanted him to do—go to law school, find a wife, have a family.

"I'm not gettin' married," he'd told Ellie more than once. He didn't see why it mattered. They had a good thing without talking about the *M* word, didn't they?

Apparently not good enough for Ellie.

She must have wanted the ring and the Mrs. in front of her name worse than he'd thought, because when he'd come back to school the next autumn, eager to tell her about his summer working for a horse breeder in Ireland, Ellie wasn't there.

At first he thought she'd just moved out of the dorms and into an apartment in town. But he hadn't been able to find her. Then classes had begun, and still she wasn't there. That was when he'd realized she might not have saved enough money to return to school. He knew she'd been working two jobs.

Though he had no money beyond what he'd saved from the pittance the breeder had paid him that summer—and he certainly would never have asked his father for money—he would have helped her however he could.

When he finally ran into her friend Leah, he demanded, "What's with Ellie? When's she coming back?"

He remembered how Leah had looked at him, then shaken her head. "Ellie's not coming back."

"Why not? Is money that tight? I can help. I—"

"It's not money." Leah hesitated for a split second, then said flatly, "Ellie got married."

The news was almost as unexpected as the sudden end of his rodeo career. Rance knew he must have stood staring at Leah, jaw hanging open, for at least a minute. Then, feeling like a fool for displaying his feelings so openly, he'd snapped his mouth shut, muttered something about "if that was the way she wanted it" and stalked away.

He hadn't asked who Ellie had married. He hadn't wanted to know. Later he heard she'd wed a guy she'd grown up with. But at the time it was enough to know how little she'd cared about him!

Obviously she'd wanted marriage more than she'd

wanted love—*his* love, anyway! Well, fine, she could have it.

If she didn't care about him, he wouldn't care about her. He wouldn't even *think* about her.

And he hadn't—except rarely—until now.

Now.

Now he looked at this older version of Ellie again. She was looking at him as if she'd seen a ghost. Her face was as white as the boy's in his truck.

And that was when he realized that the boy he'd given the ride to, the boy whose horse had been spooked—was Ellie's son!

"Ma?" Josh said now.

And at the sound of his voice, Ellie's gaze jerked away from Rance. *"Josh?"* Panic flickered in her eyes as she looked wildly around. Then "Josh!" she exclaimed as she spotted him.

"He's okay," Rance said quickly. He started to go after her, then realized how bad he smelled and stayed back. "Just took a spill."

She ran to the back of the truck. "Josh! What happened? Are you—"

"'M all right, Ma," Josh said gruffly. He struggled to his feet.

Ellie looked at the way he was holding his arm and gave a small gasp. "Oh, Josh! What have you—I told you you didn't need to—"

"I did need to," Josh said in the same stubborn tone Rance had heard earlier. "You can't do everything yourself. But *he*—" and here the boy acknowledged Rance for the first time "—spooked a skunk, an' the skunk spooked Sunny an' Sunny took off—"

"Oh, Josh," Ellie said again. Her hands trembled as she reached for him. Before she could try to lift him down, Rance stepped in and helped the boy over the side of the truck, taking care not to jar his arm.

"You stink," the boy said.

"Tough."

Ellie didn't seem to care if he smelled, she just wanted her son. "Let me see," she insisted.

"It's okay. I'm fine," Josh said, twisting out of Rance's grasp.

But clearly Ellie didn't believe that any more than he had. She didn't contradict the boy, though, just hugged him gently and brushed at a smudge of dirt on his cheek.

He came up almost to her shoulder. He had the same slender, fine-boned build she had and the same smattering of freckles on his cheeks. Otherwise Rance thought he didn't look much like her. Josh's hair was a darker brown, his eyes a deep blue. Ellie's were still the deepest green Rance had ever seen. They used to twinkle when she was amused, or grow deep and reflective when she was concerned. She was concerned now, he could tell.

So were the other two boys who had come running up as he was helping Josh out of the truck. "Josh! What happened?"

"Josh! You okay?"

Then they caught a whiff of Rance and edged away. They were younger than Josh, but they had to be his brothers. If he didn't look like his mother, they did. Their eyes were pools of dark green jade. Their hair, too, was blond—lighter than Ellie's, though Rance supposed she might have been that fair when she was a child. They were as alike as peas in a pod.

But Rance didn't dwell on that. He dwelt on the fact that Ellie had *three* kids. God Almighty! Her rancher must keep her barefoot and pregnant with a vengeance, he thought. A muscle in his jaw ticked.

Just then the door to the house opened, and a little golden-haired girl came out. "Mommy, what's wrong with Josh?"

Four?! She had *four* kids? Rance gaped.

Ellie didn't notice. Her attention was still focused entirely on Josh. "I'll call the doctor," she was saying. "He can meet us at the clinic."

"I don't need a doctor, Ma!"

"Yes, you do."

"But I gotta get Sunny. What about Sunny?"

Rance saw a momentary flicker of worry in Ellie's eyes, but she didn't betray it in her tone when she spoke to Josh. "Don't worry about Sunny. He'll come home." She brushed a hand over the boy's dark hair, then seemed to give a small shudder. "I'm just glad he didn't come before you did. It would have been..." Her voice trailed off, and she shook her head helplessly.

"It wasn't," Josh said, his tone sharp. "It didn't happen, Ma. I told you, I'm fine."

Ellie seemed to give herself a little shake. "Of course you are," she said briskly. But still she blinked as if she was fighting off tears.

"He's not hurt that bad," Rance said.

Ellie started, as if she'd forgotten him. Now she slanted a glance his way. "Rance. Thank you, Rance."

It was the first time he'd heard his name on her lips in eleven years. A thousand women had spoken his name in the meantime. They'd called it, sung it, whispered it, caressed it. And not one of them had had the effect on him that Ellie had.

Still did.

How the hell annoying was that? He'd had women prowling around his life in droves for the past few months. Even before the damn article had come out, he'd had his share. He'd never given any of them a second glance.

As close as he'd come to lying awake thinking about a woman was when he'd been offered Poppy Hamilton on a plate.

He'd almost been tempted then—because Poppy, the daughter of matchmaking Judge George Hamilton, really was everything her father said—but she had also been in love with Shane. And seeing the two of them so screwed up in their love for each other, Rance realized how little interest he actually felt.

His disinterest in any particular woman was so enduring that he'd assumed it was natural.

To feel this sudden spark of desire, this desperate awareness, for Ellie of all people—the one woman who'd rejected him and married someone else!—made him furious.

Now he stiffened. "You're welcome," he said almost formally. Then he added, "He'll be all right. But in the future, I wouldn't be asking for a man's work from a boy his age."

"I didn't—"

"She can't do everything herself!" Josh cut in.

"Where's your husband?" Rance asked. "Don't tell me he got four kids on you, then up and left!"

His words, harsh and louder than he intended, seemed to echo in the sudden stillness in the valley. Josh's blue eyes went hard and dark as steel. The other boys stared at him, their mouths open. It was so quiet he could hear when Ellie drew an unsteady breath.

"He didn't leave us," she said. Her gaze flickered up to meet Rance's for an instant before focusing on something beyond him. "Not intentionally. He's dead."

Oh, hell. Oh, God. A million desperate thoughts tumbled through Rance's mind, each less helpful than the last. He ducked his head, scuffed his boot in the dirt, then looked straight into her eyes.

"I didn't mean—" he broke off. His gaze dropped again. "I'm sorry, Ellie," he said.

She didn't answer for a moment. He couldn't blame her. What was she supposed to say? That's all right?

It wasn't all right. He'd acted like an ass!

She could say *that*, he supposed, and it would only be the truth.

"You know my mom?" Josh's accusing voice broke into the silence.

Both he and Ellie stiffened, then looked at the boy. Josh was frowning and still obviously angry at Rance's dig at his father. As, of course, he had a right to be.

Since Ellie didn't answer, Rance nodded. "I knew your mother in college."

Josh's gaze swung to meet his mother's. She ran a hand over her hair distractedly. "That's right. We did know each other. Once," she added. "A very long time ago."

Which put him very effectively in his place. But Rance couldn't really blame her. Under the circumstances he deserved it.

"I'll look for your horse," he said.

Ellie's gaze swiveled to meet his. Her eyes widened. Her mouth tightened. He could see the "thanks, but no thanks" coming.

"It's the least I can do," he said quickly to forestall it. "Really. I'd be glad to help, but I'll need to grab a shower first."

No invitation to use the O'Connor bathroom was immediately forthcoming. In fact, Ellie didn't say anything at all. She just looked at him for a long moment. He had no idea what she was thinking. Wasn't sure he wanted to know.

Finally Josh said, "Let him catch Sunny, Ma. He *oughta* help." The look on his face said that Rance ought to have to look long and hard, too.

"It's not necessary," Ellie objected. "The skunk may have startled him, but Sunny is old and not terribly adventurous. I'm sure he'll come home."

Rance was sure he would, too. But something in him wouldn't let him just turn and walk away. Was it because of what he'd said about Ellie's husband? Was it because he felt more than ever a need to make amends? Or was it some odd sense of unfinished business between them?

She'd never told him she didn't love him.

She'd never really said goodbye.

Whatever it was, he continued to press. "Fine, he'll come home. But I still owe you, Ellie. I'll watch your kids."

"*What? No!*" She looked horrified.

"Not forever," Rance said quickly. God forbid! "Just while you take Josh to the doctor."

"Oh." She looked slightly mollified, but still she shook her head. "I don't think that's a good idea."

"Why not?"

"Yeah, why not?" Josh said, just a little belligerently.

"Because...because..." Ellie was grasping at straws, and both she and Rance knew it.

"You need to concentrate on Josh," Rance said to her gently. "Don't you?"

She looked at the boy, still holding his arm hard against his body, and her eyes shuttered for a moment. Then she looked back at Rance, and Rance saw from the look in her eyes that the answer was yes.

It was pretty clear that Ellie's attention was spread so

thin that nothing got her undivided attention anymore. Not the ranch, not the cattle, not even her children.

Rance wondered how long ago her husband had died. From the look of things, it had been a while. As he glanced around now, he could see painting that needed to be done, fence that needed to be mended, a door on the barn that was listing to one side. He saw a ten-year-old who felt compelled to do a man's job, and even younger boys who were clearly intent on doing their share.

Another longer, deeper look at Ellie told him there was more to her than maturity now. Up close he could see lines of strain around her eyes. Tiny telltale creases bracketed the corners of her mouth. Some people got them from smiling. Ellie's might have begun that way, but Rance thought it a good bet that pain was what was etching them deeper now.

For one short moment he wanted to take her into his arms and soothe her, comfort her, tell her he was here now and that all her troubles would go away.

Yeah, right.

And she wasn't even inclined to want to let him use her bathroom to take a shower.

What the hell had he ever done to make her so mad at him? When he'd gone to Ireland that summer, he'd thought they'd parted on good terms. She'd been sad, of course. She'd held him, hugged him hard and she'd looked longingly at him as he'd headed for the plane. She'd stayed waiting as long as he'd been able to see her.

But in the end she was the one who hadn't come back.

She was the one who'd got married and had never bothered to tell him! She'd let him down, not the other way around!

He turned hard eyes on her now and waited, almost daring her to turn him away.

Finally she gave a jerky nod. "All right. Thank you. That's very kind."

Kind? He wasn't being *kind* damn it! But he couldn't say so. Couldn't say any of the things he was thinking. Not in front of her kids.

So he gritted his teeth. "My pleasure," he said through them. "Do you mind if I have a shower?"

She blinked.

"As your son said so bluntly, I stink."

The kids all giggled. Ellie flushed. "Of—of course. Daniel will show you the bathroom." She nodded toward one of the pea-pod boys.

Rance looked at them. "Which one of you is Daniel?"

"Me," the one on the left said. He had a tiny scar just above his eyebrow. It was the only difference Rance could see.

"I should have introduced you," Ellie said quickly while Rance reached inside the cab and grabbed his duffel with clean clothes in it. "You've obviously met Josh. These two are Daniel and Caleb. They're eight. And this—" she drew forward the little girl who'd come up to them while they were talking "—is my daughter, Carrie. She's four."

Rance looked down at this miniature version of Ellie and felt some odd, unknown emotion squeeze his heart.

"Hi, there," he said to the little girl who clutched a well-worn bear in a cowgirl outfit to her chest. He favored her with one of his world's-most-eligible smiles. "I'm Rance."

"He's Mr. Phillips," Ellie corrected firmly. "Say hello to Mr. Phillips, Carrie."

Carrie wrinkled her nose at the smell of him, but she

managed a soft, "'Lo," around her knuckle. Then, clearly not charmed, she ducked back behind her mother again.

Rance gave Ellie a rueful smile. "She's very like you. They all are," he added. "Except Josh."

Ellie didn't reply. Instead she turned back to the boys. "Daniel, show Mr. Phillips the shower. I've got to call the doctor." And she headed toward the house, almost at a run.

This was no time to panic.

Just because at this very moment Rance Phillips was standing naked in her shower, that was no reason to lose it.

She was a sane, sensible, intelligent, adult woman, after all. She was almost thirty years old. She was the single surviving parent and sole support of four growing children. And she'd managed everything since Spike had died two years ago. *Everything.*

She was strong. She was determined. She was capable.

So why were her hands shaking? Why were her palms damp and her mouth dry? Why did she fumble and drop the phone as soon as she picked it up?

"Because your child is hurt," she told herself under her breath. And indeed a quick glance over her shoulder showed her that Josh's face was still as white as the porcelain sink.

He stood almost gingerly in the middle of the kitchen, cradling his arm and watching her with his father's eyes.

She dropped the phone again.

"I'm sorry, honey," she babbled, scrabbling to pick it up and trying to reassure Josh at the same time. "I'm just...worried."

"I told him you'd panic," Josh said, disgruntled.

Him. Rance.

"I'm *not* panicking!" If she said it often enough, Ellie wondered, would she believe it?

God, she hoped so. She could hear how shrill her voice was. She could feel her hands trembling even now as she stuck the receiver against her ear. Making herself focus, making herself say the numbers under her breath, finally she got the clinic's number dialed.

"This is Ellie O'Connor. Josh has been hurt. I'm bringing him right in!" Then she ran into the bedroom to get her purse and grab a sweater. "All set," she told Josh. "Let's go."

"Pick up some tomato juice while you're there."

She spun around to see a bare-chested, barefoot Rance standing in the doorway to the kitchen. He'd obviously showered. He wore only a pair of jeans. His dark hair was damp and spiky, and he had a towel slung around his shoulders. But it wasn't the towel her eyes were drawn to—or his hair. Not the hair on his head, anyway. She couldn't seem to take her eyes off his chest.

She'd lived for eleven years with memories of Rance Phillips's bare chest. Months went by sometimes when she didn't think of it—of him. Years went by—the good years when she was married to Spike—and she didn't remember it at all. She might, if she'd been asked, have said she'd forgotten what it looked like.

The memory came back real fast.

Present reality was more impressive than that. Broader and harder muscled than she remembered, Rance Phillips's chest could only be said to have improved with age. And damn, that was the last thing she should be thinking!

"T-tomato juice?" she croaked.

Rance nodded. "Soap isn't going to do it. I got the

worst of the skunk washed off, but J.D., our foreman, once had a run-in with a skunk. Tomato juice neutralized the smell. At least that's what my old man said."

You're talking to your father these days? Ellie wanted to ask.

He hadn't been, eleven years ago. He hadn't been listening to his father, either. Rance had wanted nothing whatever to do with Trey Phillips and his demands and expectations then. And now?

She didn't ask.

"Could you pick me up a pair of boots, too? Ten D." He waggled a bare foot at her. "I'll write you a check. No way tomato juice is going to salvage mine."

Ellie nodded jerkily and ran her tongue over parched lips. "Of course." She started toward the door, then stopped, her gaze caught by the boots under the chair. Spike's boots. Josh wore them sometimes—just threw them on to go do chores. When he needed a reminder of his father.

She swallowed. "You can wear those," she said, nodding to them now. "Until I get you another pair."

Rance's gaze followed hers. He looked at the boots for a long moment, obviously registering their size, obviously aware that they couldn't be hers or the kids'. "You sure?"

Ellie made herself nod. "Of course." Why not? It would be for the best. He couldn't wear them without remembering that she had left him, that she had married someone else. "Of course," she said again. Then, "Come on, Josh. You two keep an eye on Carrie," she said to the twins.

Carrie pulled her knuckle out of her mouth, clutched her bear to her chest and scrambled down out of the chair where she'd been sitting. "I wanta go, too, Mama." She looked back at Rance. "Don't wanta stay with him. He smells."

"But—"

One look at her daughter's stubborn chin and Ellie knew this wasn't a battle worth fighting. Carrie was a force. She was as determined as Spike had ever been—more stubborn than all the boys put together. If Carrie liked someone, she liked them with a passion. If she didn't, God help them.

And if she hadn't made up her mind—which Ellie suspected was the case with Rance—nothing on earth was going to help her do it but time and experience.

The last thing Ellie wanted was to give Carrie the time and experience to find out what a charmer Rance Phillips really was.

"Fine." She reached for her daughter's hand. "You come with me. These two won't bother you," she said to Rance. Caleb was only interested in numbers and Daniel in animals. That was safe enough.

"Never met anybody got sprayed by a skunk before." Caleb eyed Rance with a mixture of awe and respect.

"We'll find Sunny," Daniel added.

"You cannot go looking for Sunny," Ellie replied firmly. "I forbid it. If one of you two got hurt—"

"They won't get hurt," Rance cut in. "Go. Now. Josh needs the doc. And I—" he grinned wryly "—need that tomato juice."

It was a pure 100% Rance Phillips grin. Ellie hadn't forgotten that, either.

Don't! she begged silently. *Please don't!*

She grabbed Carrie by the arm, put a gentle hand on Josh's shoulder and steered both children toward the truck.

* * *

She didn't look back.

Rance supposed he shouldn't have expected her to.

But that had been the way he and Ellie used to part from each other—with a smile, a kiss, a touch and, finally, that lingering backward glance, each of them trying to see who could get the last glimpse of the other.

It wasn't that way now.

Of course it wasn't! Because she didn't give a damn about him.

And he didn't give a damn about her, either! It was just a reflex, that was all.

A reflex that had stood the test of eleven years' time. He shoved the thought away and determinedly he turned back to Daniel and Caleb. "Show me what you've been doing on that fence."

The way they looked at each other, he was reminded of Tom Sawyer with a bucket of whitewash and the knowledge that a sucker was born every minute. They grinned.

"Sure," Caleb said. "Come on."

It was, as he'd suspected, too big a job for two little boys. But it was too big a job for one lone woman like Ellie also. The boards were long and heavy and unwieldy. But he could move them far more easily than Caleb and Daniel, so he did. He made them hammer the nails while he held the boards in place.

"Stay way down there," Caleb told him.

Rance nodded. He stayed downwind. The boys, tongues trapped between tight lips, foreheads furrowed with the effort of their concentration, hammered away.

And at the same time, Rance picked their brains.

"Your mother runs this whole place by herself?"

"We help," Caleb replied.

"An' Josh," Daniel added. "An' Gran'ma."

"Grandma?" Rance had heard some crazy nicknames for hired hands, but he'd never met one called Grandma.

"Dad's mom," Daniel said between thumps with the hammer. "She lives down the valley."

What about Grandpa? Rance wanted to ask, but he'd already stuck his foot in his mouth enough for one day.

"By herself?" he said cautiously.

"Yep," Caleb said. "Gran'pa died."

"What about your other grandparents?"

"They died a long time ago," Daniel said. "I don't even remember them except Mom has pictures."

"I'm sorry." Rance settled another railing against a post. "I'm sorry, um, about your dad, too. I...didn't know."

He wasn't sure why he felt compelled to bring that up again. He'd made such an ass of himself the first time that he ought to just keep his mouth shut. But he wanted the boys to know he sympathized with their loss. However much he might resent O'Connor's having swept Ellie away from him, it was clear from his children's expressions and the pain in Ellie's eyes that he'd been deeply loved and desperately missed.

"He fell off his horse," Caleb said. He didn't look at Rance. He kept his eyes focused firmly on the nail he was about to hit.

"'Cause somethin' spooked 'im," Daniel said.

The fence rail wobbled in Rance's grasp. Ellie's husband had died from a fall off his horse? A horse that had been spooked? *God.*

No wonder she'd turned white at the news of Josh's fall. And no wonder the boy had been in such a hurry to catch his horse and, failing that, to reassure his mother that he was fine.

Rance wet his lips and steadied the fence rail. "Cripes," he muttered under his breath. Then, "How long ago?"

"We were in first grade," Caleb said.

"Now we're in third." Daniel added.

So Ellie had been on her own for two years. It was a long time for one person to try to keep things going with only three little boys and an older lady to help.

No doubt when her husband had been alive, the ranch had done well enough. Small ranchers, if they were careful and frugal and lucky as hell, could still manage to eke out a living in today's cattle market. Apparently the O'Connors had.

The operative word, however, was *had*.

It didn't look much like Ellie was eking out anything anymore. Maybe the unmended fence, the peeling paint and the torn screen he'd seen on the front room window were the only problems she had. But if they were indicative of her finances and not just of her inability to keep hired help, it looked like, for all her efforts—and all Josh's—she was simply prolonging the slide into bankruptcy.

"Hel—heck of a lot of hard work to do around here," he said, lifting his eyes from his fencing task for a moment just to look around.

"We don't mind workin' hard," Daniel said.

Caleb said, "It's good for us." And the two of them looked at him squarely, as if daring him to dispute it.

Rance didn't. He'd worked hard when he was growing up. He understood the values Ellie was trying to instill in her kids. He respected them. But still he felt obliged to say, "Ranching's a big job for just one person."

"She ain't just one person," Caleb protested. "She's got us."

"An' Josh," Daniel added. "An' Gran'ma."

As if to make his point, he gave the nail an extra hard whack. It bent. He made a face. But instead of tossing it aside and taking another, he laid it on the plank and banged it with the hammer to try to straighten it. He banged at it half a dozen times to little avail.

Then Caleb took the hammer away from him and tried his hand at straightening the nail. Rance's own hands itched to grab it away from both of them.

"Throw it out," he said finally, "and use another."

"Wasteful," Daniel said.

"Mom always straightens nails," Caleb agreed.

Ellie's kingdom depended on saving bent nails? God help her, Rance thought.

"Mom says every little bit counts," Daniel told him. "It has to," he added after a moment, "or we might hafta sell the ranch."

Caleb kicked Daniel in the ankle. "We aren't going to sell the ranch!"

"I know that," Daniel retorted. "I was just sayin' we might."

"We *aren't!*" Caleb insisted. "So stop sayin' it." He kicked Daniel again for good measure.

Daniel kicked him back. "He ain't going to buy it. He's not Cleve Hardesty."

"Who's Cleve Hardesty?" Rance asked.

"He lives over th'other side of the valley," Caleb said vaguely.

"He wants to buy the ranch," Daniel put in.

Caleb kicked him again.

"Quitcher kickin'. It ain't a secret!"

"Well, Mom doesn't like us sayin' it." Caleb looked like he might quit kicking and start hammering at any moment. "She says you say these things an' they happen. So don't go tellin' the world."

"I'm not! I'm tellin' him."

"And I won't tell a soul," Rance promised quickly. "Here." He couldn't stand it any longer. He reached for the hammer and deftly straightened the nail, then handed it to Daniel who concentrated on carefully pounding it in, fortunately straight this time.

So Ellie had a vulture hanging over her, watching and waiting for her to go under? The notion made Rance grit his teeth.

"Who is this Hardesty guy?" Rance thought he knew most of the larger ranchers in Montana, but he'd never heard that name.

"He's new," Daniel told him. "He's a bigwig, Mom says. From California."

Caleb glared at his brother, no doubt for continuing to fill Rance in. But then he sighed and gave in to the inevitable. "He's from Hollywood, Josh said. A movie guy. A producer, I think." Obviously if he wasn't going to shut Daniel up, he was going to make sure the story got told right.

"Ah." Rance's mouth thinned.

"He bought Mr. Jeffers's place last year," Daniel said. "An' now he wants ours. He's waitin' till 'the price is right.'" And from the way he said it, Rance could tell that Daniel had heard someone say those exact words. "He's waitin' till Mom can't pay Mr. Murrgage."

"Who?"

"Mr. Mortgage," Caleb corrected. "At the bank. But she will," he told Rance firmly. "She said so, and she will."

"Sure she will," Rance agreed.

But he had the feeling "Mr. Murrgage" wasn't going

to be tolerant if she was late—especially if a well-heeled outsider like Cleve Hardesty was waiting in the wings with a full wallet.

He was only guessing, of course. There was no telling how bad things were for Ellie, but her kids were obviously worried. The very fact that kids their age even knew the word *mortgage* told him that she had serious financial problems.

They finished with the fence, then took a break. Caleb said he would make lemonade. Daniel said, wrinkling his nose at Rance, that they could stay outside to drink it.

The boys had warmed to him now and were chattering on—about school—how much Caleb liked math and Daniel hated it; about horses—how Sunny better come home because he was "the only real horse" they had, the others being too green or too old; about the coming branding—which would be soon—"next weekend, maybe," Caleb said. "Soon's Josh an' Ma get 'em sorted."

But then the boys stopped and looked at each other, aware that Josh's accident would change things now.

In the silence of this realization Rance said to Daniel, "Go find me some more nails." And to Caleb he said, "Help me bring those leftover fence rails over here."

"Whatcha gonna do?" both boys demanded.

"We're going to fix these steps before somebody falls through 'em."

It wasn't much, but it was the least he could do. He took what was left of the fence rails and set Caleb to measuring them to match the rotting wood in the steps. He cut them and handed them to Daniel to nail down.

They had just finished when Daniel looked up and shouted, "Look! It's Sunny!"

Sure enough, through the trees, Rance could see the

horse that had bolted past him on the mountain. He straightened up to go catch the animal, but Daniel was already on his way.

"I'll get 'im."

Rance was going to protest. Sunny was a good-sized horse, and Daniel wasn't a very big boy.

"Don't," he began, but Caleb interrupted.

"Daniel will get 'im. Don't worry. He's good with Sunny."

And it was clear almost at once that he was. As Rance and Caleb watched, Daniel moved slowly toward the horse, talking softly the whole time. And Sunny, lathered and rough with sweat, pricked his ears and looked in the boy's direction, then whickered, as if he was letting out a sigh and trotted right up to Daniel.

"See?" Caleb said proudly.

Rance nodded and grinned. "Good for him."

As Daniel caught Sunny's reins and led him toward the barn for a rubdown, Rance noticed the door again and said to Caleb, "See if you can find a hinge pin and we'll fix that barn door."

"Okay." And Caleb was off and running.

Rance sat there for a minute, watching him go. Then he finished the last of the lemonade and thought about the afternoon—about unexpectedness, about the twists and turns that came out of nowhere to nail a guy when he wasn't paying attention.

Like the accident that had ended his rodeo career.

Like the accident that had ended Ellie's husband's life.

Like the one that had brought Rance to her doorstep once more.

A feller's got to get up early an' keep his eyes open. Rance remembered his grandfather, John Ransome Phillips II, often saying that. *A feller never knows quite what's gonna happen, yes sir, so he's gotta be ready for anything.*

Anything.

Like skunks? And magazine articles? And broken arms?

Like the only woman who'd ever enchanted him suddenly appearing once more in his life?

What was he going to do about that?

What could he do?

His gaze lit on Ellie's laundry basket, sitting forgotten beneath the half-filled clothesline in the middle of the yard. Half a dozen little boys' shirts flapped in the breeze. Some even smaller little girl's jeans in pink and blue hung next to them.

Vaguely Rance remembered the washer rumbling when he'd first gone into the house to get his shower. *A woman's work is never done.* How often he'd heard that, though he wasn't entirely sure he'd believed it.

Now he did—if her name was Ellie Pascoe O'Connor.

He hauled himself to his feet and went down the steps and across the yard to the basket. He stooped and picked up one of the damp long-sleeved boy's shirts, then fished a couple of clothespins out of the bag and began pegging the shirts to the line.

He was as awkward at hanging out laundry as the twins had been with the too-big fence rails. But eventually, and after only dropping a couple of shirts in the grass, he had a full line of them. Then he reached back down and came up with something very different from a little boy's shirt.

It was a pair of panties. *Ellie's* panties.

They were cotton and serviceable, but not entirely plain. There was nothing standard-issue white about them. They were a soft peach color, low-cut and with just a thin edge of lace where they would touch Ellie's legs.

Rance's mouth went dry. His body—especially one particular part—tensed. All his male hormones, which had been for months—nay, years—quite easily ignoring the clamor of a hundred Mrs. Rance Phillips wannabes, suddenly went on alert.

His fingers, still with the panties in their grip, closed into a fist.

"I got one!" Caleb called, and Rance's head jerked around to see the boy waving something—probably a hinge pin—in his hand. "Come on."

"Um." Rance tried to answer. His voice cracked. He felt his face burn. He cleared his throat quickly, ran his tongue over his lips and tried again. "Good. I'll be right there. I er...want to finish this."

This. Hanging out the rest of the clothes in the basket. Hanging out *Ellie's underwear.*

He took a deep steadying breath. *For God's sake, Phillips, it's not like you've never touched a woman's panties before!* Which was true. But it had been a damn long time. So long ago he couldn't even remember. And these weren't just any woman's panties.

They were Ellie's.

He fumbled them, his fingers more like thumbs as he hung the panties on the line. *It's no big deal!*

Of course it wasn't. But as he hung them up, he was not quite able to look at them—and not quite able to pull his gaze away. He reached down and picked up another pair. He hung them. His breathing grew shallow.

He remembered Ellie in panties.

He remembered her young, lithe, supple body wearing nothing else. He remembered running his hands over her body, then laying her on a bed and peeling her panties slowly down her very long legs, his gaze following the movement of his hands.

He remembered tossing the panties aside and settling himself between those legs, finding Ellie eager and moist, waiting for him.

His body remembered, too—very, very well. It responded to the memory almost as fiercely as it had always responded to Ellie.

"Rance! Aren'tcha comin'?" Caleb's childish voice jolted him.

He almost dropped one of her bras in the dirt. He bent to pick it up out of the basket again and found that straightening up was a little more difficult than it had been, his body slower to deny the memory than his mind. "Just a—" he cleared his throat "—just a couple more things. Almost finished."

He hung them up hastily, barely glancing at them. He didn't need to. The feel of her lacy underthings was enough to create havoc in his mind—and in his loins.

Why the hell couldn't she wear plain dingy boxer shorts or something?

He got the last bra hung—a flimsy pale blue affair that reminded him of what it had been like to cup her breasts in his hands. He felt a hungry shudder run through his body and gave himself a shake, like a dog coming out of an icy river. Then he turned and gave Caleb a wave. "All done."

He was. All done.

His concentration was shot. He fixed the hinge pin on the barn door, but not without whacking his thumb, too.

"Have you done this sort of thing before?" Caleb asked him, his estimation of Rance clearly dropping.

Rance didn't answer that.

He oiled the other hinge pins. Then the three of them mucked out the barn.

They were just finishing when Ellie's truck came around the bend and down the hill. The twins ran to meet it. Rance stayed beside the barn, watching as the doors to the truck opened and Josh, Ellie and the little girl—what was her name?—got out.

There was a faint hint of color in Josh's cheeks now, and he had a bright white plaster cast on his lower arm. Rance was glad he was looking better, but once he'd ascertained that much, he barely noticed the kids at all.

His attention was on Ellie. She waited for her daughter to clamber out of the truck, then slammed the door and grabbed two bags out of the back. Then she turned and moved purposefully toward Rance.

He watched her walk, watched those long lovely legs moving toward him and remembered the panties. He took her jeans off with his eyes, saw in his mind her slender tanned limbs, remembered them tangling with his, opening for him. He sucked in a quick sharp breath.

She stopped in front of him. "Here's your tomato juice."

He looked at her blankly.

"Tomato juice," Ellie said impatiently. She thrust a paper sack at him. "And your boots."

"Oh. Er...right." Rance grabbed for them both as if they were a lifeline. He blinked fiercely, restoring her jeans, dragging his eyes upward to meet her gaze.

No help there. He'd always been a sucker for Ellie's eyes. He cleared his throat. "H-how's...Josh?"

"Surviving. I'm sure he'll be able to dine off the story for the rest of his life. It was a simple fracture." She smiled her relief. "Six weeks in a cast." Then her smile faded and she looked worried once more.

Rance could almost read her thoughts. He knew her first concern had been her son. But now that Josh was doing all right, she had other things to worry about.

Like the ranch. The cattle. They were still at the end of calving season. That alone would take all her time. And how was she going to get the branding done without her ten-year-old top hand?

"Mom!" Caleb shouted. "Didja see the steps? We fixed the steps!" He ran over and jumped up and down on the no-longer-rickety steps.

"Great," Ellie said, shoving a hand through her hair distractedly. "That's great."

"An' Rance fixed the hinge an' we mucked out the barn!" Daniel added.

"Wonderful." She was smiling at her sons, but it didn't reach her eyes.

"It's not enough, is it?" Rance asked her quietly.

She jerked, startled, and turned back to him. "What?"

"The stuff we did. It's great. It's wonderful…but it isn't enough."

She stiffened. "What's that supposed to mean?"

"Just that you have too much to do."

Her jaw jutted. "We're fine. I'm doing the best I can."

"I know. But it isn't going to be enough. And now you're going to be shorthanded."

"A little," she allowed. She wasn't giving him much.

"Reckon you could do with some help."

She shook her head. "We'll manage. We always have."

"A smart manager doesn't turn down the offer of help."

Ellie looked at him out of the corner of her eye. "Who's offering?"

"I am."

Her brows lifted. "Going to send me one of your hands?"

"Nope."

She cocked her head. "Nope?" she echoed warily.

"I reckoned I could stick around."

Three

No. Oh, no.

Ellie gave her head a little shake. She couldn't have heard right. She had just spent the entire afternoon assuring herself that today's visit was a fluke, that by dinnertime Rance Phillips would be out of her life again, and now he was suggesting that he stay around?

Her stomach squeezed in apprehension. She ran her tongue over suddenly dry lips. "Why?" she asked, but it was more of a croak.

He looked surprised.

His gaze left hers and traveled in a slow, clear arc around the ranch. It took in the barn door he'd fixed, the fence he'd helped the boys mend, the porch steps that no longer wobbled beneath their feet. And then it moved on to peruse the torn window screen, the peeling paint, the depleted woodpile, the young, barely broke horses she'd bought last fall. And at last it went to the pasture where she had hoped to do the branding in a week or so.

"Why?" Rance repeated her question almost conversationally, as if he knew she would argue with him if he spelled it out for her. Then he shrugged and nodded. "Well, maybe you don't need any help. After all, Daniel and Caleb are big and strong and can do anything they set their minds to. And of course, Josh can put in a full day. You've got a hired hand, I hear, too. Someone called...Grandma?"

"My mother-in-law," Ellie agreed through her teeth.

Rance gave her a sardonic smile. "Right. Top hand, is she?" The implication was clear: Rance thought having her mother-in-law as her hired hand was like having the singing nun as her line boss.

"My mother-in-law is not in her dotage," Ellie said sharply. "She can do anything I can do, better. She rides cutting horses when she's not helping me. And when she is helping me, we do fine!"

Rance held up his hands in surrender. "I'm sure you do," he said in a smooth, conciliatory manner that somehow seemed to Ellie to hide a knife edge underneath.

"Did you get your law degree?" she demanded suspiciously.

He looked momentarily taken aback. "Yeah, I did, actually."

"I thought so." The Rance she had known had been bright and quick and clever. He'd also been a smooth talker. A natural lawyer, she'd always thought, and had said so more than once. Rance had always refused to even consider it, because that was what his father had wanted him to become. Apparently he'd changed his mind—or his father had changed it for him.

"Yale?" she asked, remembering that his father had gone there.

"Harvard." The wanna-make-something-of-it Phillips jaw jutted.

She almost smiled. But she was afraid to.

In her entire life, she'd never been more susceptible to any man than she'd been to Rance Phillips. After he'd gone off to Ireland and she'd gone home that summer, she'd assured herself her responsiveness to him had been the result of youth, foolishness and having her head turned by buckets of masculine charm and a devilishly handsome, rugged face. It wouldn't happen again, she'd told herself.

She knew now she'd been wrong.

The very sight of him this afternoon had, of course, set off warning bells in her brain. But it had set off some odd hormonal resonance deep within her, as well. It was foolish, it was pointless. It was downright dangerous, this attraction she felt for Rance Phillips. But it was there, nonetheless.

And if he *had* happened upon her again merely by accident, which she was beginning to believe was the case, *why* was he offering to stick around? He obviously had a career these days. He wasn't some down-on-his-luck rodeo cowboy recovering from a broken arm and trying to put his life together, as well.

"Harvard, hmm?" she ventured after a moment. "And you passed, presumably."

He looked offended. "Of course I passed."

"Then why does a Harvard-educated lawyer want to 'stick around' here?"

He shifted from one foot to the other. He glanced in her direction, then away again. Ellie, watching this display of foot shuffling, cocked her head. "What's in it for you?" she asked him.

He kicked at a tuft of grass. He rocked back and forth on the heels of Spike's boots. He sighed. "It'd help me out, too."

What was that supposed to mean? She waited for an explanation.

It wasn't quick in coming. Rance looked out across the valley, then down at the ground. He shifted his weight from one boot to the other, and then, when she thought he was never going to speak again, he did. But he said the most ridiculous thing.

"I don't suppose you ever read *Prominence Magazine?*"

Had he lost his mind? Why on earth would she, a penny-pinching widow of a small-time Montana rancher, ever even look at a magazine aimed at the idle rich? And if she ever had—which she hadn't—so what? What did *Prominence Magazine* have to do with her tiny, rundown Montana ranch?

More to the point, what did it have to do with Rance Phillips?

She might not have seen him in eleven years, but she knew how little value he'd put on fame and fortune. He'd always rejected it the same way he'd rejected his father's dynastic impulses. She couldn't imagine he coveted it now.

"No I don't read *Prominence Magazine,*" she said finally, when it didn't look as if he was going to explain until she answered.

"Didn't think so," he muttered.

Was that a line of color along his cheekbones? Ellie leaned slightly closer for a better look. "Do you?" she asked after a moment's silence, "Read *Prominence Magazine?*"

"No, I damn well do not!"

His vehemence had her taking a quick step back. "Well, you're the one who brought it up."

He rubbed the back of his neck. "Damn fool thing," he said irritably, more to himself than to her, his gaze still fixed on the dirt. "They got no business pokin' their noses in and messin' up people's lives. The articles are stupid, anyway!"

Ellie cocked her head, totally mystified now. And curious. Ver-r-ry curious. That *was* a hectic flush of color on his tanned cheeks. Rance Phillips was *blushing!*

She rose right up on her toes, as if being taller would get him to answer her quicker. Except it didn't look like he was going to answer her at all!

"What articles?"

Rance heaved a sigh, then jammed his fists into the pockets of his jeans. He hunched his shoulders. "The ones they've been doin' about bachelors." He turned away from her and stared out toward the pasture.

It was like pulling teeth. She practically had to yank the words out of him. *"What about bachelors?"*

Rance turned, his lips pressed into a thin line. "The world's most eligible." The words came out in a barely intelligible mutter.

Ellie's eyes widened. She looked at Rance, scowling furiously at her, and she couldn't help it—the relief was too great—a laugh exploded from her. "The world's most eligible— *You?"*

"Me!" He spat the word. "Yeah, isn't it funny? In fact it's damn hysterical—unless you happen to be one of the chosen! Then your life's not your own anymore!" His scowl was fierce. He kicked at the dirt.

Ellie didn't say anything. She was still trying to swallow the giggles that kept bubbling up, but she couldn't. He was right, she was getting hysterical, but more from relief than from hearing about his predicament—though she certainly wasn't going to tell him that!

"It's a pain in the ass," he went on, apparently determined to make her understand. "People follow me around everywhere I go. They pop up at the office. They bake me pies. They call me up, send me notes, write me letters."

"People? You mean...women?" Ellie considered that. She considered the popping up, the pies, the calls, the notes, the letters. "They *propose* to you?"

He pulled off his hat and ran his hand through his hair. "Not all of 'em," he corrected gruffly. "Enough," he added honestly after a moment.

"Heavens," Ellie said faintly.

"Hell more like." Rance grimaced, then rubbed a hand over his face and said with flat certainty, "And it's got to stop. That's why I reckoned I could stick around. You could get some help. I could get some...space."

"And all the eager women will forget you?"

"I hope." He slanted her a glance. "So, what do you say?"

She wanted to say no. She definitely should say no. Having Rance around was not a good idea for a whole lot of reasons.

Unfortunately there were other reasons that recommended it. All the reasons he'd given her. The place was getting beyond her, there was no doubt about it. No matter how hard she and Sandra, her mother-in-law, worked, they couldn't seem to keep up. And she *needed* to keep up.

Cleve Hardesty had made it clear that he was ready to step in whenever she'd had enough—and the bank would get their money a lot quicker from him. They'd been tolerant and patient with her so far. After Spike had died, Jim Riker, the loan officer, had made a point of telling her that they didn't expect miracles, that if she needed to renegotiate or stretch things out, they'd understand.

But that had been before Hardesty had come to town. *And* before either she or the bank had any idea how hard it would be for one woman to keep things going. She'd coped. The first year had been tough, but together they'd managed. This year when she'd hoped things would be better, they'd actually been worse. The weather had been harsher. They'd had to feed longer. She'd had less time to spend checking fences, and more breaks had occurred. The little things—the barn door, the steps, the window screens—hadn't mattered. She'd had to let them go.

But there was no way she could let the calving go. She'd been strung out over that, checking and rechecking, worrying—occasionally helping a first-time mamma cow—for the past six weeks.

And now spring branding was just around the corner. They had to round up the cattle, sort them and get the calves branded—and they had to do it soon.

But they wouldn't be able to do it without Josh.

And the reason she was doing it at all was for Josh.

She loved the ranch, but she could live without it. The twins and Carrie could live without it.

Josh could not.

It was his legacy from Spike, the love they shared. Ellie could close her eyes now and see the two of them together—in the barn, on horseback, pitching hay, feeding cattle.

There had been no one closer to Josh than Spike. No one closer to Spike than Josh. Since the time he'd been able to ride alone, Josh had been Spike's right-hand man.

"The foreman," Spike had always called their sober, intense, responsible eldest child. And, "My partner," he'd called the boy, too, every day when he looped his arm over Josh's thin shoulders as they went out to do chores.

More than any of their other children, Josh had worshiped Spike. As soon as he'd walked, Josh had followed Spike everywhere. "Me come, too, Daddy," had been his first sentence. When Josh was two, Spike had put him on his own horse. They'd been inseparable after that.

"He's got ranchin' in his blood, I reckon," Spike had said.

"It's in the other kids', too," Ellie always replied. But while all of them liked the ranch, none of them loved it the way Josh did.

It was for Josh that Ellie was trying so desperately to hang on.

Now, though, without his help, she couldn't—unless she said yes to Rance Phillips's question.

It sounded so simple. It promised disaster; Ellie knew it. It was like giving the devil a toehold to save your shirt, then discovering that your shirt wasn't worth much once you'd ended up losing your soul.

Would she lose her soul to Rance?

Or worse?

It was a risk.

There were other risks, too. Bigger risks.

But, she reminded herself, life was a risk. Getting out of bed in the morning was a risk. And how big a risk could it actually be?

She might feel a certain hormonal awareness where Rance was concerned, but she was a big girl now. She knew better than to give her heart away again.

And hadn't he just said he wasn't interested in entanglements? He might be one of the world's most eligible bachelors, but clearly he wanted to stay that way.

So the risk wasn't that great after all. Nothing had changed.

Not really.

If she said yes, they would both have what they wanted. She would get the work completed that so desperately needed being done. And he would get his "space."

And Josh—Josh's inheritance would be safe—at least for a while.

Ellie figured Rance owed him that.

If the daydreams he'd had while hanging out Ellie's underwear had, in small measure, fueled his offer to stick around, any chance that reality would include her welcoming him into her bed was highly overestimated.

She made him sleep in the barn.

"The barn?" He stared at her.

"It's not that uncomfortable," she said. "All those nice straw bales. And I've got a couple of wool blankets in the house," she added.

"I've got my own sleeping bag," Rance told her through his teeth.

"Well, then—" she gave him a little shrug and a blithe smile "—I'm sure you'll be fine."

Fine? He kicked at the straw now, hours later, and scowled in the direction of the house where Ellie and her brood had gone to bed. Then he spread out the blankets she'd pressed on him and lay his sleeping bag on top of them. "Home, sweet home," he muttered and slid in.

Was he nuts? It wasn't the first time he'd wondered. And the answer was the same as last time: he didn't know.

Maybe. He wasn't sure.

It seemed somehow serendipitous to end up at Ellie's today—though he wouldn't have thought he'd have kind thoughts about a skunk.

Still, this felt like the same sort of turning point that the end of his rodeo career had—and *that* had begun with a broken arm.

Ellie had been there that time, too, listening, caring, loving. She'd given him faith in himself and in the future.

She'd given him love—and courage to pursue his own life and follow his own dreams.

And if she hadn't been there when he'd come back from Ireland, well, he supposed he couldn't really blame her. He'd been hurt, angry even. But he'd never actually promised her anything.

He'd never ever said, "Wait for me."

In fact every time she'd mentioned marriage—even in the abstract—he'd brushed her off. Marriage hadn't seemed like a dream then. It had seemed like the chain that would anchor him to the Phillips legacy before he had the chance to become a man himself.

He hadn't wanted to get married then—or maybe ever—and he'd never pretended otherwise. He'd been honest with her.

And so had she, he realized, when she hadn't come back. She'd told him by her actions what her priorities were: she'd married the guy whose boots he'd worn today.

They'd been too big.

Rance hadn't said so. Never would. He had no intention of trying to fill Spike O'Connor's boots—literally or otherwise.

He was just here for a week or two. To help with the calving and the branding. To give her some space and get the breathing room he needed, as well.

And to let his old man know that magazine articles and busloads of women were not the means to getting his way. There were no means by which Trey Phillips could get what he wanted—not unless, like his law degree, it was something Rance decided he wanted himself.

He didn't know if he wanted a bride.

He only knew he wanted to be here on Ellie's place for a while.

For himself. For Ellie.

She needed him.

He couldn't ever remember being needed in his life.

Rance Phillips was in her barn.

Ellie said the words over and over to herself, as if repetition might make her finally believe them. But even those times she thought she actually did believe them, she wasn't sure she wanted to.

She turned out the light in the kitchen and took one last, long look at the barn silhouetted in the moonlight. Through gaps in the old wooden siding she could see slivers of light spilling through.

Rance Phillips was in her barn. Rance Phillips was in her barn.

It would take some getting used to.

Not that it was going to last! Of course it wasn't. Who knew, after one night on the straw he might be gone before breakfast. But if he stayed—*if* he stayed—it could make a tremendous difference.

Rance was strong and capable, and he gave every indication of meaning what he said about lending a hand. Earlier that evening during supper he'd quizzed both her and Josh about the lay of the land, the size of the herd, the whereabouts of the cattle. He'd wanted a notion of how many more calves had yet to be born and where their mothers were. He nodded, made a few notes, asked to see what records she had and had studied them wordlessly while she watched and felt like a child waiting for the teacher to read her homework.

After supper, when the children were doing their own homework, he'd gone back outside, and she'd seen him in the pasture looking over the new horses. Daniel and

Josh had wanted to go, too, but she'd said no. She didn't want them to get in the habit of following him around.

She couldn't tell what he thought when he came back. She'd wanted to jump in and defend her purchases, tell him that she'd got the best she could get for what she could afford, but she didn't want to sound as close to the edge as she knew she might. So she'd kept her mouth shut, only saying "Thank you," when he chopped firewood before he came in.

"No problem," he said easily, and then he smiled at her.

Ellie didn't want him to smile!

She wanted him to doctor cattle, deliver calves, break horses, cut firewood, mend fences and then go back to where he came from, leaving her life—and her heart—intact.

She turned away from the barn now and went up the steps to check on the kids before she went to bed herself.

There were two bedrooms in the attic. The house itself had been built by Spike's grandparents in the twenties. Then the children had slept in the big attic room. Spike, an only child, had had the entire upstairs to himself. Josh, Caleb and Daniel had shared the one big room until Carrie had been born. Then Spike had divided it, giving the boys the bigger portion and making a small bedroom at the back for his only daughter.

"I can always move the wall if she has a sister," he'd told Ellie with a grin.

But she hadn't. Carrie had been only two and a half when Spike died. Other people said she was a little Ellie, but to Ellie herself, Carrie was the one, of all the children, who looked the most like him.

She stepped into the small room and looked down at

their daughter now. She was sprawled on her back, one arm flung above her head, the other wrapped around Clarissa, her bear.

When she was small, Carrie had gone to sleep sucking on Clarissa's ear, and before long the bear had looked much the worse for wear. And then the day Spike had come home from the Denver Stock Show, he'd brought all the kids new cowboy hats, including a small bear-sized one for Clarissa.

"So her ears don't get cold," he'd told his daughter, giving both her and the bear a hug.

Clarissa wore the hat now. It was getting a little shabby looking, too. And so was the cowgirl outfit that Ellie had made for Clarissa a year ago last Christmas. If she had time, she'd make Carrie some more clothes for Clarissa for her birthday. That was less than three weeks away, and she hadn't had time to even catch her breath, let alone sit down and sew.

"Maybe now," she whispered, bending to kiss the little girl and the bear. Maybe she could get some sewing done, she thought as she went quietly along to the boys' room, now that Rance was here.

While they'd been doing their homework, the twins couldn't say enough about him.

"He fixed the steps, Mom," Caleb had told her eagerly. "He let me measure!"

Daniel had said, "He let me take care of Sunny. He didn't even come check and see if I knew what I was doin'."

Ellie thought that Rance's awareness of his own lingering odor of skunk could have had more to do with that than any innate confidence in Daniel's ability to deal with animals, but she didn't argue. "That's nice."

"He's pretty cool," both boys had reported.

"I'm glad you like him." But in her heart she'd thought, *Don't get too fond of him. He won't be around that long.*

Now she tiptoed into their room and stood looking down at them, Daniel in a single bed, Caleb in the bunk below Josh's. With their straight fair hair and scattering of freckles, everyone said Caleb and Daniel were their mother's sons.

It was true that they looked like Ellie. In fact they were temperamentally much more like Spike—generous, loving and fun to have around. Caleb was logical and matter-of-fact; Daniel, gentle and compassionate. But in that, too, they were like their father. Two sides of Spike O'Connor. Two halves of one whole.

She bent and kissed them both, then straightened to find Josh raised up on one elbow, looking at her from the top bunk.

"I didn't realize you were still awake," she said in a whisper. "Does your arm hurt? I can get you another pain pill."

Josh shook his head. "It's okay." He plucked at the blanket for a moment, then said, "Is he really stayin'?"

She knew who he meant. Ellie wet her lips, then mustered up a smile. "Looks like," she said cheerfully. "I saw a light in the barn just before I came upstairs."

"Is that okay?"

"Of course it's okay." She worked a little bit more on the smile.

Josh made a face. "It'd be better if we could do it ourselves. It's my fault—"

"It is *not* your fault. You were helping when it happened." She looked at him, hoping to see some sign of agreement, but he didn't respond. "It wasn't your dad's fault when his horse bolted, was it?"

He sat straight up and glared at her. "Of course not!"

She put a hand on his arm. "Of course not," she repeated quietly. "And it's not yours, either. Life isn't everything we'd like it to be. But we'll manage, Josh. I promise we will. We'll just have Rance's help for a while."

For a long moment they looked at each other. Mother and son. She so desperate to make him believe, and he so earnest and so very, very young. She wanted, more than she could say, to give him back the hopes and dreams he'd lost when Spike died.

Josh had always been intense, always been serious. But he used to play with Spike. He used to play with his brothers.

Now all he did was work—and worry.

There would be time enough for worry when he grew up, she wanted to tell him. There would be things enough to worry about then. Someday, she thought, she wanted to give him the ranch, and he could spend the rest of his life worrying about it. But right now she just wanted to give him his childhood back.

Slowly Josh lay back and stared at the ceiling. She heard him swallow. She heard him sigh. Then, "Hope he's a hard worker."

Ellie knew who he meant. She squeezed Josh's hand lightly. "I'm sure he will be. He always was."

"When did you know him?"

"In college. Briefly," she added. "The last semester I was there. He was new. He'd been hurt—broke his arm at a rodeo and couldn't ride anymore. We had a class together."

"Broke his arm? Like me?"

"Worse. He was in the hospital."

"Oh." There was a long pause while Josh considered that. Then he said, "But he worked hard in your class?"

"Yes. And he had three other jobs just so he could stay in school." And so he didn't have to ask his father for help. She didn't add that, though.

Josh chewed on his lip. "He must have been pretty busy."

"He was."

"So you...didn't spend a lot of time with him?"

Ellie wondered where this was going. "Enough to know he worked hard," she said, trying to reassure him.

"Mmm." Josh lay back in the near darkness and stared at the ceiling again. "Just one semester, though?"

Ellie frowned. "That's right. Why?"

"He stared at you a lot."

Ellie was startled. "Stared at me?" She rose up on her toes, trying to see Josh's face. But he wasn't looking at her now, and she could only glimpse his profile.

"While you were cooking dinner," Josh said flatly. "While we were eating. When he was askin' about the cattle. He looked at you," he repeated, and there was emotion in his voice now. It sounded like an accusation.

He raised his head again, and his eyes fastened on her. "Did he like you, Ma?" Even in the dimness of the room she could see the intensity of his gaze. The concern. The worry.

"Of course he liked me! What's not to like?" She managed a grin and a huffy tone.

"Nothin'," Josh said quickly. "Nothin'. I just... wondered." He twisted the blanket in his good hand. His gaze probed hers. And Ellie tried to meet it steadily.

Finally Josh's eyes slid away. He took a deep breath and let it out slowly. Then he said, almost speculatively,

"But even if he did, I guess you couldn't have liked him all that much, huh?"

"What do you mean?"

"Because," Josh said—and his body relaxed back against the mattress again "—it was your last semester there." He smiled slightly. "You didn't stay. You came home and married Dad."

Four

The smell of coffee woke her.

Ellie sat bolt upright in bed, panicked. Coffee? Ohmigod, was it that late? Coffee meant that Sandra was already here—and that she'd overslept!

She scrambled out of bed and, not even stopping for her robe or slippers, she shot down the hall and into the kitchen. It was still dark, inside and outside. Only the light over the stove was on.

It lit Rance's surprised face.

For just a second he didn't say anything, just looked at her—at her, with her sleep-tangled hair and bare feet. At her, boobs bobbing beneath Spike's old Seattle Mariners T-shirt.

He cleared his throat. "Coffee?"

"N-no!" She wrapped her arms across her breasts and backed hastily toward the dark hallway, grateful at least that she was in shadows still. "I—I thought you were S-Sandra. My mother-in-law. I thought I'd overslept."

"It's just past five. But I wanted to get started. Hope you don't mind about the coffee...."

"Of course not! I should have thought. I'd have set the alarm earlier and got up to make you some. I usually go out and feed the horses before the kids get up, then I come in and make breakfast. But let me get dressed now and I'll fix you some."

"Not necessary," Rance said. "Just put me together a

lunch and dump the rest of this in a Thermos. I'll stop
back by and pick it up. I'll feed the horses.'' He started
toward the door, then turned back. "Tell Daniel I gave
that calf a bottle already.'' He opened the door and
headed out.

Oh dear, she'd forgotten about that. One of last week's
calves had been orphaned. Daniel had been keeping it in
the barn. Rance had had a roommate all night!

"Rance!"

He turned. It was too dark to see the blue intensity of
his gaze, but she could feel it touch her, anyway.

She hugged her arms against her tighter than ever.
"Did the calf...keep you up?''

A corner of his mouth lifted wryly. "I've had worse
roommates.''

"Thank you. Daniel thanks you. I—I'll fix you breakfast tomorrow.''

Another smile touched his lips. He dipped his head in
agreement. "I'd like that.''

And then he was gone.

And Ellie was left berating herself for being a fool
because somehow it felt as if she'd just made a date with
him.

She made another pot of coffee, pouring herself a cup
from the pot that Rance had made, then carried it with
her to the bathroom where she turned on the shower.

A morning shower was a luxury Ellie could rarely afford the time for. But today she indulged—and scrubbed
herself thoroughly every time she caught her thoughts
drifting to whatever Rance might be doing at the moment.

She didn't think about grizzled, graying Wattie, did
she? The old cowboy who sometimes came to help out
last winter had never figured in her daydreams when she
was showering or at any other time for that matter.

"Rance is just the same as Wattie," she told herself, toweling off with just the same furious energy as when she'd washed. She wished Rance hadn't been so successful with his tomato juice rinse. She could have used an olfactory reminder to stay well away from him.

Well, just remember it anyway, she told herself sharply. Then she got dressed, braided her hair and went to wake the kids.

"Is he still here?" Josh asked the moment his eyes opened.

"Already at work," Ellie assured him. "He was up and making coffee in the kitchen before I woke up."

Josh smiled. It wasn't much of a smile, but it was the first Ellie remembered seeing from him in ages.

She smiled back. "Arm okay?"

"Hurts a little. I could stay home," he said hopefully. "Help out?"

"Not on your life, bud," she told him. "Come on. Get up and get dressed. Tell Daniel that Rance fed the calf. I'll have breakfast ready by the time you come downstairs."

She heard Sandra's truck pull up while she was stirring the oatmeal. A quick glance out the window told her that her mother-in-law was taking a look at Rance's truck on her way to the house. Rance himself had come in and picked up his lunch and Thermos ten minutes ago.

"Took a look at one of those cows out yonder," he told her. "Reckon she'll be a mamma sometime this morning if all goes well. I'll just go keep an eye on her."

Ellie was glad he wasn't sitting in the kitchen when Sandra came in.

Of course they'd meet sooner or later. But somehow Ellie thought it would better in the clear light of day. She poured Sandra a cup of coffee and had it ready when the door opened. It was a morning ritual of sorts.

Sandra lived half a mile up the valley in the house she and Spike's father, Tom, had built shortly before Daniel and Caleb were born. After Tom died four years ago, Spike had asked his mother if she wanted to move back.

"Never," Sandra had said firmly. "I love my house. I love my independence. But," she'd added with a smile, "I'll always be happy to come for a cup of coffee."

In fact in the last two years, she had been coming for much more than the coffee. Without Sandra's unstinting help, Ellie would have had to sell out the year Spike died. Together, with Wattie's occasional help, they had coped.

Now Sandra accepted the cup with a smile and a glance behind her through the window to where Rance's truck was parked by hers. Her brows lifted.

"Wattie's replacement," Ellie said as blithely as she could. She put four pieces of toast into the toaster.

"Pretty nice truck for an old geezer like Wattie."

"Well, he's not like Wattie in that respect," Ellie said. "He's…younger. A little more…successful. He's a friend I went to college with."

"He scared a skunk!" Daniel informed her, bouncing down the stairs two at a time and hurtling into the kitchen.

"An' the skunk spooked Sunny!" Caleb added, coming after him.

"An' I broke my arm," Josh said, bringing up the rear.

Sandra's wide-eyed interest turned to consternation. "Oh, Josh!"

"It's not a bad break, Gran'ma. The doc said not. But Ma won't let me herd now." He made a disgruntled face. "So he's gonna do it." He looked out the door toward Rance's truck.

Sandra looked at Josh's cast, told him how brave he'd been. But then she turned her attention back to Ellie. "This man just...offered to come work for you?"

"He wasn't busy at the moment." Ellie dished up the bowls of oatmeal, put raisins on Josh's and Daniel's, and set Caleb's and Carrie's out plain. She didn't look at Sandra. "And," she added airily, "I'm doing him sort of a favor, too."

"A favor? To let him work here?"

"He was looking for a...change of pace. He used to cowboy and he wanted to do it again. Just for a while." Did she actually think Sandra was going to believe this the moment she saw Rance?

Caleb got out the milk and Daniel the sugar. Ellie set the bowls on the table and motioned for the kids to start eating. She carried the empty oatmeal pot to the sink and turned the water on. She could feel her mother-in-law's eyes on her all the while. Assessing. Speculating.

There hadn't been a man here—other than Wattie— since Spike died.

"He slept in the barn," she blurted.

Sandra's brows shot up. "The barn?"

Ellie colored furiously. "Well, we hardly have room in here!" And she didn't want Sandra thinking even for a moment that she'd taken Rance into her bed.

"He must have wanted a change of pace," Sandra said with just a touch of irony. "Unless he's used to that sort of accommodation?"

"No." Ellie started scrubbing the pot.

"Well," Sandra said briskly into the silence, "it certainly was...handy of him to agree to step in." There was a certain amount of speculation in her voice, which Ellie had no intention of addressing.

"It is, actually." She finished the pot, took the toast

out of the toaster and put four more pieces in, then passed out one to each of the boys and put the last on a plate for her mother-in-law. "I don't know how we'd have coped without Josh."

"How long is he staying? Your friend?"

"Oh, not long. Not long at all. Do you want jam on that?"

"No, thank you," Sandra said, regarding the plate in her hand with some surprise. "I ate at home. I always do, you know."

"Er, of course. Sorry. I forgot." Or maybe it was simply Freudian, giving Sandra the toast. A sort of unconscious effort to keep her mouth full and thus unable to ask questions. Ellie gave her mother-in-law a quick, apologetic smile, but she didn't take the toast back. Instead she reached for the rest and gave them to the boys. "Eat up," she commanded, then went to the bottom of the stairs and shouted, "Carrie? Where are you? Breakfast is ready!"

Small feet came pattering down, and Carrie appeared, dragging Clarissa by one leg. "I was tyin' my shoes." Carrie looked down sadly at the scrambled mess of laces. "But they gots knots in 'em."

"They certainly do," Ellie said. "In fact we might want tweezers to get them out." She took her daughter's hand and headed toward the bathroom. And as they went, she said a small prayer of thanksgiving for Carrie's inability to tie her shoes.

They had been trying to teach her for months. But Carrie was left-handed and the rest of them were not. Usually it was a source of impatience.

But, unless Carrie mastered the feat in the next ten minutes, today's lesson would keep Ellie busy—and out of the way of Sandra's curious questions—until it was time to take the boys to catch the bus.

His back was killing him. His arm ached. He didn't like the taste of his own coffee. And before the day was out, his butt was going to be sorry he'd spent so many hours in the saddle.

He'd never felt better in his life.

Or not in recent memory, anyway. Certainly not in the past four months. Probably not for years. Rance couldn't remember experiencing this same exhilaration since...well, since college if the truth was known.

Since the last time he'd seen Ellie in a T-shirt and nothing else.

You wouldn't think a widowed mother of four could look that damn good in a faded baseball shirt. But, she did. Oh yes, she did. Maybe it was the way the shirt stopped just above mid-thigh, making him wonder what—if anything—she had on underneath. Maybe it was the way the shirt's brevity accentuated her long legs, making him recall all too clearly a time in the distant past when they'd wrapped around him. Maybe it was the way the soft cotton masked, but not completely, the fullness of her breasts, making him want to slide his hands up under her shirt and cup them, nuzzle them, taste them.

Oh, God. He shifted in the saddle now, remembering, aching. Wanting. Her.

It was perverse, he supposed, wanting the one woman he'd met in the last four months who wasn't falling all over him, making herself available. Ellie seemed somewhere between shy and indifferent.

Or maybe that was *why* he wanted her. Because she was shy, not forward. Because she didn't pretend the sun rose and set on him—and his bank balance.

No, she wanted him because he could bring her cattle down, cut her firewood and mend her fences. Now there was a humbling thought. It made him smile wryly. It didn't make him stop thinking about her.

He'd been thinking about her all day.

Was he simply intrigued because he *didn't* have her? Was it the chase he was interested in? The thrill of pursuit?

God knew he hadn't pursued a woman for a good long time. It hadn't seemed worth the trouble.

It did now.

He wanted to go to bed with Ellie in the worst way. It had been a vague hunger since yesterday's encounter with her underwear. It had teased the edges of his unconscious while he tossed and turned on the straw last night.

But it had taken hard and urgent shape this morning when she'd appeared in the kitchen, sleepy-eyed and rumpled, then fled in embarrassment at the desire in his gaze.

At least now he knew she was aware of him as a man. Yesterday he hadn't been quite sure.

Now, though, he had another problem. What was he going to do about it?

They weren't unencumbered college kids anymore. And if he was still footloose when it came to relationships, she most definitely was not. Five other people had definite claims on her time.

And if his hormones clamored for him to focus on pursuing the awareness that still existed between them, real life, he'd discovered this morning, had other ideas.

He'd come back in to pick up the lunch he'd asked for—hoping at the same time for another few moments' worth of heated looks, even if Ellie was dressed this time.

But she'd been making oatmeal and packing lunches for the kids, and she'd hardly turned around when he came in.

"It's there on the table," she'd said over her shoulder. "Four sandwiches, an apple, some cookies and your coffee. Is that enough?"

"Sure, fine," he'd said. *Turn around, Ellie. Smile at me.*

But she'd just said, "If you end up still hungry, let me know and tomorrow I'll fix more." Then she'd gone to the bottom of the steps leading to the attic and shouted, "Hurry up, you guys! Oatmeal's almost ready."

At the sound of boys clumping down the stairs, Rance had given up. "I'll just go check on that calf that's coming. Thanks, then," he'd said, and headed out the door.

He'd gone back to the barn for a heavy jacket, when a truck had pulled up and parked next to his and a woman in her fifties climbed out.

She was a little taller than Ellie, with graying dark hair and a slender, lithe figure. She was, he'd guessed, the grandmother. He understood what Ellie meant now about the woman not being in her dotage.

She'd looked at his truck curiously as she passed. He didn't come out of the barn. He figured he'd have plenty of time to meet her later. And somehow, right then, as aware as he still was of Ellie's attractiveness, he hadn't wanted to meet Ellie's husband's mother.

He felt rewarded a little bit later, just as he was about to set out, when the back door opened and, shrugging into her jacket, Ellie came out. His eager body propelled him out of the barn toward the truck to intercept her, to talk to her, to get a smile from her.

But he barely got three words when the back door banged again and all three boys came hurrying toward the truck. They had plenty to say, and the twins smiled and Josh said his arm was doing okay. And then Ellie had the truck warmed up and was chivying them to get in.

"I'll be back to help pretty quick," she told him, putting the truck in gear.

As they passed by him, Daniel had rolled down the window and hung out. "Thanks for feedin' Lilly Belle."

"Who? Oh, the calf? Sure. No problem."

Daniel grinned. "Really glad you came."

Rance wasn't so sure Ellie's mother-in-law was as thrilled.

He spent the morning alternating between checking on the mother cow and working with the new geldings Ellie had bought. And if he'd hoped, somewhere in the back of his mind, that Ellie might come to the corral and join him, well, it hadn't worked out quite like that.

He'd had company, all right. But when the roan gelding decided to take exception to his rider and pitch Rance to the dirt, it wasn't Ellie who sat across the corral on the fence rail and watched him stagger up.

"Anything broken?" his spectator called.

Rance slapped at his jeans with his hat. "Just my pride."

Ellie's mother-in-law smiled. "Well, that happens to all of us now and then. I'm Sandra O'Connor, by the way."

"Rance Phillips." He took one last swipe at the dirt on his clothes, then walked over to speak with her. She watched him come, and as she did so, her smile faded. So, Rance noted, did the color in her face.

"Something wrong?" he asked her, looking up at her.

Her knuckles were white on the rail, and as he watched, she loosed her grip and climbed down. "N-no.

Just…got a little light-headed for a moment.'' She took the hand he offered. ''It's nice to meet you,'' she said almost gravely.

''You, too, ma'am.''

''Ellie said you went to college with her?'' It wasn't exactly phrased like a question but Rance understood the intent.

He nodded. ''She got me through my first semester. She was in my English class. Read all my papers. Shaped 'em up,'' he went on, trying to make it sound as platonic as he could.

''Oh, yes. Ellie was always good with words.''

''She shoulda stayed in school,'' he said without thinking, then remembered she'd left to marry this woman's son. ''I mean, well…I'm sure she had better things to do.''

Sandra took pity on him. ''Ellie's always known what she wanted to do,'' she said. Then she continued talking easily about her daughter-in-law, and Rance, finding that he was starved to hear whatever he could about Ellie, hung on every word.

Sandra asked him questions, too, and before long he'd told her quite a lot about himself. Sandra, he decided later, would have had a great career before the bench. Subtle cross-examination seemed to be her forte. Before he even realized it, he was telling her the story of his life—about his rodeo career and its precipitous end, about his decision to go to school but to do it on his own terms. He told her about being a Phillips, about the pressures and demands that had come with being the only son of one of the most prominent, wealthiest, most determined men in the state. ''Being a Phillips is only slightly less demanding than being in line for the British crown,'' he complained. ''I belong to *them,* not to myself.''

He told her he wanted more than anything to be his own man.

He told her more than he'd ever told anyone, as if they were sharing confidences.

Sandra told him what a good mother Ellie was, what a good wife she'd been to Spike, how happy she and her husband had been to have her as their daughter-in-law.

"Yeah, I can see that," Rance said. And when he thought about all the things Sandra had said and the few things he had seen of this grown-up, adult Ellie, he had an inkling for the first time what his stubborn refusal to consider marriage had cost him.

Would they have married if he'd been willing? he wondered.

It was the food for thought he took with him while he went out on the mountain to check on the cattle that afternoon. He had plenty of time to think about it—plenty of time to think about *her*. His mind's eye played over Ellie in the T-shirt, Ellie in the kitchen surrounded by kids, Ellie looking into his eyes for just one shattering moment this morning.

What would it have been like to be married to Ellie?

Did he really care?

She hadn't.

She hadn't come back to school in the fall. She hadn't bothered to wait and see if he'd had a change of heart and mind. She'd found someone else she loved better.

She'd stayed home and married Sandra O'Connor's son.

The best defense is a good offense.

Spike had always said that about football, hockey, parent-teacher conferences and rounding up a balky steer.

On the theory that it also applied to intrafamilial relationships, Ellie breezed into the kitchen as Sandra was making dinner that evening and said, "So, what do you think of my new hired hand?"

She hadn't seen her mother-in-law all day. By design. She'd been trying to figure out her strategy on how to act regarding Rance.

He was the first man to stay over on the ranch—even if he had stayed in the barn. He was the first man of her generation to breach the pleasant but distant demeanor Ellie had shown to every male who'd crossed her path in the past two years. He was the first man Ellie thought Sandra might see as a possible replacement for Spike.

Even though Ellie knew Rance wasn't interested in marriage, Sandra didn't. She didn't want her mother-in-law jumping to conclusions. And she knew that protesting Rance's lack of interest was not going to accomplish that. There was such a thing as protesting too much.

No, the best tack, Ellie decided, was to be cheerful, up-front, straightforward. Honest.

More or less.

There was no doubt in her mind that Sandra had formed an opinion by now. When Ellie and Carrie had come back from a quick trip to town for baling wire this morning, she'd seen Sandra in conversation with Rance by the corral. It had been her first impulse to rush over and push them apart. Of course she couldn't do that, so rather than stand by, tongue-tied and desperate, she'd taken herself and Carrie off for the rest of the day, doctoring cattle, bringing in the few she found near Bryce Creek and then spending an inordinate amount of time with Daniel's Lilly Belle out in the barn.

But by suppertime she knew it was time to tackle Sandra. And better to do it when they could be alone.

So she settled Carrie in the sandbox with Clarissa for

company, hoped that Josh and Daniel and Caleb would stay outdoors until dinner was ready, then went indoors to face her mother-in-law.

"He's very nice." Sandra looked up from the potatoes she was mashing. "Well-spoken. Well-mannered. Bright." The adjectives were tossed out like accusations.

"Yes, he is," Ellie said, smiling brightly.

"With a Harvard law degree. And with a home of his own. I don't exactly think he needs a place to stay," Sandra added.

Ellie felt herself flushing. "Not a place to stay exactly," she agreed hastily. "He just said he...wanted to get away for a while."

"From the women."

Now it was Ellie whose brows shot up. "He *told* you?"

"Only in passing." Sandra smiled. "Smart of him, actually, to get out before he did something he'd regret."

"Like marry one of them?" Ellie asked.

Sandra laughed. "I was thinking more of shooting one of them. Or his father."

"He told you about his father, too?" It sounded like Rance had told Sandra his life story. Had he told her he and Ellie had been lovers, for heaven's sake?

"He didn't have to tell me much about his father," Sandra said. "Tom and I knew Trey Phillips from way back. Hard not to know one of the biggest ranchers in the state."

"I guess," Ellie mumbled. She turned away, got the plates from the cupboard and started putting plates out on the table.

"Wash your hands," Sandra said.

Chagrined, Ellie did. She didn't say anything else as she set the table. She couldn't think of anything to say.

It was actually better than she'd expected, she assured herself. Sandra liked him. She didn't seem to think Ellie was trying to replace Spike with someone else. Everyone was being very mellow. Maybe, Rance being who he was, Sandra had realized right away he wouldn't be interested in Ellie.

But just as she thought it, Sandra said, "Yes, I like your Rance Phillips," and set the mashed potato pot down with a thump.

It was on the tip of Ellie's tongue to say *he's not* my *Rance Phillips!* But she remembered about overreaction and protesting too much. Instead she smiled her agreement and said, "Mmm."

"Nice of him to help out. We can use a man's help."

"Yes, well, don't start depending on it," Ellie warned her quickly. "He's not going to be here long."

"No?" Sandra seemed surprised.

"Of course not. As you've just pointed out, he's certainly got a life beyond riding for our brand. This is just an interlude."

There was a pause as she let Sandra digest that. Then her mother-in-law asked, "Are you going to let him go?"

That brought Ellie up short. Her brows drew down. Her fingers tightened briefly around the spoons in her hands. "Of course I am."

Sandra just looked at her. Outside Ellie could hear Daniel and Caleb arguing and Carrie singing a hopscotch rhyme. Beyond that there was the steady thunk of an ax into wood.

"You're going to let him mend the fence, help with the branding, cut the wood and walk away?" Sandra asked, her voice carrying a tone of quiet challenge.

"Of course," Ellie said impatiently. "What else am I supposed to do?"

Their gazes met again for just a moment.

Then Sandra went over and started to make the gravy. She mixed the flour-and-water paste, then began to stir it into the beef drippings. She didn't look at Ellie. "I'd say you're going to have to tell him eventually," she said almost conversationally.

Time seemed to stop as Ellie stared at the worn red-and-white oilcloth on the table. *Tell him*... Sandra's words echoed in her ears. *Tell him*...

"Tell him?" she echoed faintly.

Sandra turned her head slowly. The gravy bubbled and steamed unattended as their eyes met once more.

Sandra's were warm and compassionate and caring, and she smiled with a mixture of resignation and infinite gentleness as she said quietly, "When a man has a son, Ellie, he has a right to know."

Five

Ellie gasped. "How did you—" She broke off and stared at her mother-in-law.

Sandra smiled slightly. "You've only got to look at him. At the two of them."

Ellie felt as if the ground had been cut from under her—as if she'd been holding back a flood for years, only to be swept away by a wave she hadn't even seen coming. "It's that easy? But—*he* never said! *He* doesn't know!"

He couldn't know! Surely if he did, he would have said.

"He just sees Josh, not himself," Sandra pointed out.

"But—" Ellie shook her head "—it's that...obvious?"

"Certainly it wouldn't be to everyone. People in general wouldn't probably notice. After all, Josh has Spike's coloring. The dark hair, the light eyes. For all anyone knows the rest of him must be from someone on your side. They aren't looking for anything else. You were married to Spike when Josh was born. Spike never told them differently. They have no reason to think he's not Spike's natural son."

"But *you* knew? I—I didn't know that you knew," she said faintly.

Of course Spike had always been close to his parents, and there was no reason he shouldn't have shared such knowledge with them. But if he had, he'd never told Ellie. And in almost eleven years, Sandra had never once intimated that she had any idea Josh was not her blood kin.

"Spike never said Josh wasn't his," Sandra said gently. She finished with the gravy and poured it into a bowl. "As far as he was concerned, Josh was every bit as much his son as Daniel and Caleb were. But he was living at home with us while you were in Bozeman at school. We knew—or thought we knew—what your relationship was.

"When the two of you came to us and said you were getting married, that you were pregnant, well, we thought it was possible that you'd slept with Spike and he'd gotten you pregnant, but it didn't seem likely."

Sandra regarded her daughter-in-law with gentle understanding. "We didn't think you'd sleep with a man if you weren't in love with him. Especially not Spike. He loved you too much for you to trifle with his feelings. At least that was the way we saw it. Spike was your friend."

Spike had always been Ellie's friend. He'd been her best friend and her greatest confidante—from the time she'd been five and he'd been six, and they'd shared a tent when they'd gone with their fathers to move cattle to the summer range.

From shared secrets to scuffles and wrestling matches, from how to rope a balky steer to how to get a boy to kiss you, no one had ever known Ellie like Spike had. And no one had known Spike like Ellie.

But sometime long ago she'd realized that Spike's love for her was different than her love for him.

"I...wouldn't," Ellie whispered now. "I didn't." She bent her head. I—" She stopped, couldn't say the words.

"Loved Rance," Sandra finished for her when Ellie's courage failed.

"Yes," Ellie admitted. She twisted her fingers together. "At the time, anyway." Then she lifted her gaze to meet Sandra's. "But he didn't love me."

"Don't be too sure," the older woman said promptly, startling her again.

Fiercely Ellie shook her head. "He didn't want me! He didn't want to get married. He certainly wouldn't have wanted the baby. He was completely antimarriage. Antikid. We were reading Coleridge—*The Rime of the Ancient Mariner*—when I found out I was pregnant. I was so scared. I didn't know what to do."

The panic she'd felt was so strong that even thinking about it now brought it right back to her.

"I hoped, if I told him, he'd think it was wonderful, that he'd tell me it was all right, that we'd get married and live happily ever after. So that night when we were studying, I brought up babies. I said something about having children someday, and he looked horrified. 'I don't want kids,' he told me. 'I'm trying to make my own life. Talk about albatrosses,' he said."

The memory of that night could still send a shudder through her eleven years later. Her dreams had died that night. There had been no room for question. No doubt about how he felt.

"I couldn't tell him then," she said. "He would have felt cornered, hemmed in, tied down. He would have 'done the right thing'—it's the way he is—but he didn't want marriage and, unlike Spike, he would have ended up hating me and Josh both!"

She stood quite still in the middle of the kitchen, remembering how terribly alone she'd felt in those days. Later that week Rance had met her at the library, ecstatic over an offer to go to Ireland for the summer and work for a horse trainer. He'd seen his world opening up again.

"The world *I* want to live in," he'd told her, supremely satisfied. "Not the world my old man has cut out for me."

Ellie couldn't cut out a world and force him into it, either. So she'd rejoiced with him as best she could. He'd taken her not-quite-wholly disguised sadness as an indication that she wished she was going along.

"I wish I could take you," he'd said. "God, we'd have a blast. Maybe we can." He'd warmed to the idea, his enthusiasm bubbling over. "Think of it, Ellie," he'd said, twirling her into his arms. "Ireland—all summer. You and me! What do you say? Want to come?"

And crying inside, Ellie had shaken her head and pulled away from him. "I've got to work, Rance. I can't play this summer. I have…responsibilities."

"Sometimes you sound like my old man," he'd grumbled.

Sometimes she'd felt like an old woman—panicky and fretting, certain that the world was spinning out of her control. She'd seen him off in May with a smile and a wave and the last bit of courage she could muster. She hadn't cried until she got back in her car. She was still crying three hours later when she got home.

Spike had been quick to notice. Spike always knew when something went wrong. "Tell me," he'd said, putting his arms around her, drawing her into a gentle embrace. "Tell me, El."

And she'd told him. She'd hiccupped and sniffled through the story, aware that she was destroying his image of her, but unable to pretend.

And when she had finished, Spike had said, "Do you

want him? I'll go get him for you if you really want him.''

And there had been no doubt in her mind that he would. Spike would have moved heaven and earth for her, and she knew it. Just telling him had made her feel better. And braver.

So brave she'd shaken her head. "I don't want him," she'd said. "I don't want a man who doesn't want children to be the father of my child."

"Would you settle for me instead?"

The words had been so unexpected that even today the very memory of them could send a shiver right down Ellie's spine. At first she hadn't believed them, had thought she'd dreamed them because marrying Spike would certainly be a far, far better ending to this than she deserved. She hadn't answered.

But then he asked her again. "Would you marry me, Ellie?"

And before she could do more than open her mouth, he went on, "I'd like to be a father to your child. I love you, El. I always have. You know that." There had been urgency in Spike's voice. He'd taken her hands and crushed them between his own work-roughened ones. "I do love you. And I'd love your child. Our child," he'd amended.

She'd told him he was crazy. She reminded him that he was not quite twenty-one years old. How could he know such a thing? How could he be willing to make a commitment like that?

"I love you, Ellie," he said again. "That's not going to change."

"I love Rance," she'd admitted, forcing herself to be honest, not wanting to hurt Spike then, but knowing that if he wasn't fully aware of her feelings, she'd end up hurting him more later.

She'd seen the flicker of pain on his face. But then he'd nodded. "I figured that much. But could you learn to love me?"

"I already do love you. Just not the same way."

"I'll settle for being loved in my own way." Spike rubbed his thumb along the edge of her hand. "I think we can make it, El, if you want to." He looked into her eyes, his light blue gaze so intent and pure that Ellie couldn't have said no to save her life.

In fact she thought that Spike's love had saved it for her.

He didn't see why they should tell anyone that their baby wasn't his. "It's nobody's business but ours," he'd said. "What good would it do?"

None. Ellie had certainly agreed with that. And Spike couldn't have been a more devoted father. He couldn't have been a better husband, either. They hadn't been married a year before Ellie knew she'd made the right choice.

The love she'd felt for Rance had been strong and intense and passionate. It had swamped her like a storm at sea. She'd had no defense against it. She'd had no defense against him. But it hadn't been the sort of love that would survive a screaming baby, 2:00 a.m. feedings, frosty morning calvings, dipping cattle prices and three more children in six years.

What would have sent Rance around the bend, Spike thrived on. And they were the things Ellie thrived on, too.

"Spike was the best husband any woman could have ever had," she told his mother now, tears brimming. "I loved him."

Sandra crossed the room and put her arms around Ellie. "I know that. *He* knew that." She gave Ellie a gentle squeeze.

"He loved Josh," Ellie said in a croaky little voice.

Sandra smiled. "He loved Josh more than anyone," she agreed. "Partly because Josh was so like him—and partly, I think, because without Josh he might never have gotten you."

And then the tears came. Ellie couldn't stop them. Blinked. Sniffled. Bit her lip furiously. All to no avail.

And Sandra held her. "Don't cry," Sandra said, patting her back. "Not for that. Cry because you miss him. Cry because he was a wonderful man and he didn't get his full three score and ten. But don't ever cry because you think you shortchanged him. You never did, Ellie. He loved you all. And you loved him." And now Sandra blinked back her own tears. "Spike had what he wanted. He was a happy man." She gave Ellie one last squeeze and stepped back to look deep into her eyes. "Happier than Rance."

Outside, Ellie heard footsteps on the porch. "Hey, Mom," Josh called. "Dinner almost ready?"

She cleared her throat hastily. "Almost," she called back. Her eyes were still locked with Sandra's.

"Tell him, Ellie," Sandra urged.

If she thought it would be better for any of them, she would, Ellie knew. But all she could see ahead was pain and resentment if she did. Rance was no more ready for the truth now than he had been eleven years ago. And Josh? She didn't even want to think what the knowledge would do to Josh.

"I can't," she said.

* * *

A part of Rance expected that he'd have his fill of cowboying in a few days' time.

There was nothing that enthralling about getting up before dawn, wrestling around in the mud delivering slimy calves from ungrateful mother cows, chopping firewood until your back spasmed and your arm was about to fall off and landing on your butt in the dirt three or four times a day while you broke a horse that seemed more likely to break you.

There was nothing inherently appealing about his mattress, either. Rance didn't think he'd ever get used to sleeping on straw.

But Ellie needed his help. And no women pestered him. And every day he had the pleasure of gorgeous scenery, plenty of daytime solitude and all the fresh mountain air he could breathe.

Still, when it became obvious that he wasn't likely to get near Ellie's bed, he thought that his desire to hang around would wane pretty quickly.

He was wrong.

He had always liked arguing a case, thinking up angles, making himself aware of all the reasons for and against something, applying himself. It was the challenge of his law career that he found most appealing.

He got to do the same thing here on a daily basis arguing with Josh.

They didn't talk about law, of course. They talked about ranching—about breeding and feeding and land use and weather. The kid knew more about running a ranch than a lot of grown men did. And after the first few days, he didn't hesitate to express his opinions whenever Rance tried to tell Ellie how he thought she should be doing something around the ranch.

At first Rance was taken aback. Most boys his age

were seen and not heard. But Josh was determined to have his say, especially if it was something Spike had felt strongly about. The kid must have committed to memory every theory Spike O'Connor had ever expressed.

Rance found himself making outrageous statements just to get Josh riled and ready to debate. Now he looked forward to their almost daily verbal encounters.

"Do you always have to argue?" Ellie asked him more than once.

"We're not arguing, we're discussing," Rance always told her. "The kid is sharp," he added when Josh wasn't around. "And stubborn."

But sometimes it was a little annoying to have everything he said contradicted by Josh's "Well, my dad said..." followed by Spike O'Connor's pronouncements on ranch life.

Cripes, you'd have thought Spike O'Connor was some damn oracle.

But he couldn't help admiring Josh's interest and, seeing it, he understood better Ellie's determination to hang on to the ranch for him.

"He loves it," she'd told Rance once.

Rance could see that. Josh loved it far more than the other two boys. But Rance had a good time with them, too.

In fact they were more fun than Josh was. Caleb loved logic puzzles, and when Rance found that out, he started giving the boy simplified ones he remembered from a logic class he'd had in his pre-law training. Almost every day Caleb came up with the right answer. When he didn't, he and Rance had spirited discussions about how to get it.

Rance and Daniel had spirited discussions about cows.

Not about their feed or their breeding, like he did with Josh, but about how much formula Lilly Belle, Daniel's orphaned calf, had taken on any given morning, and how much she ought to have in the afternoon, and if Rance had ever known anyone who had raised a cow as a pet.

Their discussions reminded Rance that he actually had once hand raised a calf when he'd been no bigger than Daniel. One of the cowboys had been deputized to look after it and check on it by Rance's grandfather.

His own father was the one who had encouraged him to step in and take the responsibility on. Trey had even come out to the barn and sat feeding the calf with Rance late into the night. All that had happened so many years ago that Rance had completely forgotten it until Daniel had asked.

The kids all asked a lot of questions. But in the end, none of them more than Carrie.

If Caleb and Daniel were eager to befriend him, and Josh was just as eager to argue with him, Carrie was in no hurry to make up her mind about him.

The first four days he was there, she didn't say anything to him at all except the briefest answer possible to any direct question he might ask her.

The fifth evening he was sitting on the back porch, taking a break from wood chopping and telling Caleb and Daniel about a bear he'd seen the past spring in the Absarokas, when Carrie, who'd been standing in the kitchen door listening, said, "I got a bear."

It was the first thing she'd volunteered since he'd come.

He turned to her and saw that she had the everpresent Clarissa dangling by one leg from her hand. "Will you introduce me?" he asked her gravely.

Carrie settled the bear upright in her arms and, with

equal seriousness, said, "This is Clarissa." And then to Clarissa she said, "This is Mr. Phillips."

"Rance," Rance corrected, because Ellie wasn't listening.

Carrie hadn't said anything else, but she'd come and sat down beside Caleb to listen to the bear stories. He made it a point to anthropomorphize them a little more for her. He even found himself creating a character, "Lone Bear," who was looking for a friend.

"Clarissa would be his friend," Carrie said to him.

The next morning Rance gave her two horsehair bracelets he'd been braiding in the evenings to take his mind off the fact that he was not then and presumably never would be in Ellie O'Connor's bed.

"One for you," he said, squatting down in front of her and slipping it over her wrist. "And one—" a very small one "—for Clarissa."

Carrie looked at them, her mouth a soft little O. Then she looked at him. "Thank you. Say thank you," she said to the bear.

Rance shook the bear's well-worn paw. "She thanked me," he said. Then he sat down on the porch steps next to her and said, "Let me tell you another bear story. This one's about a bear who goes around a mountain and into a cave..." He picked her up and set her on his lap. "Look, I'll show you..."

"She's your slave for life," Ellie told him the next day after Carrie determined to follow him around every time he got off his horse. "What did you do?"

"It's all that world's-most-eligible charm." Rance grinned. "I gave her a horsehair bracelet. And I taught her to tie her shoes."

Ellie's jaw dropped. Her gaze sought Carrie who was running after the boys in the yard. Sure enough, her shoes were tied. "How on earth? Do you know how long we've been trying?"

Rance shrugged. "I told her a story." He demonstrated with his hands, pretending they were holding laces. "There was this bear, you see. And this mountain. And the bear went around the mountain looking for his friend. And then he went into a cave and found her and—" he made a pulling motion with his fingers "— they shut the curtains and had a very good time."

Ellie's face turned bright red. "It was a rabbit," she said, "and the story was not salacious when I heard it."

"Hey, it worked, didn't it?" He laughed. "Besides, I'm left-handed."

It was every bit the break from routine—and women—that he'd hoped it would be. It was better, in fact, than he had any right to expect.

It would have been great—if he'd had Ellie.

But after a week of herding and sorting cattle, of chopping wood and mending fence, of telling stories and teaching shoe-tying and arguing breeding and feeding calves, he still spent every night on the straw in the barn by himself.

When he'd agreed to it, he'd been thinking in terms of stopgap measures. A place he could stand to sleep while waiting to get into the house and—he hoped—into her bed.

But it didn't take him long to see that that wasn't going to work.

There wasn't any way to sort of ease his way in. There was no extra room in Ellie's house. Every bedroom was taken. All three boys were in one. The little girl was in another, barely bigger than a closet. And even though

Ellie had one to herself, Rance wasn't fool enough to think he was going to get an invitation to share it.

It hadn't taken him long to realize how very much Ellie had loved Spike. Whatever feelings she'd had for Rance—and once he'd dared call them love—Rance had to admit they'd been short-lived. No doubt they'd passed as soon as she'd come home for the summer.

She didn't say that in so many words. She didn't have to. Her love for Spike was in everything she did every day.

In fact, if he hadn't known better, sometimes he would have thought Ellie wasn't the woman he'd known in college at all. Though she was obviously grateful for his help, he got the feeling anybody's help would have sufficed—and maybe even been preferable.

She seemed awkward around him, ill at ease. There was certainly nothing in her manner that made him think she was glad her new hand was a man she'd once professed to love. She would probably have been happier with any remotely competent cowboy the cat had dragged in.

Of course she didn't have a cat.

She couldn't afford to feed one.

That was something else he understood—that finances around the O'Connor place really were tight. The motto was one his great-grandfather would have appreciated: do it by hand, make do, or do without.

Ellie did a lot of all three.

Rance would have liked to have made things easier for her, but one thing he remembered very well—and one thing that hadn't changed—was Ellie's pride. She was grateful for his work. She wouldn't be grateful for his money.

Not even if it would free them up a little time to spend together, Rance thought grimly.

He was just a little bitter about that.

Maybe he was spoiled. After all, he'd spent the past few months fending off what seemed like every woman in the western hemisphere. And now, when he finally found one he'd once actually had feelings for—and felt surprisingly strong feelings for still—she didn't appear to be the least bit interested in him!

Trey would have said it served him right.

Which just proved again that Rance and his father had never agreed on anything.

"You want somethin', you got to go after it," Trey always said.

Rance would have liked to see his father go after Ellie!

She'd tell him to make himself useful and chop wood or weed the garden.

Well, Rance had chopped more wood than he'd thought possible. And he'd worked harder than he remembered ever working in his life. But as tired as he was, he still couldn't sleep. He laid awake every damn night, aware of her movements in the bedroom of the house across the yard.

He didn't suppose she knew he could see her through the thin shade on her bedroom window. If she had known, she probably would have painted the window black or doused the lights!

Instead every night she treated him to the sight of her lissome silhouette moving from one side of the room to the other. Some nights he got to watch as she slipped off her shirt or pulled her sweater over her head. He could even tell when she'd shed her bra and was walking naked behind the shade.

It drove him nuts.

He watched, anyway.

He had become a voyeur, a peeping Tom, a lustful, frustrated man who hadn't had a woman in so long he couldn't recall. He was so aware of her, it hurt. And it did him no good at all.

But for all that she wandered around behind her shade in varying degrees of undress, as far as Rance could tell, she never slept.

Either that or she never turned the lights off.

At least, they were always on when Rance finally buried himself in his sleeping bag and let his dreams and frustration take over the night.

Ellie was the subject of both.

It was insane. Laughable. The old man would bust a gut laughing if he knew that his son—who'd refused to even look at a busload of gorgeous women all hankering after him—was himself yearning after a widow who didn't even seem to like him anymore.

Well, she'd liked him once, he consoled himself as he folded his arms under his head and stared up toward the rafters in the dark. She'd slept with him all those years ago, hadn't she? She'd even said she'd loved him.

Then, he reminded himself.

Not now.

Now Ellie hardly even looked at him, much less smiled at him. Or if she managed a smile, it was obviously forced. And yet...

And yet.

There was the way he sometimes *almost* caught her glancing his way. If he looked quick, he sometimes thought he'd seen her just avert her gaze. And there was the way she pulled back fast if their hands touched when she was handing him a mug of coffee or a plate of stew.

Was she remembering when more than their hands had touched?

Was the reason the lights were on at all hours that Ellie was having trouble sleeping, too?

Rance shrugged his shoulders against the straw beneath his back. He flexed his shoulders, clenched his toes. Maybe thoughts of him out here in the barn were keeping her up, the same way thoughts of her naked in her too-big-for-one-person bed were driving him up the wall.

What if she was just waiting up over there, wondering how to get him to come to her?

What if she wanted him and couldn't manage to say so? What if he went to the house right now and opened the door? What if she smiled at him? Held out her arms to him? Invited him to...

He couldn't get out of his sleeping bag fast enough.

He stopped just long enough to comb his hair and run a hand over his jaw, then wish he had running water in the barn. There was considerably more than a five-o'clock shadow on his jaw at half past midnight.

But maybe Ellie would think his whiskers were sexy.

Or maybe she would be too busy kissing him to notice.

He hurried across the yard and up the porch steps. It wasn't until he reached the door that he hesitated. Usually he went right in.

But usually she was expecting him for a meal or to take a shower. He didn't want to surprise her.

He tried to see in the window, but the shades were drawn, and the angle from which he had to peer only gave him a slice of the sink. She wasn't standing at the sink.

He put his hand on the knob. The door was unlocked. He knocked, anyway.

If she really didn't want him, he would see it on her

face, and he could make up some excuse about forgetting to brush his teeth.

Want me. The words hammered in his head. He shifted from one foot to the other, waiting, listening for footsteps.

She didn't come.

He tapped again. Louder. Maybe she had the television on, though he couldn't hear it. He couldn't hear anything except the wind in the pines on the hillside and the muffled sounds of cattle.

She didn't come.

He jammed his hands in the pockets of his jeans. He rocked back on his heels, then tapped his toes. *Aw, the hell with it,* he thought, and eased open the door.

"Ellie?" He said her name softly, not wanting to wake the kids. He stepped into the empty kitchen. "El?"

Closing the door and moving as quietly as he could without taking his boots off, Rance crossed the kitchen. "Ellie?" he called again softly.

She couldn't be waiting in bed for him, could she?

His heartbeat quickened. He stepped into the doorway to the living room and stopped dead.

Ellie wasn't in bed, but she was fast asleep. She was half sitting, half lying on the sofa, a piece of bright blue cloth and a needle and thread on her lap, as if she'd simply fallen asleep while sewing.

Which, Rance thought, damn it all, she probably had!

So much for making love with Ellie O'Connor.

She was clearly too tired to do anything at all. He was surprised she hadn't fallen asleep in her dinner some nights. She worked twenty hours a day, for heaven's sake!

Even now, asleep, she looked tired. There were dark smudges beneath her eyes. He would have liked to run his thumb over those smudges, erasing them, making her the eager innocent he'd once known. But there was no way to do that. No way to turn back the clock.

And, truth be told, he liked Ellie the way she was.

Oh, not as tired as she was. But the woman she was. The woman she'd become in the past eleven years. There was a strength in her, a determination, a purposefulness that he admired. It amazed him how a woman as delicate as she looked could be as resilient as she was.

It was actually comforting to see that she wasn't superhuman, that she sometimes got *too* tired, that she sometimes couldn't accomplish everything she put her mind to.

Rance moved quietly across the room, coming to stand over her where he could actually indulge himself and look his fill.

Ellie had always been pretty. But there was more than prettiness in her face now. There was gentleness, warmth, caring—character. She was a woman for whom life had not been easy, Rance knew that well enough.

And yet she looked almost happy as she slept.

"Are you happy, El?" Rance whispered. He reached out a hand and brushed a lock of hair away from her forehead.

For an instant, at his touch, her brows furrowed, and he held himself quite still, afraid that she would wake. But then her forehead smoothed again and she smiled once just slightly as she shifted, trying to get more comfortable. The piece of blue cloth slipped off her lap.

Rance picked it up, taking care to pick up the needle and thread along with it. He held it up, studying it. It looked like a dress—a doll-sized dress. Not, not a doll. A bear. She was making clothes for Clarissa.

As if she didn't have enough to do, he thought to himself as he set it on the table beside the couch.

"You need sleep, not sewing," he told her in barely more than a whisper. And then, before he could think twice about what he was doing, he bent and slid his hands under her, scooping her up in his arms.

It was an indication of just how tired she was that she didn't even wake up. Instead she simply leaned her head against his shoulder, her fingers clutching at his shirt-front, and she slept on.

He carried her to her room. Her hair brushed against his mouth. He could kiss the top of her head.

For an instant he did. Couldn't help himself.

He'd never been in her bedroom. He went in boldly now. He crossed the room and, bending down, laid her gently on the bed.

She sighed and smiled slightly, but still didn't wake up.

He wondered if he ought to undress her. But he wasn't sure she was exhausted enough to sleep through that. And he wasn't sure what kind of damage control he'd have to do if she woke up to find him peeling off her jeans.

He didn't dare even slide the covers down and tuck her between the sheets for fear of waking her. Finally he just undid the top two buttons of her shirt—only to make her more comfortable, he rationalized—then lifted the blankets on the far side and covered her with them as best he could.

It wasn't much, but it was better than leaving her on the sofa.

So much for pipe dreams about sliding into the bed next to her, making love with her and keeping her warm that way. He wasn't going to get it. Not tonight.

But one thing he couldn't resist. He bent and pressed a light kiss to her lips.

A shadow fell across the bed.

"What're you doin' to her?"

The harsh childish voice caused Rance to jerk back. He spun around to see a pajama-clad Josh standing in the doorway. The boy looked at him accusingly.

"I found your mom asleep on the sofa," Rance said. "And I carried her to bed."

For a moment Josh didn't say anything, just looked at him. And the way he looked made Rance feel very much like a teenager all over again, caught with his hands in Mary Jane Beasley's shirt.

But then he pulled himself together. He was an adult, not a teenager. He was interested in this woman. "I was kissing her good-night," he said.

Now Josh took a step into the room. "You don't need to do that," he said firmly.

"No. I suppose I don't," Rance said. "But your mother has very kissable lips, you know."

He shouldn't have said it. It was almost as if he was trying to have another of those arguments he had with Josh. As if he was playing devil's advocate. Or the devil himself.

"It don't mean you gotta kiss 'em," Josh said furiously. He jerked his head toward the door. "Get outa here. Now."

The boy's anger was palpable. And Rance felt equal parts foolish and regretful. He rubbed a hand against the back of his head, nodding and heading toward the door at the same time. "It's okay, Josh," he said gently. "I was only giving her one kiss. That's all."

The boy didn't answer. He didn't move, just kept his

gaze fixed on Rance unblinkingly as Rance eased his way out of the room.

"She fell asleep on the couch. I came in for…a glass of water. I found her there. She was exhausted. Obviously. She works too damn hard." He couldn't keep all the emotion out of his voice, but he tried to keep it down. "I figured she needed as much rest as she could get, so I carried her into the bedroom, put her down and kissed her good-night. That's all."

The boy didn't even blink, but slowly his gaze turned. He looked at his mother, then he lifted his gaze, looking for a moment toward a photo on the dresser just beyond the bed. It looked like a wedding photo to Rance. Finally Josh's gaze moved back to meet his. There was an ache in his eyes so deep it hurt Rance to look at it.

"I've known your mother a long time, Josh," he said quietly. "We're old friends. Old friends are allowed a good-night kiss."

He wasn't sure if he was convincing the boy or not. He just knew he didn't ever want to be responsible for pain that harsh. "Ask her, if you're worried about it," he said at last.

"Maybe—" Josh cleared his throat "—maybe I will."

The boy followed him to the living room. Rance remembered to get his glass of water. He gulped it down and set the glass on the counter, all the while feeling the boy's eyes on him. Then he opened the door, paused, looked back and gave the boy his due. "You're a good man, Josh O'Connor."

"Huh?"

"You're takin' care of your mother. Good for you."

Was he?

It didn't seem like it sometimes. Not well enough, anyhow, Josh thought as he stood at the window in the darkened living room and watched from behind the curtains as Rance took a slow, lazy walk toward the barn.

If he'd been taking care of his mother right, he wouldn't have let Sunny spook and throw him. He wouldn't have broken his arm. He wouldn't have let a lecher like Rance Phillips move in on her—much less have encouraged him!

But how was he supposed to know Phillips had had eyes for his mother?

Josh wasn't used to thinking of his mother as a *sex object*. Even thinking the words *sex object* made him shift from one foot to the other and shrug his shoulders against his pajama shirt because it suddenly felt too small.

He was almost ten and a half years old. He knew about sex. He knew what went where. What kid raised on a cattle ranch didn't?

Sometimes lately he even thought about it. Not about cows and bulls. About girls—like Megan Stevens and Katie Kyle in his class at school.

Not about his mother! Josh couldn't imagine anybody thinking things like that about his mother.

But Rance Phillips did.

Josh's fingers tightened on the curtain as he watched Rance disappear into the barn. Would Rance have gone back to the barn if Josh hadn't come looking in his mother's room? Or would he have woken her up? Slid in bed beside her?

Josh let go of the curtain and shook his head, as if he could dislodge the thought. Of course not! And even if Rance had thought about it, his mom wouldn't have let him.

Would she?

Josh was sure she wouldn't.

At least he was pretty sure she wouldn't.

But she liked Rance. He could tell that from the way she watched him sometimes when he was saddling his horse, telling stories to the kids, or dipping his head under the tap to cool off. She'd stand there watching, and she'd get a funny kind of look on her face.

She never had that look when she was watching him or the twins or Carrie. Josh had only seen it a few times— and only when she'd been watching his dad.

She used to go out with Rance—before she'd married Dad.

Did she want Rance like she'd wanted Dad?

She missed Dad. Josh knew that. His mom was lonely. He knew that, too. Sometimes he found it hard to believe a person could be lonely in a house this small with so many people in it.

But he knew it could happen, because sometimes he felt lonely here, too. Caleb and Daniel were twins. They had each other. Mom and Carrie were girls. They had each other. But he, Josh, had no one.

Not anymore.

Once he'd had his dad.

He shut his eyes and pressed his fists against them. He shouldn't be thinking about his dad tonight. It hurt whenever he thought about his father. It was like there was this great aching hole where his father once had been.

He'd spent eight years of his life watching his dad and doing everything just the way he did. Usually his dad called him Josh or Bud, but sometimes he'd called Josh Chip—as in "chip off the old block."

When he'd been old enough to understand that meant he was just like his father, Josh's chest had swelled with pride.

He could still remember that feeling, could still remember standing straighter when his father said the words. He could still remember the feel of his father's hand, firm and steady on his shoulder or rough and teasing, ruffling his hair.

It wasn't the same when his mom ruffled his hair. She did it softer, as if she might hurt him if she rubbed his head really hard. It hadn't ever hurt when his dad had done it. Josh reached up now and scrubbed his hand roughly through his hair. Like that, he thought, swallowing hard against the lump in his throat.

But that wasn't it, either. Not really.

No one did it like his dad had.

No one ever would again.

Six

Rance was careful around Ellie after that.

With Josh's eyes on him, he was circumspect, proper. Everything that Josh could possibly want him to be.

He was frustrated as hell, too. Nothing new about that.

He was sure Josh would be pleased as punch if he knew, but he was equally determined the boy would never find out.

It occurred to Rance more than once over the next few days that maybe nothing at all would ever happen between him and Ellie. Maybe his dreams and fantasies would come to naught. Maybe all you got in life was one single shot. And as far as Ellie was concerned, he'd already had that.

It was beginning to look that way.

Well, then, so be it.

At least he'd done some good for her these past couple of weeks. He'd got her cattle down and sorted. He'd delivered three calves. He'd got her fences mended and her wood chopped. Yesterday, when a hard rain had made him less inclined to spend more time outside than he had to, he'd even helped strip wallpaper in Carrie's bedroom.

"You don't have to do that," Ellie protested. "Take a nap. Read a book. Watch television. You don't have to work every minute."

But he'd wanted to. Not just work. He wanted to spend time with Ellie.

So he did. And he felt the same proprietary interest in the kids and in the house that he already felt about the ranch.

For all the good it would do him.

Because before long he was going to have to leave. He had a court date coming up—a case he had to try, one that he couldn't postpone or fob off on Lydia. He'd talked to Jodi about it earlier in the week, and she'd assured him that it was hard-and-fast in the schedule.

"Monday afternoon," she'd said. "You will be here?"

"I'll be there," Rance had promised. But not without regret. He would have to leave Sunday evening, after the branding.

Doubtless that would make Ellie happy.

She'd been more distant with him than ever since the night he'd carried her to her bed. She'd never mentioned it to him, of course. Maybe she didn't even know for sure he'd done it. Maybe she thought she'd sleepwalked.

Or maybe Josh had told her about the kiss.

He'd hoped for an unspoken acknowledgment, a little eye contact at least. But she'd barely looked in his direction and went out doors as quickly as he came in them.

Finally last night Rance had broken down and stopped Josh as the boy was on his way to the tree house. He asked Josh if he'd spoken to his mother about what happened.

The boy had given him another of those looks of searing disapproval. But then he'd shaken his head. "I wouldn't," he said stonily.

Obviously even bringing up such a thing to his mother was distasteful. One more person who'd be happy to have the branding over and see Rance Phillips's back.

Still Rance didn't want to go.

Even on a day like today—a day when the rain still

came down, shoved down the valley by an increasingly sharp north wind and he couldn't hole up inside by a nice warm fire because one of the last of Ellie's pregnant cows was trying to deliver—he found himself reluctant to think about leaving two days later.

You like it here? He asked himself, hunching his shoulders and turning his collar up against the rain. *You like this?*

Well, maybe not this. But once the calf was delivered, once the chores were done, he did like the thought of tramping up the steps to the warm, waiting kitchen. He did like the notion of sitting around the supper table with Ellie and the kids, of the chatter and the questions and, after, sitting with them all in the living room, playing checkers with the boys or telling stories to Carrie, while Ellie worked on the books or sewed or read in the rocker by the fire.

"C'mon, Bossy, we haven't got all day," he muttered to the straining cow.

The cow gave him a baleful look. She made a pained lowing sound. He got off Sunny and checked the calf. It was big, but he thought she could manage. He wished he knew more about her.

The rain turned to sleet. The sleet stung his face. He got back into the saddle and moved on, checking on the other cattle, trying to stay warm, trying to keep Sunny warm and moving.

The next time he checked, things were no further along. The cow was straining more, accomplishing less. He considered trying to get her down to the barn. If he was actually going to have to deliver this calf, he'd rather do it there than in a wet, frozen pasture.

But he knew from her labored breathing he'd left it too long. She was in no shape for a mile jaunt at this point. She'd be having the calf right here—and like it or not he'd be helping.

He got his rope and squatted at the nether end of her. "Okay, sweetheart. You got a little problem, but nothin' we can't handle together. You wait till I get ready, then you push and I'll pull, and we'll have this critter out in no time."

He stripped off his gloves and reached toward her. She swatted him with a tail full of rain and nameless muck.

He swiped it away and set to work.

He wasn't even aware when it started snowing.

The last thing on earth Ellie needed right now was a teacher in-service day.

Two days before her finally scheduled branding—a day when the wind had been whipping rain, then sleet, then snow past her windows since early morning—she did not need a day with no school and four children underfoot.

She didn't know if it was because of his broken arm or for some other reason she had yet to fathom, but Josh, who was usually the most independent of her children, had been, these past few days, more underfoot than everyone else.

He hadn't even wanted to go to his friend Matt's birthday party this afternoon. "I don't think I'll go. You might need me," he'd said to her last night when she'd reminded him.

"Not go?" Ellie had been equal parts puzzled and aghast. "Of course you'll go. Why ever wouldn't you go?"

"The brandin's comin' up," Josh said. "I oughta help get ready, even if you won't let me ride." It had been a sore point between them since she'd informed him that she wasn't having him in the middle of roping and tying and branding with a broken arm.

"You can keep the tally," she'd told him.

He hadn't thought it much consolation.

"There will be other years when you can do the rough stuff," she'd promised. It was a promise she was fairly sure now that she'd be able to keep. Thanks to Rance.

Without Rance's help they would be in nowhere near as good a shape as they were. She owed him a tremendous amount, and she knew it. She thought Josh knew it, too, and that he was both grateful and annoyed that he had to be grateful, when he'd have preferred to do things himself.

At least, she guessed that was what was bothering him.

He was so closemouthed these days, she really couldn't tell. He was either underfoot, staring stonily at her and Rance, or he was up in his tree house, glowering down. When Spike had built the kids that tree house, he'd said, "They'll need a place to go where they can think—a place of their own."

Ellie thought Josh was doing entirely too much thinking—she just wasn't sure about what.

The one thing she did know was that he needed to go to Matt's party. He needed to remember that he was ten, not forty. He would only get to be a child for a few years. And whether he wanted to or not, she was determined that he was going to enjoy them.

"You're going to Matt's," she told him. "You deserve a break, Josh." And at his continued disagreement, she hauled out the big guns. "Your dad would think so, too."

Sandra agreed when she arrived. She also made an offer Ellie couldn't refuse. "I'll take Josh in to Matt's," she said, "and I just happened to notice that there's a new Disney film playing in town that I wouldn't mind seeing.''

There was a sudden stillness in the kitchen.

Sandra looked at the hopeful eyes of her grandchildren, then said to their mother, "I wonder if you'd mind if I took Daniel and Caleb and Carrie, too?"

Ellie didn't mind.

In fact, Ellie was thrilled.

It would give her a chance to wash the walls in Carrie's bedroom. It would give her an opportunity to work on the outfits she was making for Clarissa. Carrie's birthday was just a little more than a week away now.

She was expecting a freshly painted bedroom and dalmatian puppy sheets for her birthday. She wasn't expecting new clothes for Clarissa. If Ellie could get them done, the gingham dress and the bright blue cowgirl outfit would be a lovely surprise.

Her children needed more lovely surprises.

And she could definitely use this time alone. She just wished she didn't have to be alone with her thoughts, as well.

Her thoughts, far more than she wanted, revolved around Rance.

He was doing so much for them, she felt guilty. And yet she couldn't tell him not to. She wanted him to stop so she wouldn't be beholden. And she didn't want him to stop because she needed his help—and she wanted him there.

That was the part she didn't like to think about.

It was something else that could get the guilt going—this wanting Rance the way she did. It had done her no good at all the last time she'd wanted Rance, she reminded herself. She'd loved him, she'd given herself to him—and he'd been only too happy to walk away.

It would happen that way again if she was foolish enough to let him see how much she still cared about him. She did her very best not to.

But it was hard.

Some nights she had the most erotic dreams. Not about Rance specifically. They weren't that blatant—as if her subconscious knew she'd be shocked and would resist frantically if it came up with anything that obvious.

They just made her edgy, hungry—in capital letters, AWARE.

She thought he might have put her to bed one night, too. But she wasn't sure. She remembered sitting on the sofa working on Clarissa's cowgirl outfit, nodding off once or twice and pricking her thumb with the needle every time she jerked back up straight and tried to stay awake. And the next thing she remembered, she woke up in her bed.

Dressed.

On top of the comforter, with the other half pulled over her, as if she'd been tucked into a sleeping bag.

The question was, who had tucked her?

And there was only one answer. Rance.

The thought made her face go warm and her body go soft. She didn't want that to happen. She didn't want to think about Rance anywhere near her bedroom—even if she was asleep. But her body didn't seem to be paying much attention to her mind these days.

Had he put her to bed?

She wanted to ask him. She absolutely, positively could not.

But she'd watched him out of the corner of her eye for the past few days, trying to get a notion of whether he really had done it. But it was hard to tell when she didn't dare look him full in the face.

It would be a good thing when he left after the branding, as he'd told her this morning he was planning to do.

The words, when they came, had been a salutary dash of reality. Of course he was leaving! She hadn't ever expected him to stay, had she?

Of course not, she assured herself now, poking the needle through the gingham of Clarissa's dress and staring out into the increasing snowstorm.

She'd always known he would leave. But he couldn't leave, she thought, getting up and going to the window to look up the road for any sign of him, if he didn't get back in the first place.

It was well past four. She'd enjoyed the afternoon's solitude.

But now she was worried about Rance.

A little rain never hurt anyone, she'd assured herself when he'd left this morning to make a circle of the herd, to check the couple of heifers who still hadn't calved, to round up a couple of strays and repair a break in the fence that Early Smith, one of her neighbors had called to tell her about.

In fact she hadn't really thought much about the weather. She'd just been so aware of him there in the kitchen, his tousled dark hair tempting her fingers to smooth it, that she'd been only too glad once he'd gone.

She'd thought he might come back by midday. Since most of the cattle were within relatively easy reach of the ranch house now, once he got the strays, he didn't have to stay out in the weather—unless he wanted to.

Maybe he did. Maybe he was avoiding them, eager to have the time he'd spent with her over, desperate to be gone. After all, he didn't know the kids weren't home and they'd have some peace in the house today.

And maybe it was just as well he didn't know, Ellie thought.

There was such a thing as too much temptation.

By midafternoon, when the rain had changed to sleet and then, quite abruptly, to snow—fairly heavy snow— she spent more time going to the window to look for him than she did sitting in the rocker by the fireplace.

It didn't seem fair that she should be in here enjoying a nice fire and a quiet house while he was outside in the cold and wind and snow, doing work that by rights should have been hers.

She paced the floor, bounced on her toes, went to the window every few minutes, craned her neck and squinted, trying to discern Rance, riding Sunny, coming back home.

He didn't come.

The phone rang, and she jumped, then snatched it up, as if it might somehow be him on the other end of the line.

It was Matt's mother. "I know I said I'd bring all the kids home after the party, but I was wondering if you'd mind," she said with a somewhat desperate laugh, "if it didn't end until tomorrow?"

"Are the roads that bad?"

"Bad enough," Matt's mother replied. "And, to be honest, the three boys who live out in the country are the ones who get along best with Matt so I don't mind having them stay over. What do you think?"

"I think it's a great idea," Ellie said. Not just because of the weather, either. It would be good for Josh to spend more time with his friends, to realize that life on the ranch could continue without him having to work there all the time. Perhaps he would rediscover the joy of being a child.

"We'll bring him home tomorrow then," Matt's mother promised and hung up.

Ellie went back to the window. No Rance. She turned on the radio to get the weather forecast.

"A sudden fast-moving storm," the newscaster called it. "In and out. It'll be gone before you know it. Look for a foot of new snow."

The phone rang again.

"Well, we've made it back from the movie," Sandra said, "but I slid into the ditch right before the turn up to the house."

"Are you all right?" Ellie demanded.

"We're all fine. And we've got a pizza in the oven. But I won't be bringing anyone home tonight."

"But——" But Ellie knew there was no arguing with a car in the ditch and a freak spring snowstorm.

"Enjoy," Sandra urged her.

"It will be just me...and Rance," Ellie said a little faintly.

There was a long pause on the other end of the line. Then Sandra said, "How handy."

Ellie knew what her mother-in-law meant. *Tell him.* Her stomach churned at the thought. Worse, it churned at the worry that he still wasn't anywhere to be seen.

Surely the same thing that had happened to Spike hadn't happened to him.

It was the one thought she'd been trying desperately to keep at bay all afternoon. She remembered all too clearly the worry that she'd felt when Spike hadn't come home that day. But then she'd thought he might have hurt himself, broken a leg, been a long way from home.

She'd never let herself think of the worst possibility.

Now she couldn't help it.

She grabbed her jacket off the hook by the door, pulled

on her boots, then hurried out to catch Peaches. The old nag would hate being made to do anything in this weather. But she was sturdy and reliable.

And Ellie couldn't wait any longer.

Her voice blew past him on the wind.

He thought he was hearing things, dreaming. He thought he might very well perish out here in the storm alongside this damnable cow.

He supposed he really shouldn't blame the cow. It was his fault for not seeing she was having trouble sooner. If he had, he could have got her to the barn. He would have had Ellie there then—or Daniel. Someone with smaller hands. Someone who could reach in and grab that leg that was laying wrong. Someone who could save this cow—and her calf—before they froze to death or died from complications in the birth.

"Rance!"

It was clearer now. High and pure on the wind. But he still didn't believe it. He was kneeling hunched on the ground at the business end of the cow and a quick squint over his shoulder didn't show him any angels singing on high—and that was the only company he expected.

"Rance!"

Her voice was strong and sharp and, it seemed, almost right next to him. He stopped struggling with the calf and looked around. Ellie was maybe twenty feet away from him, pushing through the snow atop her swaybacked old sorrel Peaches.

He straightened up, unbent painfully. All his joints ached. His hands and arms were raw and cold. "God," he said, "am I glad to see you!"

She was off the horse in a second. "What's wrong?"

"Calf's got a leg back. The mother's too small. I can't

turn it. She isn't going to last much longer. Think you can do it?''

"Of course," Ellie spoke without hesitation, already stripping her gloves off.

With Ellie's smaller hands, what had been impossible for him, was just a matter of waiting until the contraction abated, then carefully easing the obstructing leg around.

Rance held the cow's tail out of the way. He crooned soothingly to her. He tried to stay between Ellie and any hooves that might come flying in her direction.

"I think I got it," Ellie breathed after a moment. She was kneeling, too. Her hair was whipping into his face. "Okay, sweetie," she murmured to the exhausted cow. "Your baby's ready to come now. All you've got to do is push."

But the cow was too tired by this time. "We'll use my rope," Rance said. He played it out, and Ellie, knowing exactly what to do, went back in to slip it around the calf.

"A cowboy's forceps," Rance remembered his grandfather calling his rope. "Move out of the way now," he told Ellie. "I'll pull."

She scrambled aside and let him take her place. Then she knelt next to the cow, rubbing her and stroking her. "It'll be all right. It'll be all right."

And on the next contraction, when the cow did what feeble pushing she was still able to do, Rance pulled, as well. A slick, unmoving calf landed almost in his lap.

Instantly Ellie was clearing its mouth, rubbing it, coaxing it. "It's breathing," he thought she said, but her words were blown away by the wind.

And then it twitched. It jerked. It struggled to move in her arms. And Ellie sat back on the ground, grinning.

Rance grinned, too. He laughed. He said, "We did it! *You* did it!"

And Ellie looked straight at him for the first time since he'd set foot on the ranch as she said, "I could never have done any of this without you."

Rance hauled himself up. Then, with the calf still lying between them, and the wind howling around them, and the snow coming down on top of them, he leaned over and kissed her.

It wasn't a passionate kiss, though God knew there was passion in it. It wasn't a hungry kiss, though Rance knew he'd been starved for her for what seemed like years. It almost wasn't sexual at all.

It was an affirmation—of life, of hope, of what they could accomplish together.

And then the calf wriggled, and the cow moved, and they broke apart—aware of each other—and aware that, for now, there was time for nothing more.

Rance put the calf where the cow would know it was alive and could lick at it. Then he hauled Ellie to her feet. She stumbled as she came up and fell against him. His arms went around her to steady her. He held her in the circle of them—and she didn't pull away.

She leaned lightly against his chest, watching the cow nudging and bathing the calf. "We need to get them into the barn."

"As soon as she can move," Rance said. "I'll carry the calf. You're shaking. You must be freezing. Why don't you go on back to the house?"

Ellie shook her head. "I'm fine." But he felt a breath shudder through her even as she spoke. "I don't want to go back right now. I'll come when you do."

They settled the cow and calf in the barn. They fed Daniel's Lilly Belle, then fed and brushed the horses. It was all very methodical, purposeful, proper. They did it all without speaking.

Then together they went up to the house and into the kitchen.

The silence was deafening.

Rance looked around, then frowned at Ellie. "Where is everybody?"

She told him.

"They're...gone? All of them?" There was a note of something in his voice. Doubt? Wonder? Urgency?

She wasn't sure—of anything—except she felt it, too.

"All of them," she agreed. "Until tomorrow."

She took off her jacket. She took off her hat. She shed her boots. And then she stood, sock-footed in the kitchen, and she didn't run from him.

Probably she should have. Probably there was no probably about it!

But she didn't run because she couldn't. She'd been running from Rance since he'd come back into her life. She felt like a pin who'd been resisting and resisting a magnet, all the while being drawn closer, being pulled inexorably in. She was too close to hold back any longer.

Her resistance was gone.

"You need a shower," Rance said hoarsely.

"Yes."

"So do I."

"Yes."

Their eyes met. Their fingers touched. Curled. Held. But Rance didn't lead. He waited.

That was what decided her. His waiting gave her courage. His leaving it up to her was what she needed, to have the choice to say yes or no.

She said yes.

She wanted him. It would be sex, she told herself. Not love. Not love like she'd had with Spike. But the moment she thought it, she knew it wasn't true.

There was love in whatever she felt for Rance still. Of course it wasn't love like she and Spike had shared. Once she'd told Spike she couldn't love him the way she'd loved Rance. But the way she had loved him had been better. It had grown deeper, stronger, firmer than anything she could have imagined.

The loves were different, she decided. They didn't—couldn't—compare. But they were both a part of her.

Rance had given her a son. He had, in fact, given her the whole rest of her life through that gift. Without his having left her expecting a child, she never would have turned to Spike. She never would have known the depth of Spike's love, the joys of not only Josh, but of Daniel and Caleb and Carrie. She never would have been the woman she'd become.

She had all that because of him. And she would have this night of love to remember, to share, to hold in her heart with her other dearest memories.

Spike she would hold in her heart forever.

Tonight, because she loved him, too, and always would, she would hold Rance in her arms.

They shared the shower.

They undressed each other slowly, wordlessly, marveling with their eyes and lips and light finger touches the beauty of each other's body. They ran the water, hot and hard. They played with the spray, laughed and lingered. She soaped his back and he soaped hers. Then somehow the soap seemed to take on a life of its own. Ellie found herself following it up the length of his legs, around his hips, and as his fingers dug into the hair on the top of her head, she pressed kisses to his thighs. She felt him shudder. His legs trembled.

"God Almighty, Ellie." The words hissed through his lips. "You're gonna be the death of me." And then, he drew her up hard along the length of his body, bringing her mouth into line with his. They kissed again, slowly, deeply, desperately.

And both of them knew that kissing was no longer enough.

"Not here," Rance whispered. "Not here. Let's do this right."

Ellie wanted just to do it! The heat of her need seemed in danger of consuming her. And even though Rance's body was hard with need for her, he seemed in no hurry to assuage it.

He took a towel and slowly, quite deliberately he dried her off. The soft terry seemed to bring all her nerve endings alive wherever he touched. And he touched everywhere. He made her shiver with longing for him. Her fingernails dug into his shoulders when he knelt to dry her. His hair brushed against her naked thighs as he parted her legs to dry them. And she heard herself whimper when he touched his tongue to the inner side of her knee.

"Rance!" She tugged at him, tried to bring him to his feet, to wrap her arms around him. But he wasn't ready yet. He was still touching her, drying her—teasing her. "Rance!"

"Hmm?" He looked up at her then, his blue gaze dark and lambent with desire, but also twinkling with just a hint of mischief. "Did you want something, El?"

She almost laughed. She did stifle a groan. Then, when he got to his feet and started to lead her out of the bathroom, she shook her head. Two could play that game.

"My turn," she said.

He looked confused.

"You dried me. Now I get to dry you."

He didn't argue. But he did begin to look a little desperate as she took another towel and began to softly stroke his skin. She dried his shoulders and his arms. She dried his neck and his chest. "Raise your arms," she told him.

He did. But he also ran his tongue over his lips. "Hurry up," he said.

Ellie smiled and shook her head. No, she wasn't going to hurry. At first she'd been eager, almost frantic. But now she realized that would be foolish. She didn't have forever with Rance. She had one night. And she was going to make it last.

She bent and picked his foot up. She dried between his toes. She ran a finger up his hair-roughened calf. She felt him tense.

"Ellie," he said, strangled.

She looked up at him, smiling with her eyes. "You wanted something, Rance?" she teased, echoing his earlier line.

"You know damn well what I want."

She nodded. "So do I." She breathed the words against his legs. She ran the towel up between them, following the words. She touched him, stroked him.

"Ellie!" He pulled back sharply. His breath came in quick, desperate gasps. "I didn't mean hurry like that! You do that and it's gonna be all over before we get started."

"But I have to dry you, to warm you. You were freezing."

"Was. Now I'm dry. And so damn hot, it won't take a match to light my fire." He grasped her arms and pulled her to her feet. "Enough," he whispered against her lips just before he kissed her again.

And Ellie whispered back, "Not nearly."

But she let him lead her out of the bathroom, and then, wrapped in the comforter from Ellie's bed, they went to the living room and lay before the fire.

It was no hotter than they were. It burned no more brightly than the desire Ellie saw in Rance's eyes and knew was reflected in her own as they touched and stroked and nibbled. She tried to take her time, to savor and anticipate, to make it last.

But her body burned for him, and his was on fire for hers.

The time to go slow had passed.

His fingers found her slick and warm and ready. Hers found him hard and urgent with desire.

"Now?" she breathed and opened for him.

"Now," he agreed, sliding between her legs and easing himself into her body—as he'd already eased his way into her heart and into her soul.

Where he belonged.

She didn't know where the thought came from. She didn't question its appropriateness there. She no longer hoped, as she had when she was younger, to have Rance forever. She only knew that tonight she'd made the right choice—to show him the love she felt and would undoubtedly feel her whole life long.

Tears sprang to her eyes as she drew him in and hugged him tightly to her. She ignored them, let them fall. They didn't matter. The future didn't matter. The past didn't matter. Only loving him this very moment mattered.

Her whole body clenched around him, shivering through a climax he shared.

"Ah, Ellie," he murmured against her ear when at last they lay quietly together, their passion spent, their hearts slowing down, the real world coming back between them. "Ellie." He said her name again, then pressed a kiss into her neck, then another and another along her jawline. He rolled onto his back and pulled her on top of him, snuggling her close in the cocoon of the comforter.

"Perfect," he breathed. "You're perfect. This is perfect. The whole world is perfect tonight."

For an instant, Ellie knew, he was right. They had shared perfection.

Was she supposed to ruin it now? How on earth was she supposed to tell him that Josh was his son?

Loving Ellie should have satisfied him.

Spending the night in her arms, holding her in his, making their bodies one, should have sated his appetite. It should have freed him to move on, to put the past behind him and face the future with calm confidence and renewed purpose.

It did not.

It made him want Ellie more than ever. It made him want not only to make love with her again and again. It made him want a life with her—and her kids.

He wanted love, a wife, a home, a family. Everything he'd thought he would never want. He had run off to hang on to his freedom, to remain forever unencumbered, a single man—on his own.

Now he had that. He had all the freedom in the world to walk away from Ellie. In fact he had to leave.

And all he wanted to do was come back.

The day of the branding dawned clear and cold. The day before had brought balmy spring breezes that had softened and melted most of the snow. Now things were ready to go. Three of Ellie's neighbors showed up to help out. They took Rance's direction without question, because both Ellie and Sandra deferred to him.

It wasn't near the work that the branding on the Phillips spread had been. But it was more satisfying to Rance because he'd been fully and completely the one in charge. And because, when they were all finished, and the bawling babies were mothering up again, and the neighbors were all around sharing the after-branding meal, he could see Ellie moving around talking to her neighbors, laughing with them, smiling all the while.

It was over. The branding was done. The ranch was still on its feet.

"Jim Riker," Ellie told him after everyone was gone, "one of the guys who helped out today, also works at the bank. He said he'd hold Cleve off or point him in another direction. He thinks I'm doing well." She smiled at him again. There was a light of satisfaction and peace in her gaze and just the barest twinkle of mischief. "He doesn't know I owe it all to you."

"My pleasure," Rance assured her. It had been, too.

And then she drew herself up and faced him almost formally. "I want to thank you, Rance, for all you've done. I don't know what we would have done without you."

Her tone surprised him as much as her words. He'd been standing there, waiting for her to touch him, to kiss him, to slide her arms around his waist and hug him.

He'd been waiting for her to ask him to stay.

He felt like he'd been handed his hat.

It was what he'd said he wanted, wasn't it? he asked himself. It was what they'd agreed to when he'd come. She'd give him a "bolt-hole," and he'd stick around through the branding and help her out.

She'd fulfilled her part of the bargain. He'd fulfilled his.

One look told him that she wasn't going to change the rules now—even if they had made love.

He looked at her closely. For an instant—only an instant—she looked back. It was long enough. She'd held herself with total restraint since yesterday morning when the kids had come home. She'd never betrayed, by the slightest hint, that they'd spent the night in each other's arms.

But they had—and they cared about each other, too.

He might even dare to think they loved each other. He could read her a little better than he'd been able to read her all those years ago when they'd first loved. He was older now, smarter, less self-absorbed.

She hadn't said anything. She never would. He understood that now. But he had seen the way she watched him without wanting to. He had seen the way her hand almost brushed his, then pulled back, when he passed. He had seen the small unspoken things that told him he mattered to her.

He wanted to matter.

Now he took her by the arms and drew her close—not caring if Sandra was standing in the window watching, not noticing if Josh was gritting his teeth in the attic window or the twins and Carrie were looking on open-mouthed.

"I'm going now," he told her before his lips touched hers. "I have to."

"Of course." She was trying to sound matter-of-fact. She sounded desperate.

"Of course," Rance said mockingly. "But you can bet your bottom dollar, sweetheart, I'll be back."

Seven

He wouldn't be, though.

Ellie was sure of it. His words were just Rance's way of being polite, the same way a man who had no intention of making a second date would still say to the woman, "I'll call you."

He wouldn't come. He wouldn't call. The interlude was over for both of them. The real world beckoned. In Rance's case, she knew, it even *demanded.* She'd heard his side of the phone calls he'd made to his secretary this past week.

She'd heard him say, "Never mind where I am. It doesn't matter."

It didn't matter.

Or it wouldn't once he was back home.

And that was fine with her. She'd never expected anything else. It only made her glad—in spite of Sandra's disapproving gaze—that she hadn't told him about Josh.

When there was no future, there was no point at all in raking up the past.

"Where the hell have you been?"

It was a litany Rance heard wherever he went—when he got back to the ranch, when he went down to the barn, when he walked into his office, when he turned up in the courtroom. His father, his foreman, his secretary, his partner, his clients and, not surprisingly he guessed, seven or eight weary young women who looked like they'd been waiting for weeks, all wanted to know.

"Getting my head together," he said to them all. "Regrouping. Sorting out my life."

"Good," they said, one and all, then waited expectantly as if, now that he'd done it, things would—*he would*—get back to normal.

He tried.

God knew he had plenty of work to do—both on the ranch and in the office. It was all work he was interested in. But not as interested as he was in thinking about Ellie.

Mostly he thought about Ellie.

He thought about making love with her. He thought about stripping wallpaper with her. He thought about all the time he'd spent with her—and her family—and he tried to put that together with the rest of his life.

It was a stretch.

He'd been so firm for so long about not wanting any strings—so determined to resist any thought of settling down, of getting married, of having a family—that thinking about it now caused him a major mental adjustment.

Oh, he'd thought about it once or twice before—like when Judge Hamilton had offered Poppy up—but never terribly seriously. And he'd never regretted a lot that it hadn't happened. He hadn't regretted not marrying Ellie eleven years ago.

At least for the past eleven years he hadn't.

Now he began to realize what he might have missed.

He was thinking about marrying Ellie.

He was also thinking about calling her. He'd wanted to call her since he'd left. But he hadn't. He wasn't sure what to say.

Now he was pacing in his office late Wednesday night, not thinking about the witnesses he had to cross-examine tomorrow—which was what he ought to have been thinking about—when the phone rang.

Jodi was long gone, leaving the answering machine to catch all the calls. Rance wouldn't answer any of them, but he always listened on the off chance that one of them might be Ellie calling him.

It never was. This one wasn't, either. But it did catch his attention.

"Hey, bud," a cheerful masculine voice said to the machine, "I know you're in there. I can see you pacin' around the room."

Rance snatched the phone off the hook. "Shane?" He took three strides to the window and jerked the blinds back.

A cowboy with a cellular phone to his ear grinned and waved at him from across the street.

"Get up here," Rance commanded, beckoning through the glass.

"You ain't gettin' me in any law office, bud. I've seen all I want to see of them for one lifetime. C'mon down."

Rance glanced at the paper in his hand, at the notes strewn all over his desk, then back out the window at Shane. It wasn't a contest. "Be right down."

They went to Sully's down the street. It was a good, honest bar that had never seen a fern and on Fridays had its share of fist fights.

"The real thing," Shane called it as they bellied up to the bar and took long pulls of draft beer. Then, wiping his mouth on the back of his hand, he cocked his head and got straight to the point. "What's this about you goin' AWOL?"

"Who told you that?"

"Your old man. He called lookin' for you."

Rance scowled. "Interferin' old coot. It's his own fault

I left, you know. He's the one responsible for that tour bus.''

Shane grinned. ''There's fault and there's fault. Wish somebody had sent me a tour bus full of lovely ladies.''

''No, you don't,'' Rance said firmly. ''Or you wouldn't have Poppy.''

Shane considered that. ''I wasn't in any all-fired hurry to tie the knot.''

''No, but if half the world's women were shoved down your throat, I reckon you'd have swallowed.''

Shane's mouth tipped in a rueful grin. ''Well, when you put it that way…'' He cocked his head. ''You gonna swallow?''

''Not them.'' Rance finished his glass and thumped it with such vehemence on the bar that the bartender hurried over. Rance, embarrassed, waved him off.

''Who?'' Shane asked.

''What?''

''Not them, you said. So, who?''

Trust Shane, who generally wouldn't see a truck bearing down on him at high noon, to catch the unspoken qualification in Rance's words.

He shrugged, unwilling to answer when he hadn't sorted it all out yet.

''Marriage scare you?'' Shane asked.

''Of course not. I just never thought I'd get married.''

''Well, it's got a fair bit to recommend it.'' Shane gave the sigh of a satisfied man.

''Of course, if you're married to Poppy,'' Rance said.

''That's true. But I reckon she wasn't the last good woman. There's probably one or two left.''

''There is,'' Rance said at once.

Shane grinned. ''Thought so.''

Rance felt an unaccustomed heat climb his face. He

decided to shove his glass toward the bartender after all. When it had been refilled, he took a long swallow, then asked, almost conversationally, "It didn't scare you, gettin' married?"

"Hell, yes, it scared me. I wasn't lookin' to get married to anybody. And then, when I found out Poppy was Hard-A—" he grinned and corrected himself "—George's—daughter, I thought, no way! I'd probably still be runnin' if you hadn't come after me and told me to get my butt back home." He reached out and punched Rance lightly on the arm. "One more thing I owe you for, bud."

It was always easy to see what other people ought to do—especially a basically uncomplicated guy like Shane. Rance wished his own life was that simple. "I'm glad it's working out."

"Oh, hell, yes. Not that we don't have our set-to's. Poppy's damn stubborn. Bad as her old man sometimes. But, hey—" Shane shook his head "—she loves me. And there ain't many women who'd even tolerate me. I figure I'm the luckiest bum in the world."

Rance figured he was, too. He'd known Shane Nichols for a lot of years, and he'd never seen Shane happier. Marrying Poppy and settling down to run the Hamilton spread definitely agreed with him. He and Poppy's old man actually seemed to hit it off these days. Of course, Shane didn't have Rance's pressures. Or his problems. Or his father.

He drew a deep breath, then raised his glass. "To you," he said, "and Poppy."

Shane clinked his glass against Rance's, then gave him a wink. "And to you and the future Mrs. Phillips, whenever you get the guts to marry her."

* * *

Ellie felt hollow every morning, like she had after Spike had died—as if there was a hole in her life, as if something major was missing.

But that was nonsense. Nothing was missing. The children were all present and accounted for. Sandra turned up every morning like clockwork. Things were humming right along, better than ever.

She didn't let herself think about Rance.

Much.

Just every waking moment.

You're a fool, she told herself firmly. It was nothing but foolishness to lie awake at night and remember the way it had felt to have his arms around her. It was insanity to think about his lips kissing hers. It was the height of idiocy to dry herself after a shower and actually stand there thinking how much better the towel had felt when Rance had been the one doing the rubbing.

If she'd known she was going to go this far overboard, she would have resisted, she told herself.

As if you could have, her more honest self countered.

She tried not to think about that. She had her memory. That was what she'd wanted, wasn't it? Of course it was. *So be grateful and stop mooning around,* she chided herself.

She tried.

It didn't help that Daniel and Caleb and Carrie talked about him constantly. They were like little lost souls now that they didn't have Rance to follow around and ask questions and pester all day.

It was ridiculous! He hadn't been here *that* long. She said so rather sharply when Daniel was pouting because Rance wasn't there to help him with his fractions one night.

"Well, I hate fractions. An' I miss Rance," Daniel said stubbornly. "I wish he'd come back."

"Well, he's not going to." She was determined to force realism on her children, even if she still dreamed about him herself.

"Ever?"

How could a mother look into eyes that deep and trusting, eyes that had known a lot of hurt in eight years, and deny that Rance would *ever* come back.

He might, after all, someday...even if she didn't want him to.

"No time soon," she hedged.

Daniel brightened. Then he stabbed his well-used eraser at his math paper and his smile faded. "Not soon enough," he said glumly.

"I want him to come to my birthday," Carrie said. "Do you think he'll come for my birthday?"

Ellie picked her up and gave her a hug. "I don't think so, sweetie. But there will be so many kids here, you won't miss him."

Carrie wriggled to get down. "Will, too."

Only Josh, bless his heart, seemed to be immune.

He actually seemed glad Rance was gone, even though it meant more responsibility fell on him. He didn't seem to mind. He even whistled when he went to feed the horses these days.

"You're certainly cheerier about having to get up and at 'em anymore," Ellie said to him late that week.

Josh shrugged. "It's my job."

She should have left it at that, but perversely, and maybe because she wanted someone else to express relief that Rance was gone, she pressed on.

"I'd have thought you'd have been glad to have help.

He did a lot," she added. She didn't have to say who she meant. They both knew.

"I reckoned you missed him," Josh said, almost accusing.

She wondered if he suspected what had happened the night he was gone to Matt's birthday. Sometimes the way he looked at her...half lost, half searching...made her think that he might.

But he never said anything. And he never brought Rance up unless she did. Sometimes she thought he looked so much like Rance she was amazed that if he looked in the mirror he couldn't tell.

Until Rance had come back into her life, she'd never given much thought to how much Josh was like him— in looks and in temperament. They were both unholy stubborn. They both were opinionated, argumentative and right ten times out of ten. They had high expectations for everyone, including themselves. And they couldn't be pushed. Nowhere. No how. No time.

And yet, he was just as much a product of Spike's love and devotion. He had Spike's ready grin, his willingness to take on anything, to do the best he could, to go the extra mile.

Ah, Josh, she thought, watching him go out the door and across the yard, wearing Spike's old cowboy hat and walking with Rance's easy, rolling gait.

He was such a combination of the two men she loved that sometimes her heart ached just looking at him.

"The tour bus was a bad idea." Trey Phillips was popping the tab on a beer can when he spoke, and his words were so astonishingly unexpected that for a moment Rance thought he was hearing things.

The old man had been gruff upon Rance's return. He'd

said, "Where the hell have you been?" and, not getting a satisfactory answer, had stalked off, saying, "Some folks have work to do—taking up slack for those who don't bother doing theirs."

Rance's hands had curled into fists, but he had forced himself not to respond. They'd made brief and desultory remarks on the few occasions their paths had crossed in the ranch house living room and kitchen for the next few days.

Tonight, though, Clara the cook's night off, they seemed to be stuck with each other. Rance had been wondering if he ought to stay at the office and claim to be working late. God knew he could spend hours on the paperwork alone that he'd left behind. But he hated paperwork—even more than he hated the thought of dinner with his father.

And he *wanted* to be at the ranch. It felt somehow closer to Ellie, though it wasn't.

Now he propped his backside against the kitchen counter and took a deep, wary breath.

"Quantity isn't the answer," Trey went on, his voice muffled as he bent over and peered into the refrigerator. He took out last night's roast and several plastic containers of leftovers. Then he turned to face Rance. "Quality's the name of the game." He beamed, as if he'd just answered the final Double Jeopardy question.

Rance just stared at him.

Trey opened a beer and handed it to him. Then he lifted his own can in a toast. "To Stephanie."

Rance, the can halfway to his lips, stopped dead. "Stephanie? Who's Stephanie?"

"A woman of quality," Trey said. "Bright, beautiful blonde. Legs from here to Missoula. Mount Holyoke honors grad. She works for Owens. She's a CPA." He whistled as he put the leftovers in pans and set them on the stove. "Why don't you slice that roast?" he suggested.

Rance thought that offering him a knife was not the smartest move his father had ever made. He stayed right where he was, silent as a stone. He just stared at the old man, didn't even move.

Finally Trey noticed. He put the pans on the stove to heat, got plates out of the cupboard and set them on the table, took another swallow of beer, then glanced over at his son. A frown line appeared between his brows as he met Rance's stare. "What?"

"Who's Stephanie?" Rance repeated with deadly calm.

"I told you," Trey blustered. "A glorious girl. Puts me in mind of your mother when she was that age. I'd take her out myself if I hadn't already promised you to her." He put knives and forks and spoons alongside the plates, slanting a narrow glance in Rance's direction to see his son's reaction to that.

Rance felt a muscle in his jaw twitch. His fist curled so tightly around the beer can that it began to crumple in his hand.

"Not marriage," Trey said, noticing the crumpling sound. "I didn't promise marriage, boy. I just said dinner."

"No!"

The force of that one word was enough to make Trey take a quick step back. But then he stopped and planted himself firmly to meet Rance, glare for glare. "Why not?"

"Because I don't want to. *I* didn't ask her. You think she's dating material, you take her out!"

"I'm not in the market for a wife! You are."

"I am not!" *Not anymore.*

Trey went stock-still. His gaze narrowed. He looked at Rance closely. "Is there something you're not telling me?" he asked, and he seemed suddenly rather pale.

"What?"

"I mean, well..." Trey swallowed awkwardly. "You're not...gay, are you?"

Rance groaned. "No, Dad, I'm not gay."

Trey's relief was palpable. "Well, then, for God's sake, what's the problem? It's only dinner."

"I don't need you finding me a woman," Rance said firmly, but at Trey's intense scrutiny, he found his gaze sliding away.

Trey picked up the butcher knife and began to cut the meat himself. He focused on it, not even looking at Rance. "Found one of your own?" The question was casual, the intent was not. Every fiber of Trey Phillips's being seemed to be waiting, primed for Rance's reply.

He would have liked to say no.

But he wasn't ashamed of his choice, damn it! And he didn't want his father to think he was.

If he married Ellie, she was going to have to go nose to nose with Trey Phillips for the rest of her life. He couldn't hide his feelings now.

But he couldn't tell his father her name, either. The last thing he wanted was the old man meddling in this. He thought Ellie would say yes. If the way she'd loved him was any indication, he had nothing to worry about. But he hadn't asked her yet.

"Maybe," he said now.

"*Maybe?*" It wasn't a question; it was a yelp. "My God, boy! Don't you know your own mind?"

"I know my mind," Rance said stubbornly. "I don't know hers yet."

"Well, she'd be a damn fool to turn a Phillips down!"

"In your opinion," Rance said drily.

Trey just looked at him. Rance knew the meaning of the look—that Trey's opinion was the only one that mattered.

"Tell me about her," Trey commanded.

"No."

"Afraid I won't approve?" Trey lifted a brow mockingly.

Rance tipped his beer and took a swallow. "Actually, I'm afraid she won't like you."

For a moment Trey looked startled. Then he laughed. "I'll be looking forward to meeting her."

Ellie was elbow deep in five-year-olds.

They'd played pin the tail on the donkey, London Bridge is falling down, and find the potato in the garden. They'd sung a thousand verses of "There's a Hole in My Bucket, Dear Liza" and twice that many of "Row, Row, Row Your Boat." They'd picked their own toppings and had garnished their own tiny individual pizzas, which were now baking in Ellie's oven—but not fast enough.

"When can we have the cake?" one five-year-old asked, tugging at the leg of her jeans.

"An' ice cream?" asked another.

"An' when do I get to open my presents?" Carrie whispered in her ear.

"Soon," Ellie said to the first child, the second child and then to Carrie. "Soon."

But definitely, as far as Ellie and everyone else was concerned, not soon enough.

Birthday parties were not Ellie's forte. The boys had never wanted them.

"Games?" they'd said. "Favors? Yuck."

They'd just wanted each other to wrestle to the ground,

a little cake and ice cream and maybe a trip to a movie on Saturday afternoon. But Carrie had had her heart set on a "scrumptious party" ever since she'd been to Ashley Dean's fifth birthday last Hallowe'en.

"We dipped for apples," she'd told her mother, eyes wide with excitement as she'd climbed into the truck, wearing a nylon net tutu over her jeans. "An' we made costumes an' dressed up, an' we had a parade, an' prizes an' dancing!"

"Dancing?" Ellie had echoed doubtfully.

"It was swell." Carrie had given a little bounce on the seat of the truck. "I want a party like that."

There was no way on earth Ellie could have come up with a party to rival the Dean extravaganza. But when Carrie kept asking, she found herself committed to at least having Carrie's preschool friends over for the afternoon.

It escalated from there. Of course there had to be games, Carrie decided. And prizes. And food.

"Cake," Ellie agreed. "And ice cream."

"Ashley had chicken à la king," Carrie looked at her mother hopefully.

Ellie suppressed a gag.

"How 'bout pizza," Caleb, bless him, had suggested.

"Oooh, yes!" Pizza was Carrie's favorite.

Ellie didn't remember how on earth pizza had become, over time, individual pizzas with individual garnishes. She supposed it might have come from the day she'd run into Ashley's mother in the grocery store and had been a little airier about party plans than she'd had any right to.

"Do you want me to come out and help you?" Ashley's mother, a vivacious, terribly competent transplanted Californian called Melanie, had asked.

The last thing Ellie wanted was some ultracompetent party giver helping her paltry efforts. "Just drop Ashley off and come and get her," she'd said.

"Will do," Melanie agreed cheerfully. "But if you find you've bitten off too much, don't hesitate to let me know, and I'll help."

She would call in the Marines first, Ellie had thought then.

And she might have to, she thought now as she watched as half a dozen little boys pretended to sword fight with plastic tubes and wrapping paper roll cores. One thumped another on the head. That one took a round-house swing at a third.

"Watch it," Ellie cautioned. She caught a whiff of the pizzas in the oven, yet wasn't sure she dared leave the fledgling knights long enough to get them out. The girls were climbing the fence and trying to balance on it. Mostly they were teetering and falling off.

Ellie held her breath. She needed reinforcements. Badly. When she'd scheduled the party, she hadn't known Sandra would be getting a root canal this afternoon.

"I can cancel," her mother-in-law had offered.

But Ellie knew the pain of an abscessed tooth. "No," she said firmly. "I can manage."

Perhaps she'd overstated things a bit. She sniffed the air. The pizzas were burning.

"Watch those boys with the swords," she commanded Josh, who was sitting on the porch looking bored. He was there under protest, anyway.

"Why can't I just come for the food?" he'd asked. "I don't wanta mess with a bunch of kindergartners."

"They aren't even in kindergarten," Caleb, drat him, had reminded him.

Ellie could have shot them both. And Daniel, too, she thought, looking around for him now and not seeing him.

"Just watch them," she said to Josh again. *And, please God, don't let anything happen!* Then she made a mad dash for the kitchen.

She needed ten hands. Why had she ever decided letting fifteen five-year-olds make individual pizzas was a good idea?

She grabbed two pot holders, flung open the oven door and began hauling them out as fast as she could. The ones closest to the door were still pretty edible. When she got to the ones farther back, she understood where the burning smell had come from. They all had a certain "blackened" look.

She tried scraping off bits of burnt pizza crust as she arranged them on a platter. As she did so, she heard a truck pull up outside. *Please,* she thought, *don't let it be Ashley's mother!*

Melanie had looked around doubtfully when she'd dropped her little darling off earlier that afternoon, as if she wondered what she was letting the little girl in for.

"Sure you don't want me to stay?" she'd asked.

"Quite sure," Ellie had replied, smiling through her teeth.

"Whatever you say," Melanie said. "But I'll stop back early just in case."

Ellie glanced at her watch now as the door opened

behind her. Drat the woman! she thought. Oh well, it couldn't be helped.

She picked up the tray, pasted a cheerful, welcoming, totally hypocritical smile on her face as she turned around. "Ah, Melanie, you're just in time for—"

"Rance?"

The platter of pizzas hit the floor with a crash.

Eight

She could have looked happier to see him.

She could have thrown her arms around him, instead of throwing a whole cookie sheet full of pizzas into the air. Rance thought she was looking at him as if she'd seen a ghost, or a two-headed monster—or Cleve Hardesty on her doorstep with the deed to the ranch.

"Hey, El, it's not that bad, is it?" he said with a grin.

But when she continued to look stricken, and her gaze moved between him and the mess on the floor, he had to rethink the homecoming he'd been planning.

"I guess maybe it is," he said with a grimace. But then he bent and began to clean up the mess. "Look, I'll just clean it up and it will be fine."

He expected her to help him. She didn't move. She looked like she was about to cry.

He scrambled to his feet. "Don't," he said, putting his arms around her. "Don't cry, El! For God's sake—for *my* sake—don't cry!"

"Hey, Mom! They're about to mutiny," Josh yelled from the yard. "Bring on the pizzas!"

"Oh, God." At least Josh's desperation galvanized her. Ellie looked around frantically. "What am I going to do?" Then she looked back at him. "What are you doing here?"

It sounded so much like an accusation he didn't think now was exactly the time to propose.

"Well, it is Carrie's birthday, and I was invited." He grinned at her hopefully. Was this the woman who'd loved him so desperately just a week ago? The woman who had made him rethink and then change every resolution he'd ever had about getting married and settling down?

"Oh." Her face cleared. "Yes, of course. But I didn't think—" She broke off.

"But you didn't think I'd come?" Well, he supposed she might not. After all, he'd left her once before. But they'd been little more than kids then. And he hadn't said he'd be back that time!

This time he had—and he'd moved heaven and earth and five court dates to get here, as well. But before he could tell her any of that, Josh burst into the room.

"Food! We need food." The boy looked as if he were being pursued by all the hounds of hell. "They're gonna eat me alive if you don't bring on those—hey!" He spied the mess of pizzas on the floor. "What happened?" Then his gaze nailed Rance accusingly. "What'd you do to her?" Then he turned to Ellie. "Mom, what's wrong?"

"Nothing," Rance said firmly, "that a loaf of bread and some peanut butter and jelly won't fix. Get the jelly," he commanded Josh.

Ellie looked horrified. "We can't feed them peanut butter and jelly!"

Rance spread his hands and looked at her, waiting for whatever she had that was a better idea.

But she just looked around helplessly for a moment, then shrugged and reached for the bread. "What's Melanie going to say?" she murmured.

"Who's Melanie?"

"Never mind. You're right. Of course you're right. We have to feed them something. It's just— Get a grip, El," she commanded herself. Then, giving herself a little shake, she grabbed a knife from the drawer and began slapping on the peanut butter.

Outside, the mutterings of small, hungry children grew louder.

"Mom, they're gonna come in here," Josh warned at the door.

"So go entertain them."

"Me?" Josh looked appalled, shook his head and started backing up.

"Then find Caleb and Daniel and tell them to! Where *are* Caleb and Daniel?" she muttered distractedly.

"They were down at the corral when I drove in," Rance said.

"The corral? What were they doing? Ruckus is in there, and he's still skittish. I don't want them messing with him."

The words were barely out of her mouth when more footsteps pounded across the porch.

"Ma!" Caleb came running. "Daniel's hurt!"

"What!" Ellie dropped the peanut butter knife and whirled toward the screen door.

Caleb's face was flushed as he gasped, "Ruckus kicked 'im!"

Ellie shot Rance a stricken look. "He's not supposed to be messing with Ruckus!"

No, he wasn't. The roan gelding was a handful even for Rance, though he'd got him in pretty good shape before he'd left. In any case it was too late to worry about that now.

Rance beat her out the door, striding past the clamoring horde of five-year-olds, whose interest in their stomachs was momentarily diverted by this new disaster. By the time Ellie caught up with him, he was kneeling in the corral beside Daniel. The boy's face was chalk white and he had dusty hoofprint on his bright yellow T-shirt.

"Nailed you in the ribs, did he?" Rance asked, running his hands over the boy as he spoke. "That all?"

Daniel nodded. "Wasn't his fault." His words came out in a wheezy little gasp. "One of those kids moved fast an' scared him."

"Is he all right? Oh, Daniel! Where does it hurt?" Ellie reached them now and crouched beside them, brushing Daniel's hair away from his forehead.

"'M all right," he tried to reassure her. He even managed a grin, but it ended in a gasp when Rance pressed lightly on his ribs.

"Don't! You'll hurt him!" Ellie cried, trying to slap Rance's hand away.

"I won't hurt him," Rance said. He slid his arms beneath Daniel and scooped him gently up. "Open the gate," he told Josh.

Josh did, herding the little kids back as they began to crowd around. Then he and Caleb blocked them while Rance carried Daniel through the gate.

"I can carry him," Ellie said, running alongside, and when Rance didn't hand him over, she directed, "Put him in the truck. I'll call the doctor. I have to take him to the doctor."

Rance glanced pointedly at the small sea of children who'd been flowing after them from the corral to the truck. "I don't think so."

Ellie turned around, seemed to see the children for the first time, then pressed her hands to her cheeks. "Oh, Lord. What am I going to do?"

"Feed them peanut butter and jelly sandwiches and ice cream and cake," Rance said calmly.

"But Daniel—"

"I'll take Daniel. Won't I, pal?"

And Daniel at least looked up at him with trusting eyes. "Sure."

Where were they?

The party had ended. The kids had departed. The mess was cleaned up. The kitchen floor shone. Carrie had declared her birthday "super" beyond her wildest expectations because, "Even Rance was here, Mommy!"

And now it was past seven o'clock and *still* they weren't home.

"I didn't think Rance would come," Carrie confided as she lay in her brand-new dalmatian-covered bed and beamed at her mother who sat on the edge of the bed.

"I didn't, either," Ellie admitted. It had been the biggest shock of the day when she'd looked up and seen him standing in her kitchen. Her heart had lurched at just the sight of him—as had the cookie sheet full of pizzas. It was probably just as well, in the long run, that it had happened, Ellie thought now. The kids had actually enjoyed their peanut butter and jelly sandwiches—and cleaning up the mess had covered up her confusion at seeing Rance again.

It would never have done to have acted on her next impulse, which had been to throw her arms around him. That was what she'd wanted to do, heaven help her.

Why had he come?

"He brought me Lone Bear," Carrie said happily. She was hugging Rance's present in one arm while she hugged the newly dressed Clarissa in the other.

The bear Rance had brought her was a near perfect masculine match for Clarissa—same size, same soft brown fur, same soulful brown eyes. The only difference was his two intact ears—and the chaps, bandanna and jaunty black felt cowboy hat.

"He looks 'zackly like I knew he would," Carrie said, giving the bear a squeeze. "He is my best best present. An' Clarissa loves him."

So did Carrie—that was all too clear. Something Ellie refused to put a name to squeezed at her heart, and she leaned down and gave Carrie a kiss. Carrie's arms, still full of bears, came up to wrap around her mother's neck and hugged her tightly.

"This was my best best birthday, too," she said. Then as they pulled apart, she yawned, then smiled and said, "See? I tol' you parties were wonderful."

Ellie would have begged to differ. But she knew better than to argue with a contented five-year-old. "I'm glad you had a good one," she whispered. Then after another kiss, she stood up. "'Night, lovey."

"'Night," Carrie whispered back. She rolled on her side and snuggled both bears against her chest. She was asleep before Ellie got out the door.

Josh wasn't quite so pleased. He was watching television when she came back downstairs, but he looked at her when she came into the room. "What's he doing here?"

Ellie didn't ask who he meant, just as she didn't probe the surliness in his tone. She was wondering the same thing, but she didn't say so. "He came for Carrie's birthday," she said as if she'd expected Rance all along.

Josh grunted. "When's he leaving?"

Ellie wondered that, too.

He hadn't come back for another night's stand, had he? He had to realize that that had been a one-off, a single, desperate, passionate night.

She could not—*would not*—have an affair with him!

And she would tell him that, too—*if he ever came home!*

While Josh watched his television program, she paced the kitchen. She glanced at her watch. Surely they couldn't be at the doctor's all this time! She had called to tell them Rance was bringing Daniel and had hoped someone would call her back with news. But no one had.

Usually the office closed at five-thirty. She rang up. Of course they were gone. The hospital! Had they put Daniel in the hospital? They couldn't have! Could they? She called the hospital. Daniel wasn't there.

Where *were* they?

And then, just before eight-thirty she saw a pair of headlights come around the bend in the road.

She was out the door and running to meet the truck, standing where it would park before it came to a stop. "Where have you been?" Her voice was shrill, almost furious, as she yanked open the door. "Are you all right?" she demanded, reaching for Daniel.

"'M fine," he murmured, blinking, and she realized she'd awakened both boys. "Jus' one broken rib," he told her sleepily.

"One broken rib?" She looked at him, then at Rance who was looking at her, too. "Then where have you been all this time?"

"We went to dinner," he said. His voice was low and flat and, as a result, made hers sound all that much louder.

"Pizza," Caleb said cheerfully. "Pepperoni."

"With a broken rib? You took him out for pizza when he had a broken rib?"

Rance shrugged. "I thought it would be a better idea than bringing him back here where a hundred kindergartners could poke him and ask questions."

There was some truth to that, of course. But still...!
"You could have called!"

Rance didn't answer that. He seemed curiously remote.
Maybe dealing with injured children brought that out in
him. Probably it did, Ellie decided. Or maybe her yelling
at him was making him retreat into a shell. Good. Then
maybe he would go away without propositioning her.
Maybe she wouldn't have to tell him she wouldn't have
an affair with him after all.

The boys slid out of the truck. Daniel winced as he hit
the ground. His arm was in a sling, bound against his
chest.

"Did they tape it?" she asked Rance.

"No. He's just supposed to keep his arm as immobile
as possible. It will hurt. There's not much they can do
about it." He handed her a bottle that she guessed was
pain medication. "No more tonight," he said.

"Right." Ellie herded the boys toward the house. They
were more awake now. Caleb was talking about video
games. "Rance let us play 'em at the pizza place," he
said. "We got eight quarters each. I won most."

"Well, my arm hurt," Daniel said.

"Yeah, but I beat Rance, too," Caleb said. "He wasn't
payin' attention."

He didn't seem to be paying attention now, either. He
had wandered out into the living room where Josh was
watching the end of his show.

"Bedtime," Ellie said. She chivied them toward the
stairs. "Say good night, guys."

"'Night," Caleb said cheerfully. "Thanks for the
pizza and games. It was fun."

"'Night," Daniel said a little more quietly. "Thanks,
Rance. I was glad you were there."

Rance smiled at him. "I'm glad I was, too," he said equally gravely.

Then Josh edged past him, and Rance said, "'Night, Josh."

For a second Ellie thought Josh might not answer. But then he glanced back. "'Night," he said, and there was finality in his tone.

The two of them exchanged a long look. Ellie noted that it was Josh who looked away first, and continued up the stairs.

Ellie started after them, then hesitated. "Carrie's already asleep," she said, "but she loved her bear. It was very kind of you." She gave him a smile. It was her best attempt at a polite smile—a smile that said, *Please go now. I don't want to have to spell this out for you.* "Excuse me. I need to get the kids to bed."

Rance nodded, but he didn't move toward the door. He looked at her, his expression hooded. "I'll wait. We have to talk."

Ellie didn't want to talk. She didn't want to have to admit she'd made a mistake in loving him. She didn't want to have to lie and say she wished he'd go away, when really she wished he'd stay forever. But forever wasn't an option.

Forever had never been an option. She'd just been too young and stupid to realize it all those years ago.

It's the price you pay, she told herself. She should have known there would be a price—for this loving just as much as there had been for their loving in the past. A different price, to be sure. But nothing she did ever came without cost.

She took her time with the boys. Avoiding the inevitable, she knew. But she justified it by telling herself that she hadn't been with Daniel at the doctor, so she needed to be with him now. And she did need to hear everything the doctor had told him, though she would make sure to get it again from Rance before he left—and she would doubtless call the doctor herself in the morning.

Daniel did not seem to have been traumatized by being sent to the doctor with Rance. "He said he knew how much it hurt," Daniel told her when she had him tucked into bed. He looked up at her with serious eyes. "He's had broken ribs before. An' a broken arm. He said his hurt so bad he almost cried. He said I was real brave, Mom."

"You were, sweetie." Ellie tucked the blanket a little more snugly around him, then bent to kiss him goodnight. "Very brave indeed."

"It was easier to be brave with Rance there," he said after a moment. "Even when the doctor was pokin' me, I stayed still. I didn't want him to think I was a crybaby." It wasn't the doctor he was talking about and Ellie knew it.

She touched his hair lightly, then gave his hand an extra squeeze and got up, careful not to jiggle the bed. "If you need anything in the night, you just shout or send Caleb down," she told him.

"'Kay." Daniel chewed his lower lip for just a moment. "I'm glad he was there."

Ellie nodded. "I am, too." And that, at least, was the truth.

"Me, too," Caleb chimed from the other bed.

She smiled at them both. Then her gaze went to her oldest son. Josh was lying there, his head propped on one elbow, as he looked at her. He didn't say anything—just looked.

Ellie tried a smile. He didn't respond. She wanted to say, *Don't be like this. He'll be gone in the morning.* But she didn't. This was adult business, no matter how adult, Josh, at ten, thought he was. She kissed his cheek. "'Night, Josh."

"'Night." He looked away.

Josh could hear his brothers whispering below, talking about beating Rance at some stupid video game and how maybe Daniel would do it next time because then his ribs wouldn't hurt so much.

There won't be a next time, he wanted to shout at his brothers. Because right now—right this very minute—Mom was going downstairs to tell him to go away.

Josh felt sort of squirmy, wiggly, guilty knowing that—and knowing the way he felt was part of the reason she was doing it. He'd seen her sometimes when she looked at Rance—and he knew she didn't dislike him.

No. It wasn't just that she didn't *dislike* Rance. Josh knew she liked him. A lot.

But *he* didn't like Rance. He didn't like anybody who came nosing around, trying to take his dad's place. There wasn't anybody on earth who could take his dad's place!

"So don't even think about it," he muttered now under his breath.

"You awake, Josh?" Caleb said aloud. "You wanta come with us next time?"

"No!"

There was a moment's startled silence at the intensity of his reply. Then Daniel, ever the peacemaker, said, "It's okay. You don't have to."

"More quarters for us," Caleb said cheerfully.

"Caleb," Daniel chastised him.

"Well, I was only sayin'—"

"Shut up," Josh said fiercely. "Just shut up, both of you!"

* * *

Rance was in the living room when she came back down the stairs. He stood by the fireplace, studying the family photos on the mantel. *Good,* Ellie thought. *Take a good look. Realize my position, and you'll know I can't have an affair.*

She wiped her hands down the sides of her jeans, drying suddenly damp palms. At the sound of her footsteps, Rance turned around.

"I really am very grateful you showed up today," she began briskly, trying to put them on a casual-friendship footing so she could get him out the door with the least acrimony possible.

"It was very thoughtful of you to bring Carrie the bear. And I don't know what I would have done with all those kids after Daniel got hurt if you hadn't been here." She was babbling and she knew it, but the intent way he was looking at her made her feel the need to fill all the silence with every bit of sound she could manage.

"I was…happy to do it." He sounded almost formal, too. Then he raked a hand through his hair. "We have to talk."

Quickly, almost desperately, Ellie shook her head. "We have nothing to talk about." She picked up the afghan from the back of the chair and began folding it, not looking at him. "Once was it, Rance. We can't do it again."

"It?" he echoed, confused. But then he must have realized what she meant, because he made a small harsh sound and said almost bitterly, "Once wasn't it, though, was it?"

She pressed the folded afghan against her chest. "What do you mean?"

His blue eyes challenged her. "We made love eleven years ago."

"That was different. That was then." She put the afghan down and went into the kitchen, needing to get away from his gaze, even though she knew he would follow her.

"Different how?"

"We were young." She didn't look at him, focusing instead on filling the coffeemaker for morning. "Foolish. Irresponsible. We didn't have commitments. Now we do. At least *I* do." She did look at him then, so he could see how seriously she felt. "I can't play games now, Rance. I have kids."

"Do I?"

His question was so unexpected, for a moment she almost didn't hear it. And even when she finally processed the words, she didn't understand. Not at first. Then her fingers clenched on the coffee scoop, and she turned her head to see Rance standing there, feet slightly spread, fingers lightly curled, looking intently, straight at her.

"Do you what?" she asked carefully, needing to be sure.

Rance sucked in a slow breath. "Do I have a child?"

Ellie strangled the coffee scoop. "Why on earth would you ask me a thing like that?" Her heart was pounding so hard and fast she thought he must be able to see and hear it from the other side of the room.

"Because Josh isn't Joshua, is he?" Rance said quietly. "He's John. John Ransome."

Ellie went absolutely still. Now she wasn't even breathing. *This couldn't be happening. Not now. Not after everything else.*

"And," Rance went on in the same quiet voice, "because the new nurse at Dr. Cummings's office thinks the twins look like you and Josh looks like me.''

''Spike—''

''Doesn't look like me. The doctor asked if I was Spike's brother. When I said no, he said he didn't think so, that Spike didn't look at all like me.''

Ellie didn't say anything to that. What could she say? She just looked at him, and then down at the counter— at the coffeemaker, which had looked safe, when in fact, nothing and nowhere had been safe. She wished the world would open and swallow her up before he could ask what she knew he was going to ask her next.

But the world didn't open, and the ground didn't swallow her. And into the silence she heard the words she'd feared hearing for the past ten years.

''Is Josh my son?''

She stared at the floor, then at Rance's boots, at his knees, at his belt buckle. But she couldn't bring her eyes up further. ''Yes,'' she said at last, in a voice so quiet that she knew he couldn't really hear her. She cleared her throat and lifted her eyes, meeting his stormy blue gaze. ''Yes, Josh is your son.''

Rance didn't say a word. He just looked at her.

And Ellie could do nothing but look back at him, trapped by the intensity of his gaze. A part of her wanted to run, wanted to hide, wanted at least to lower her eyes.

But she didn't. She had nothing left to hide.

Besides, since he had asked, she owed him honesty. And she owed herself—and Josh—the conviction that she'd made the best decision she could have made for all of them at the time.

''Why didn't you tell me?'' His voice was still quiet, but hollow, too. Hurt almost.

Damn it! He had no right to be hurt. It wasn't as if he'd wanted a child!

"You *know* why I didn't tell you! Think about it," Ellie said. "You didn't want to get married. You said it over and over again. Every time I brought up the notion of marriage or kids, you didn't want to hear."

"You knew...then?" Now he sounded accusing. And angry!

Angry? That made her mad, too. "Yes, I knew. Oh, not the first time I brought up the idea. I think I was just dreaming youthful girlish dreams then," she said with self-deprecating scorn. "And you handed me a dose of reality pretty darn fast. But yes, the last time I mentioned it—the time you said that kids were an albatross you wanted no part of—" she went straight on, ignoring his wince "—yes, then I knew."

For a long time he didn't speak. Just stood there, his fingers curling into fists and uncurling again. A muscle twitched in his jaw. His eyes flashed fire and pain and a million other emotions that Ellie refused to acknowledge. He wasn't going to make her out to be the bad guy in this! She'd done the best she could. She'd done what she had to do.

She kept her gaze steady on him, refusing even to blink, not permitting herself the smallest waver. This was harder by far than anything she'd thought she might have to tell him tonight. This was the hardest thing she would ever have to tell him.

But she could do it. She had to.

And still he didn't say a word.

Just as well, Ellie thought. There was nothing at all Rance could say now that she wanted to hear. Finally she realized she was holding her breath—had been for she didn't know how long. She let it out shakily. She loosed her grip on the afghan. She ran her fingers through her hair.

"I—I've had a long day, Rance. A hard day. I need...I need to go to sleep." She looked away from him then, to gaze pointedly at the door.

He didn't seem to hear her for a moment. He didn't move, just stood there, as if he'd been turned to stone. And then, at last, he nodded. He crossed the room, moving like he'd aged fifty years. "Fine. We'll talk in the morning."

No, Ellie thought. *We won't. We've said all there is to say.* But she wasn't going to argue with him now. She couldn't argue.

She followed him to the door and opened it, holding it wide. "Thank you for helping with Daniel." *Ah, Ellie,* she could almost hear Spike drawling, *polite to the end. That's my girl.*

Not that Rance noticed. He didn't even look at her, and only grunted absently on his way out.

Ellie shut the door after him, then stood watching in the darkness, waiting for him to get into his truck, waiting for the truck to head over the hills and far away.

He didn't. He opened the back, took out a sleeping bag and headed for the barn.

It didn't change anything.

It changed everything.

It didn't matter.

It mattered more than he could imagine.

He'd been going to ask her to marry him, anyway. So what difference did it make whose child Josh was? Rance asked himself that over and over.

For whatever reasons he didn't know, it made a world of difference.

He had a son.

When he'd confronted her with the question, he made it sound as if he'd accepted it without batting an eye, when the pieces had fallen together in the doctor's office that afternoon. In fact, he'd felt poleaxed, as if all his moorings had been cut from beneath him.

He had a son.

Every assumption that he'd made about his life in the last eleven years had been, in that single moment, shot to hell. Fundamental things that he'd been certain were true, weren't true at all. He who had prided himself on remaining unattached, unencumbered, uninvolved with the future of the human race, had already unknowingly done his part. He had unwittingly perpetuated the Phillips dynasty.

He had a son.

A son that Ellie had kept from him. A son that she'd given to another man to raise. A son who, to be honest, didn't even seem to like him very much.

Rance didn't sleep a wink all night. He sat, he paced, he prowled, he stewed. He thought about how he might never have known—about how if that skunk hadn't been where he was, if Sunny hadn't bolted, if that damn magazine hadn't written that article, if his father hadn't come up with that flaming tour bus—

Cripes, the old man would be over the moon!

And he would think it was all because of him. Rance ground his teeth.

It had nothing to do with the old man, he decided. It had nothing to do with the Phillips dynasty.

It had only to do with himself and Ellie.

And Josh.

And Daniel, Caleb and Carrie.

In the end it came right back to doing what he'd come

to do in the first place: marrying Ellie—for yet another reason. And the sooner the better.

It was true then. Nothing had changed.

He waited until the boys had all gone off to school the next morning. He saw Sandra drive up, look at his truck speculatively, then go inside and almost at once return with Carrie and the bears. She put them into the truck and drove away.

She left Ellie alone. For him.

Rance sucked in a breath, squared his shoulders and crossed the yard. He climbed the steps, opened the door and walked in.

Ellie stood facing him.

"I didn't come back to bring the bear yesterday," Rance said without preamble. "I came back to marry you."

Ellie's eyes widened. She stared at him. She didn't look nearly as pleased as she ought to.

Rance wondered if she wanted him to get down on one knee. Well, he wasn't going to. He might love her, but he was hurt and he was mad as hell at her.

He would propose, however. He owed her that much.

"Will you marry me?" he said.

She said, "No."

Nine

"No?"

If there was one thing Rance hadn't counted on, it was finally getting around to asking a woman to marry him and having her tell him no.

No? He was shocked. Astonished. Stunned. "What do you mean, no?"

Ellie blinked, as if his amazement was amazing in itself. "Just what I said," she told him with the calm of the flaming Dead Sea. "No." And then she turned her back on him to put a load of wash in the washing machine, as if he'd ceased to matter, as if she could just shut him out!

"You have my son." He said the words in measured firm tones.

"He's my son, too." She put the laundry in, not looking at him until she was finished. Then she glanced over her shoulder and said with pointed emphasis, "He was Spike's son, too. Josh adored his father."

"*I'm* his father!"

"There's more to fatherhood than simply donating sperm."

"I didn't damn well 'donate' sperm! And you didn't give me a chance to do more!"

"This is all my fault, is it? Well, maybe it is. But I had to think about what was best—for him, for you, for me. You didn't want a child. You didn't want to perpetuate the family dynasty. Remember?''

Rance remembered. He didn't want to, but he did. Every single word. "That was then," he argued.

"And this is now," Ellie agreed. "And as far as I can see, nothing has changed."

"Of course it's changed! I just told you, I came back to marry you!"

Ellie looked at him. "Just like that," she said, giving her fingers a little faint snap.

"You love me! Damn it, I know you love me!"

"Yes." Ellie didn't deny it. But she didn't look especially happy about it, either. "And even eleven years ago it wasn't enough, was it?"

He stared at her, nonplused. "What do you mean, it isn't enough? Do you think I don't love you? I do." He threw the words down like they were a gauntlet.

They lay there between them, almost tangible. Ellie seemed to be staring at some point halfway between them for a very long time. Then she looked at him again. "And that's not enough, either, now. Is it?" she asked him.

His brows drew down. "Why not? What isn't enough?"

"There's more than me and you involved in this."

"The kids, you mean? What about them? Daniel and Caleb and Carrie like me well enough. I don't think they'd mind."

"Josh would mind."

"*What?*"

She lifted her shoulders. "Josh doesn't want me finding a replacement for his father."

"He told you that?"

"In so many words."

"In how many words?"

"You sound just like a lawyer."

"I *am* a lawyer."

Ellie shuddered. "Don't remind me." Then she muttered, "Sorry, I shouldn't have said that."

"Why? Do you think I'm going to take you to court? Sue you for custody, maybe?"

Her face went paper white.

"I didn't say I was going to do it!" Rance snapped. "Stop looking at me that way."

But even though she breathed again, it took her color a while to begin to return. She turned on the wash and sank down into one of the kitchen chairs. "You wouldn't," she said shakily.

"No," Rance said through his teeth. "But that doesn't mean you're not going to have to tell him."

She didn't answer that. She seemed to be concentrating on simply getting enough air. He waited, just watching her breathe, biding his time. They weren't done with this yet.

"You are going to have to tell him, Ellie. Or I am."

"No!"

"Then *you* are." He stood in front of her, squared off for a challenge, determined on this point at least.

Ellie ran her tongue over her lips. She pressed her fingers against her eyes. "He loved Spike," she said softly. The words sounded as if they were being torn from her. "Of all the boys, Josh was the one who..."

"I know that," Rance said. "Don't you think I've seen it? I only had to talk to him for ten minutes to know that everything he and I did while I was here, his fath— Spike—could have done better!"

"Well, it was true!" Ellie's temper flashed.

"I don't doubt that. I just—" His fingers closed into fists. He wanted to hit something. There was nothing whatsoever to hit. "He's my son, too, El," he said hoarsely at last.

Her shoulders slumped. Her fingers knotted. "I know." She drew a breath. "I know."

"So tell him."

"It will hurt him."

"Too bad. Sometimes the truth hurts. It doesn't mean we shouldn't have to face it. I know he won't be happy. Tough. He can damn well get over it! Maybe he can even learn to like it if he tries hard enough."

"The way you learned to like doing whatever your father wanted?"

He felt like she'd punched him in the gut.

It wasn't true. He wasn't doing what his father had always done! He wasn't. This had nothing to do with him being like his father. It had to do with finding out he *was* a father—and then facing what he had to do about it.

He was grown up now, for God's sake. He had a degree, a job, a life—a sense of who he was at last. He was prepared to be a man and accept his responsibilities.

And that was all it was. Wasn't it?

Or—the question came to him as he turned his back on her and walked out—was this one more example of his selfishness?

It would have been so easy to let him have his way.

Ellie sat in the kitchen, her world in shambles around her, and thought how simple things would have been if she'd just said yes. The ranch would survive if Rance took it over. The children would have everything they could ever need—and more. Josh would have the legacy that should rightfully be his.

It would be so simple.

Not quite.

Because life wasn't that simple. Ellie herself wasn't that simple. She couldn't bring herself to just jump at his offer, though she was honest enough to admit that if he'd made it eleven years ago, despite what she said now, she would have taken it.

She had grown up in the meantime, just as he had. She knew that whatever love she felt for him was important, but it wasn't enough. And as for his loving her—well, she wasn't even sure, despite his protest that he'd been going to propose even before he found out about Josh, that love had anything to do with it.

Sex. She would believe it had to do with sex.

But they couldn't build a marriage based merely on sex and on Rance's determination to have his son. She knew what made a good marriage. She'd had one with Spike.

If she was ever going to marry again, she was determined it would be the same kind of marriage. And it would last—the way her marriage to Spike would have lasted—if they'd been given world enough and time.

Sorting it out in her head like that helped. It gave her resolve. It gave her courage. She went out the door after him.

He hadn't gone far. He was standing by the corral watching Ruckus. He turned when she came up to him. He looked at her, but apparently he didn't see what he wanted to see because, wordlessly, he turned away again.

"I do love you," she said. "You were right about that. I loved you eleven years ago. It's why I let you go without saying a word. I knew tying you down would make you hate me—and the baby."

He opened his mouth to speak, but she forestalled him.

"I didn't want that then. I don't want it now. You think you want me and Josh and you'll take on the rest because it's part of the deal, but I don't know that you really want any of it. It's certainly not what you were saying when you came a couple of weeks ago. Then you were hiding out—trying to avoid getting trapped into the very life you're telling me now that you want.'' She paused for breath.

He didn't interrupt her. He looked at her, waiting for her to get to the point.

''I knew Spike could do it because he always had done it. He'd been my friend for years and years—''

''You want me to wait years and years?''

She shook her head. ''I doubt it will take years and years. I think you'll know pretty soon. And I will.''

His gaze narrowed. ''Spell it out, Ellie.''

She pressed her lips together, then nodded. ''You have money. You have prestige. You have power. They're nice. They're not important. Not to me. Not to my family. Love and support and care—just being there and helping like Spike did—that's what's important.''

''Put up or shut up. Is that what you're saying?''

''I guess it is, yes.''

Their eyes met, locked. Rance seemed to gather himself together even as she watched. He looked stronger. Sterner. Taller. More powerful than ever.

He gave her a curt nod, and she felt as if he'd picked up the challenge she'd tossed down.

Then, ''Tell him,'' Rance said, almost as an afterthought.

Ellie expected he would do one of two things.

Either he would go away and marshal his formidable financial and legal forces and the next time she would hear from him would be a one-hundred-percent linen letter with a watermark and a demand for sole custody of

Josh or he would decide it wasn't worth the trouble, that it made a whole lot more sense to go away and forget the whole thing.

She was ready to do battle on the one hand. She held out a tiny ray of hope on the other.

She was not at all prepared for the third option—the one that he took.

He moved back into the barn and dug in.

Rance wasn't quite as sanguine about his move into the barn as he gave her the impression of being. It was his legal training. Never show your hand. And never ever let 'em know when you're bluffing.

He didn't even know if he was bluffing himself.

God knew it would be easier to go away. Ellie would never come after him. She would never even ask him for support. He could give it, of course—would give it—behind the scenes, and unless someone else ferreted out the reason, Ellie would never give him away.

But he didn't go. He stayed. He wasn't sure why. Stubbornness, maybe. Willful irritation at being rebuffed. Not many people had told Rance no in his life. He wasn't used to it. He didn't like it.

And—and this gave him pause for considerable thought—maybe she was right. Maybe he didn't have it in him to be a husband and father. Maybe when things got tough, when the demands were too irritating, niggling and annoying, he wouldn't want to bother. Maybe when push came to shove, he'd shove off.

It wasn't a particularly flattering picture. He didn't like thinking he might. But he'd never tried it, so how did he know?

He thought he'd better find out.

He was used to the barn. And now that Lilly Belle had

been reunited with her bovine colleagues, and the calf he and Ellie had delivered was also big and strong enough to be out following its mother around, he and Sunny had the accommodations to themselves.

He dumped his sleeping bag and a duffel full of clean jeans, shirts and underwear. He found a place for his laptop computer and cell phone. He hadn't expected to be using them in the barn, but if that's what it was going to take...

He looked up at the house. Ellie was hanging out a load of laundry. Her bras were flapping in the breeze again, taunting him.

There were no kids around. The coast was clear. Everything in him wanted to take advantage of the moment. "Carpe diem, isn't that what they say?" he muttered. "Seize the day."

Except he had a fair idea what making a move on Ellie would get him right now.

He seized a bridle and began to put it on Sunny instead.

She had to give him credit.

He was hanging in. He drove back and forth to his law office twice a week, which was no small effort. She saw him wrangling cattle and talking on his cell phone at the same time. Sometimes, when he had to be in court in Billings, he didn't get back until the wee hours of the morning.

But he always came.

Carrie was delighted.

She confided that she had missed her Lone Bear stories. And every night found her sitting on Rance's lap while he concocted another one. Pretty soon Carrie was telling the stories herself. And during the day it seemed to Ellie that half her daughter's sentences now started with the words, "Rance said…"

The twins were equally thrilled to have him back. As far as Daniel was concerned, Rance was his best friend. Having been through the broken ribs with Daniel, and being willing to admit how much his own broken bones had hurt, Rance was a man who could be trusted.

He also seemed to know exactly how much Daniel could do without hurting his ribs. He encouraged the boy to do what he could, even spending time with him picking out Ruckus's hooves, when Ellie wouldn't have let her son near the horse.

"Daniel won't be afraid if you don't make him that way," Rance told her.

Ellie knew that was true. But it wasn't always easy to do. Life seemed pretty fragile to her these days. But she tried to keep her mouth shut whenever Daniel and Rance went to deal with Ruckus.

She was having to keep her mouth shut a lot, it seemed.

She was tempted, every time she saw Caleb hovering around Rance, eager to get his hands on Rance's laptop computer, to say, "Don't pester him now, Caleb. Don't bother him."

But then she told herself that dealing with an inquisitive eight-year-old was something Rance would have to do if he got his wish and married her. Let him find out how many "Can I try now?"'s and "Why does it work like that?"'s and "Will you show me how?"'s it took to drive him round the bend.

It turned out that he had far more patience with that sort of thing than she did. She came downstairs one evening after putting Carrie to bed to find Caleb studiously punching numbers into the computer.

"What are you doing?" she asked.

"Adding up billable hours," Caleb said.

"You let Caleb add up your billable hours?" she demanded later that night, confronting Rance in the kitchen.

He shrugged easily. "My secretary checks his addition. He hasn't made a mistake yet. And you heard Mrs. Magruder. She said he was the best in the class when it came to adding fractions. She'd never known a child to pick it up so quickly." He grinned.

And Ellie, heaven help her, couldn't argue with him. She'd heard the very same words out of Mrs. Magruder's mouth at their parent-teacher conference just last week. She just hadn't realized how Caleb had been developing his competence, though!

She was still having trouble coming to terms with the fact that Rance had gone to the conferences.

"You're not their father," she'd told him when he'd announced his intention of coming along.

"Not yet," he'd agreed. "Not the twins', anyway." An arch of one dark brow reminded her of what he didn't have to tell her—that he was Josh's father.

She was still trying to get around to that.

He hadn't been pushing her. After their initial conversation, Rance hadn't said another word about when she was going to tell Josh who his father was. They both knew he didn't have to.

Ellie thought about it every waking moment.

At first she hesitated because Josh wasn't thrilled that Rance was there at all, and she thought that maybe if he spent a little more time in Rance's company, he would like him better and would be happier about the news.

But Josh did his best to avoid Rance—except when he could interrupt any one-on-one time that she and Rance might have together. Then he was right there, horning in.

Rance didn't say anything about Josh's surliness or about his interruptions. He kept his temper, even when it was clear that Josh was deliberately trying it. He did his best, Ellie had to admit. And his being there certainly made things easier on Josh chorewise.

But Josh was never glad that Rance was around. And instead of getting easier to broach the subject, the longer she put it off, the more difficult it got.

After her first chances had passed, the others that presented themselves didn't seem as good; or they didn't provide her with enough time to explain her reasoning. Ellie began to think that she would never have time enough or an opportunity good enough to explain her reasoning.

Nothing she was going to say would be anything Josh would want to hear.

His mother wouldn't answer a straight question anymore.

At least, not when the question was, "When's he leaving?"

Josh asked it. A lot.

The day after Carrie's birthday, when he got up and found Rance still there, he'd asked it very pointedly. His mother had said, "Oh, I don't know," in a kind of nervous, hurried way, and then she'd thrust his lunch sack at him and said, "Hurry. Grandma's waiting to take you to the bus. You're going to be late."

Rance had still been there when Josh came home. He was working with Ruckus in the corral. And Daniel, his arm still in the sling, hurried over to watch, taking Caleb with him. Josh had turned his back, walking into the house alone.

His mother had been sitting at the table writing out bills. And he'd asked her again, "When's he leaving?"

And she jumped when he came in, and looked at him as if it was a big surprise that he was standing in the kitchen just like he did every day at four o'clock in the afternoon. "Oh my," she said. "Time's just gotten away from me." And she leaped up and started fixing dinner.

It wasn't until later that he realized she hadn't answered his question.

He asked it again that night when she kissed him before he went to sleep. Then she waved her hands a little, like she didn't quite know what to do with them and she said, "He has a little time so he thought he'd stay and help out for a while."

It wasn't much of an answer. The real answer, Josh began to understand as the days went past and Rance's truck stayed where it was, was that Rance wasn't going anywhere.

He dug in and settled down.

In the barn.

"Doesn't it seem funny to you that a guy like him would want to sleep in our barn?" he asked Caleb and Daniel one night after the lights were out and the three of them were still awake.

"Not really," Daniel said, just as Josh should have known he would. "We got a nice barn."

"His house has gotta be better," Josh argued.

"But it isn't near us," Daniel said logically.

It was that particular logic that Josh didn't much want to think about. It meant that Rance had his eye on their mom.

Josh kept his eyes on both of them. He didn't surprise them in any kisses anymore. He didn't even see them touch each other—except maybe by accident. And whenever that happened, he knew it was an accident, because his mom jumped back as if she'd had boiling water dumped on her.

Every once in a while Josh got his hopes up. The first time he came home from school and Rance's truck wasn't there, he started grinning. He even let out a little whoop. His relief lasted until Caleb asked their mom where Rance was.

"He had a court case today," she said. "He'll be back tonight."

He was.

Several other times the truck was gone, too. And sometimes it wasn't back by the time the boys went to bed. But it was always there in the morning.

Rance always came back.

The weird thing was, though, that sometimes Josh thought his mother wasn't any happier about Rance being there than he was. She was edgy. Distracted. Usually she knew exactly what he was thinking before he even thought it. Now she didn't even seem to hear what he was saying when he talked to her out loud.

That was Rance's fault, too. It had to be.

"Why don't you tell him to go away?" Josh asked finally one afternoon when he came home from school and found his mother in the living room, staring at a picture of his dad and him on his dad's horse, Bunker.

At the sound of his voice, she jerked around and shouted, "Stop sneaking up on me like that!"

Josh stared at her in shock. And then she pressed her hands against her cheeks and took a couple of shuddery breaths.

"I'm sorry," she said. "Oh, Josh. I didn't mean to yell at you. You just...startled me. I was...thinking about something." She crossed the room and put her arms around him, and he didn't pull away. He let her hug him. He even gave her a hug back.

"About Dad?" he said. It was only halfway a question.

"About Dad," she agreed. "And…and other things."

"Rance." That wasn't a question at all.

"He's a good man, Josh."

Josh gritted his teeth and shrugged out of her arms. He hunched his shoulders and turned away from her.

"He is," she said with a little more insistence.

"Didn't say he wasn't," Josh replied gruffly, refusing to look at her. "But he isn't Dad."

"Of course not. But—"

He whirled around to face her. "I don't want him tryin' to be Dad!"

"No, of course not." And then she ran a hand through her hair and said quietly, "Josh, no one can ever replace your father."

It should have reassured him. It didn't.

Maybe because the more time went on and the longer he was there, the more Rance did dadlike things. He spent time with Daniel and Ruckus, helping Daniel get over his wariness with the horse and teaching Ruckus good manners. It was the sort of thing Dad would have done. If it had been Dad doing it, Josh would have hung around, watching and learning. He never bothered when Rance did it.

There were things about horse training Josh wanted to know, but he didn't ask. He would never ask Rance.

He didn't accept Rance's offer of his laptop computer for typing his social studies report, either. "Your handwriting is as bad as mine," Rance told him with a smile.

Josh didn't want anything of his to be like Rance's—

not even his bad handwriting. "I can't type," Josh said flatly.

"But thank you, anyway," his mother said for him, giving him a pointed and expectant look.

Josh scowled. But when her foot started tapping, he shrugged. "Thanks." He didn't look at Rance when he spoke. And he said it soft enough that maybe Rance didn't even hear him.

He probably wouldn't care, anyway. He didn't need Josh when he had Daniel and Caleb and Carrie eating out of the palm of his hand.

Caleb didn't say no to the use of the laptop. In fact he spent most evenings fooling with the stupid thing. "Wanta see what I can do?" he asked Josh all the time.

Josh said, "No."

"He's got a couple of pretty cool games on it."

"I said no!" Josh stomped up the stairs.

Behind him he heard Carrie say, "Josh is sure crabby anymore, isn't he?"

Josh wouldn't be, he wanted to yell, if Rance would go away and leave them alone.

"How come you don't like him?" Daniel asked that night after the lights were out. It was a typical Daniel question. Daniel always wanted everybody to like everybody else.

"Never said I didn't like him." Josh folded his arms under his head and stared at the ceiling in the dark.

Daniel grunted his disbelief. "Like you had to."

"Maybe he's scared to admit it," Caleb said.

Josh bristled. "I'm not scared. I *don't* like him," he said, goaded.

"Why?"

"'Cause he's hornin' in. He wants Mom. He thinks he can just take over an' be our dad."

Daniel pushed himself up. "He thinks *that?*"

"Really?" Caleb breathed, sitting up, too.

"Yeah." Josh's jaw tightened.

There was silence from below.

Then he heard one of them take a breath and let it out, like a long sigh. And finally "Well," Daniel said, settling back down again. "That'd be pretty cool."

"Yeah," Caleb agreed. "Cool."

Josh wanted to break their heads.

He supposed he couldn't blame them. They had been barely six when Dad died. They didn't remember very much about what it was like to have a real father, so they were just willing to settle for what they could get. Carrie, of course, had been much too young. She could be forgiven.

It was only Josh who remembered—who looked at his dad's picture on the tall oak chest of drawers every night before he went to sleep, who still talked to him even though the answers were getting harder to hear.

It was Josh who wouldn't let himself forget.

It was like a storm on the horizon. You could see it coming from a long way off. There was always plenty of warning. But sometimes, even knowing it was going to happen, you couldn't get out of the way.

It was like that between Josh and Rance.

Ellie supposed telling Josh that Rance was his father might have defused things. On the other hand, every time she thought about doing it, it seemed more likely to just create a tornado where none had existed moments before.

So she didn't.

But she didn't know how much longer they could go on this way, either. Rance wouldn't hold his peace forever. He'd given her days—weeks, in fact—*three!*—and she hadn't been able to speak the truth.

But she hadn't been able to tell Josh what he wanted to hear, either. He'd wanted her to say that Rance was leaving. She couldn't do it. Rance would leave when he felt like it. Or maybe never. It was beginning to look that way.

Josh wanted her to tell him that Rance didn't matter to her. She couldn't do that, either. Because she couldn't lie.

But every day now it felt like she was living a lie.

"Rance knows, doesn't he?" Sandra had asked her the day after Rance came back.

And Ellie had had to admit that he did. "But Josh doesn't. I don't know what I'm going to do about Josh."

"That's a tough one," Sandra said. She gave Ellie's shoulder a gentle squeeze in commiseration.

She had no idea how tough, Ellie thought.

End of the semester parent-teacher conferences almost did the job for her. Rance came along. Josh thought she ought to tell him to stay home. But she could not.

"He doesn't have any right to be there," Josh railed. "He's not my dad!"

Everything in her wanted to shout once and for all, *Yes, he is!* But how could she do it then, when Caleb and Daniel were out in the truck already waiting with Rance and unless they got moving they were going to be late.

Ellie gave Josh's shoulder a squeeze. "Don't be like that," she pleaded. What else could she say?

She could almost see the anger roiling in him after that.

It didn't help that Caleb and Daniel's teacher had only the most glowing things to say about both boys. From Caleb's uncanny ability with fractions to Daniel's wonderful report on seals, she waxed poetic on the talents of the O'Connor twins.

And after the conference she looked at Rance, then at Ellie, and took Ellie's hand in hers to pat it. "I'm so glad things are working out for you."

Josh's teacher was much less happy on all fronts. "He doesn't seem interested," she told Ellie. "He stares out the window. He doodles on his papers. He doesn't get his work done. He didn't even turn in his major social studies paper."

Ellie listened politely. Out of the corner of her eye she could see Rance sitting up straighter, listening, too, his eyes not on the teacher but on Josh. Josh seemed to slide lower in his chair.

"Perhaps it's just a bad patch," his teacher said at the end of the conference. "Sometimes these things happen. And then, quick as that, things turn around again. I know it was hard for Josh after his father's death, but for most of this year, he did really well." She gave Josh a hopeful smile which he didn't return. "Perhaps," she said to Ellie and to Rance, "he just needs a little vacation and he'll come back in the fall all ready to go. In the meantime, you can give him a little extra encouragement at home."

As they were leaving, Rance muttered something about the kind of encouragement *he* thought Josh needed. Ellie shot him a hard look. Josh just stared straight ahead. He didn't say a word.

They went out for ice cream after the conferences. Josh stood with his back to them, licking his ice cream cone and staring out the window. Caleb and Daniel chattered eagerly, telling Rance about their plans for summer. They had great ideas for a tree house. The one Spike had built for them had fallen into some disrepair. Caleb and Daniel wanted to fix it up, and they wanted Rance to help them.

"Yeah, sure. I'd like that," Rance said.

Ellie saw Josh go absolutely rigid. He almost seemed to shake right where he stood. *Oh, Josh. Don't.*

She knew what he was thinking. She knew the tree house, just the way it was, was the way he wanted it to be forever. Spike had built it—and because Spike had built it, in Josh's opinion, it should never be changed.

Before he could speak, though, she jumped in, asking about an upcoming rodeo, determined to change the subject and forestall the explosion.

It worked. Then.

It didn't work the following weekend. Daniel and Caleb had been invited to a Saturday-night, end-of-the-school-year sleepover at a friend's house in town. Josh's friend, Matt, wanted him to go with their family on a weekend camping trip. Without even asking Ellie, Josh said no.

"But I thought you loved camping," Ellie said, surprised when she found out from Matt's mother that Josh had declined.

Josh shrugged. "Sometimes."

Ellie looked at him, trying to figure him out. She'd hoped that summer vacation would make him happier, but it didn't seem to. She knew what would make him happier—Rance leaving. But that didn't seem to be happening, either.

"Josh can come with us," Sandra said. She'd invited Carrie to her house for dinner and to spend the night. "We can rent a movie, make popcorn. Have a party. What do you say?"

Josh just shook his head. "No." Then he saw Ellie looking at him, tapping her foot. "Thanks, anyway," he added.

Ellie thought she heard Rance gritting his teeth, but she couldn't be sure.

The kid was a jerk.

A stubborn, obnoxious little jerk.

Josh had been, in Trey's words, "cruisin' for a bruisin'" ever since Rance had come back to the ranch.

At first Rance had been inclined to cut him a little slack. The boy obviously resented him stepping in and doing the things Spike had done. Clearly Spike had been a good father, and the kid didn't want just any old jerk taking his place. Rance could appreciate that—to a point.

They'd gone way past that point now.

If Ellie had told him the truth right off, he would be over it by this time, Rance assured himself. But when he stopped judging long enough to look at things from Ellie's point of view, he could see that telling Josh while he hated Rance's guts wouldn't be an easy task.

He tried to make it easier for her. He tried to make Josh like him. He didn't even have to try with the other three kids. They thought he was the best thing since Santa Claus. Josh still hated his guts. He could see it in the way the kid looked at him whenever he came into a room. And he knew the boy was going out of his way to make sure that he and Ellie were never alone.

"I'm worried about Josh," Ellie had told him a couple of weeks ago. "He keeps waking up and coming downstairs in the middle of the night."

"Coming downstairs?" Rance had frowned. "Why?"

"Well, to the bathroom, I guess. But twice I woke up and found him standing in the doorway of my room."

Rance's teeth came together with a snap. "Checking to see if I'm in your bed."

Ellie's face flamed. "He wouldn't—! *We* wouldn't!"

"*I* damn well would," Rance said. "And you know it. I want to marry you, Ellie. I want to be in your bed."

But she had shaken her head and turned away. But he didn't think it was because she didn't want it, too.

It was because of Josh.

That was why he wasn't going camping with Matt's family this weekend. Rance was sure of it. If all the kids were gone, there would be no one to keep Rance out of Ellie's bed. Josh wouldn't be having any of that.

He didn't want to be anywhere Rance was—that was intuitively obvious—but he wouldn't let them out of his sight just the same. There was no way he was going to let them have a chance to do what he was sure they would be doing if he left them alone.

"Well, then," Ellie said after the most tension-fraught dinner Rance could ever remember sitting through, "isn't this nice, just the three of us?" She had a brittle smile on her face as she turned to Josh. "What would you like to do?"

The boy just shrugged. He didn't even look up.

Rance had had enough. "Answer your mother," he said sharply.

Josh's head jerked up in surprise. He shot Rance a hard glare. "I don't know," he said to his mother. His tone of voice left a lot to be desired.

"How about a game of Chinese checkers?" she suggested.

"Naw, that's stupid."

Rance bit the inside of his cheek to keep from saying anything.

"Monopoly?"

Josh snorted. "He already owns the whole state."

Ellie's smile faltered. "Josh," she began gently.

"He does!" Josh's temper flared. "An' now he thinks

he can just walk in here and take us over, too. Well, you might want his money! I guess you might even want him!'' He stood up and shoved his chair back. ''But I don't know why! He's not like Dad! Did you just forget about Dad 'cause he's dead an' you're not? Don't you care anymore?''

''Josh!'' Ellie looked stricken.

Rance shot to his feet, flattened his palms on the table and glared at the boy who stared defiantly back at him. ''Don't you ever accuse your mother of not caring!'' he said through his teeth. ''Don't you throw your father's death in her face! You have no right! None. Apologize to her. Now!''

''Rance.'' Now Ellie was trying to gentle him.

But Rance was beyond gentling. He'd had it with ungrateful brats. He'd had it with sulky, selfish children. He ignored her, kept his eyes fixed firmly on Josh.

Josh's eyes were flashing just as angrily as his. ''Don't tell me what to do! What right do you have to tell me anything?''

''All the right in the world,'' Rance said. ''You're my son.''

Ten

"**I**'m sorry. I lost my temper. I—" Rance raked his fingers through his hair "—I just reached the end of my rope," he said shakily. "I'll go after him."

Josh was fast disappearing down the steps and across the yard. He was running, desperate and angry, but Ellie knew Rance could catch him. Still, she shook her head. "No."

"He'll run off."

"No. He won't. At least I hope he won't. I…I think he'll go to the tree house."

"The tree house? Why would he do that? There's a whole damn forest up there for him to lose himself in."

"I know. But Spike—" she had trouble saying his name "— Spike used to tell the boys, especially Josh, that the tree house was *their* place—that it was off limits to parents. He told them we'd never intrude, never come in unless they invited us. He said it was important that they had that. He said it was safer that way—that there would be times when we'd all need space, and that it would give them a place to go to cool off." She prayed Spike was right.

Rance looked half impressed, half doubtful. "Well, I hope he's right. But I'd be in the next county now, if I felt the way Josh does."

Ellie smiled faintly, appreciating his honesty. She

knew it had to hurt to have seen the furious denial on Josh's face. "He doesn't hate you," she said gently.

"You could have fooled me."

"He's just loyal. He was Spike's right-hand man. 'The foreman,' Spike always called him. Odd as it might seem, of all the kids, Josh was the one who was most like his da—" she stopped "—like Spike."

"Like his dad," Rance corrected harshly. He stalked to the door and stared out. "Spike *is* his dad. He might be my son, too. But Spike is Josh's only dad."

Ellie could hear the pain in his voice, and she wanted to assure him that wasn't true. "I...I should have told him when you first asked me to. I kept hoping you two would get along better. I kept waiting for the right opening. It's my fault. I'll go."

"I'll come with you."

"No. I'm the one who needs to talk to him. He won't listen to you. I'm the one who has to explain, to make him understand."

"Understand?" Rance snorted. "Don't you believe it."

"I have to try," Ellie said urgently. "He's hurt and he's angry and it's my fault. I have to try."

It was a lie.

Josh knew it was a lie.

Why else would a guy who didn't even like him say such a lousy thing? Rance knew it would hurt him where it mattered most.

Josh huddled against the wall of the tree house, hugging his arms around his knees and pressed his eyes against the soft denim of his jeans.

It was a lie!

"Josh?" He heard his mother's voice down below. She sounded worried, nervous.

Let her worry, he thought, hugging his knees tighter. But then he thought, it wasn't her fault. *She* wasn't the one who had lied. She hadn't said he was Rance's son. She knew it wasn't true!

Maybe she was coming to tell him that it was all right, that she was sending Rance away, that she didn't like him anymore because he was a liar.

Because he *was* a liar!

"Josh! Are you up there, honey?"

Still he didn't answer. He couldn't make his voice work. It felt all froggy and awful, and he knew he would cry if he tried to say anything. He had almost cried before he'd got out of the house. That was why he'd run.

He'd yelled, "That's a lie! You know it's a lie!" And then he'd hiccupped, and he'd felt his throat start to close, and he'd known he would do something stupid like burst into tears if he stayed there one more second.

There was no way on earth he was going to let a jerk like Rance Phillips see him cry. He shifted uncomfortably as he thought how close he had come to disgracing himself. His movement made the floorboards creak.

"Josh." His mom didn't sound so frantic now. She must have heard the boards move and figured he was here.

He was glad she hadn't climbed up to look. Dad had always said they wouldn't do that. When his dad had built the tree house, Josh had been five, and he hadn't quite understood what Spike had meant when he'd said, "A guy needs a bolt-hole, some place he can go to sort things out."

Later he'd figured it out. But he'd never figured he'd need it like this.

"I need to talk to you, Josh."

He didn't answer. He still wasn't ready. He could still hear those awful words, "You're my son," in Rance's voice over and over, echoing in his head. He put his hands over his ears as if that could shut them out. But they didn't go away, no more than the memory of his mother's stricken face did.

She'd looked as awful as she had when his dad had died. White-faced. Gut punched. The way Josh had felt when he and Matt had fought once, and one blow from Matt's fist had pounded all the air out of him.

Josh felt the tree shake and he uncovered his ears. He could hear his mother climbing up the footholds, but she didn't come all the way.

She stopped and said, "I won't come in, Josh. Not unless you invite me. But we really do need to talk."

Josh cleared his throat. "T-talk to him," he rasped bitterly. "Tell him what a liar he is."

There was silence from below.

Josh's throat tightened again. He swallowed hard against the lump growing there. "Tell him," he insisted, and hated it when his voice broke.

There was another movement from below, but she didn't get down. It felt more like she was settling in. "I'll talk to Rance later," his mother said at last. "Right now I have to talk to you."

"So talk," Josh said grudgingly. For a long moment she didn't say anything—so long in fact that he felt sorry for forcing her to talk to him while she hung on to the steps his dad had hammered into the tree. "You can come up."

She came up. He took her hand when she crawled through the narrow opening and helped her climb in. She still looked very pale, except for sort of bright spots of color on her cheeks, like she'd been running hard or something.

"Thank you." She sat down beside him in the narrow space, and he could feel her eyes on him, probably seeing his blotchy face and red eyes. He didn't look at her. His fingers curled into fists against the tops of his thighs.

"What Rance said," she said quietly, the words coming slowly, "is true, Josh."

His head jerked around. He stared at her. Then he started to push himself up, to scramble away from her. But she reached out a hand and caught his arm, holding him there. He struggled against her, tried to pull out of her grasp, but she held on tight.

"Will you listen to me?" she said.

"No!"

"Please, Josh. This is my fault, not Rance's."

"It's *his* fault if I'm his kid," Josh spat. "I may be dumb, but I know that!"

"You're not dumb," his mother said. "Come here and sit down. Let me tell you. Let me say what I should have said a long, long time ago."

He didn't want to hear. He didn't want her to say any of it. "Dad's my dad," he whispered brokenly. And though he sat down beside her and tried to be still and steady and calm, he couldn't stop the tears. Not all of them. They leaked out the corners of his eyes and ran down his cheeks. He swiped angrily at them with the sleeve of his shirt.

"Dad is your dad, Josh," she agreed softly. "In every way that really counts, Spike O'Connor is your father." She paused, and Josh thought for a minute he'd missed something that would make it all make sense. But then she added, "But he did not get me pregnant, darling. Rance did that."

Josh didn't answer. He didn't move. If he held himself really still, he thought maybe the words would wash right over him. They wouldn't matter any more than water in a river, sliding over the rocks and going away. Far away.

"We were in college together, like I told you," his mother said. Her voice was kind of soft and shaky, and he wanted to tell her to stop talking because it sounded like it hurt her too much. But he sensed that she was like that water he was thinking about. That whatever she was going to tell him, she couldn't dam it up anymore. It was just going to spill out no matter what either of them wanted.

"We...cared for each other very much. I loved him, Josh. I loved Rance Phillips." Her voice got firmer when she said that. Stronger. As if she wanted him to know that she meant it. "I...slept with him. And I got pregnant with you."

Josh didn't move. He heard the words. Felt them. Not just beating on the outside of him, but hitting him somewhere inside, too. Deep inside—like near his heart maybe. It hurt there. He swallowed, trying to make the hurt go away. He squeezed his eyes shut, but that didn't help, either.

He wanted his dad. He wanted his dad to be there, to put strong arms around him and crush him hard against his chest, the way he had when Josh was little and had slammed his fingers in the truck door. "I'll hold you so tight you can give the pain to me," Spike had told him.

And whether or not Spike had felt the actual pain, Josh had known his father shared it. He needed to share it now—the same way he'd needed to share the pain of his dad's death.

It felt like they were taking his dad away all over again.

And then he couldn't stop the tears. He sniffled and fought and blinked and coughed. But the coughs turned to sobs and his shoulders shook.

Then his mom had her arms around him and was holding him tight—maybe not as tight as his dad—but tight. Her tears slid down past his ear and lingered on his cheeks, mingling with his own.

It didn't make him feel better, but at least he didn't feel quite so alone.

Rance was pacing a rut in the dirt floor of the barn.

He prowled up and down, back and forth, pausing every time he came near the door, to look toward the tree house. He itched to go after Ellie, to find Josh, to talk to him—to *do* something. He wasn't used to having to sit on his hands, to let someone else handle things—not when his future hung in the balance. But now he had to.

He'd promised Ellie.

So he muttered. And paced. In the beginning he'd paused by the door long enough to watch while she called Josh's name. He couldn't believe the boy was there, but then he saw her start to climb up the wooden rungs. She went up two, then stopped and called Josh's name again.

He's not there, Rance wanted to tell her. *Stop standing around wasting time. Just stick your head in and check.*

But she didn't. She waited. And waited. He thought he'd go nuts.

Finally, though, damned if she didn't get some sort of answer, because she looked toward where he was standing in the barn door, gave a thumb's-up sign, and then proceeded to climb the rest of the way in.

That had been ages ago. Hours. Days, it seemed.

Long enough for Rance to wear a heck of a rut in the dirt. He scowled out the door, up at the tree, paced some more, wishing he smoked so he'd have something to do with his hands.

Then, at last, when it was nearly dark, he saw a pair of jeans-clad legs begin to descend the ladder, and Ellie landed on the ground.

Rance started toward her, but Ellie waved him off.

He frowned at her, but she shook her head and, sighing, he retreated into the barn once more.

It took her forever to get there. But the minute she stepped inside the barn, he reached for her and pulled her into his arms.

It was the first time he'd held her since the night they'd made love. He'd barely even been given a chance to touch her since he'd come back. She was shaking as she came to him, and he wrapped his arms around her and held her close.

"Are you all right?"

She nodded. "I think so." But he could feel her shivering. She didn't speak for a few moments, just stood there in the circle of his arms. He could have stood that way forever. But finally she spoke.

"It was— Oh, God, Rance I felt so awful. It was so hard! I knew I was hurting him, and it was the last thing I wanted to do."

"I'm the one who hurt him."

"No." Her arms tightened around him for just a moment. "Well, only at the last instant. It started before that. It started years ago when Spike and I didn't tell him the truth. I had to explain all that. And I...I don't know what I just did to his relationship to his da—to Spike."

"His dad," Rance said.

She looked up at him, her eyes questioning. Rance gave a small shrug. "Spike was his dad. I know that. It's true what you said about sperm not making a father."

Her gaze softened, and she hugged him again. "You love him, too."

"Yeah. Not that he's exactly made it easy," Rance said gruffly. "But then, I didn't make it easy, either."

Ellie leaned her head against his shoulder. "Nothing was easy. I don't even know if I managed. He was so quiet. I tried to get him to ask me things so I'd know what to tell him, but he didn't. Not much. Not many." She looked up at him again. "I told him I loved you. He wanted to know if you loved me."

"I hope you told him yes."

"I told him...I thought you did."

"I did. I do." He kissed her, needing her desperately. And she kissed him, too. But far too soon she pulled away. "I can't," she said. "Not now. Not while Josh is—" She stopped and shook her head.

"I'll talk to him." He started toward the door of the barn, but Ellie caught his arm.

"Not now," she said. "He...needs a little time."

Rance hesitated.

"Please. You can talk to him tomorrow. He might be more ready to listen then."

Frankly Rance doubted whether Josh would ever be ready to listen to him, but he nodded, then glanced toward the tree house. "He's staying there tonight?"

"Yes."

"*Will* he stay?" It was true what he'd told Ellie about being in the next county if someone had sprung something like this on him.

Ellie nodded. "He promised. Spike promised him we'd never intrude without asking. I kept that promise. Josh will keep his, I'm sure."

Rance bent his head. "Fair enough." He took her hand and drew her back into his arms once more. He kissed her again, tenderly, achingly, needing her with every fiber of his being—and knowing that, however much she wanted to stay with him, she wouldn't.

He wouldn't have her tonight. She couldn't stay wrapped in the comfort of his arms when Josh was hurting.

"I'll talk to him tomorrow," he said. "First thing in the morning."

So much for plans.

Rance had just come in for breakfast—and Josh wasn't even down from the tree yet—when Ellie noticed a black pickup she didn't recognize. It came over the rise, down the hill and through the gate toward the house.

She craned her neck. "I wonder who that is." She glanced at it again curiously through the kitchen curtains as she laid rashers of bacon in the frying pan.

Rance didn't give a damn. He'd been awake all night, pacing, prowling, trying to figure out what to say to Josh—to his *son*. It was harder by far than any opening or closing argument he'd ever done.

Maybe he should just go down to the tree house right now, wake Josh up and start talking. That way the kid might be still sleepy enough that Rance could get through most of it before he woke up enough to ask questions.

Coward, Rance chastised himself. Okay, so he wouldn't do that.

He cracked his knuckles and continued to pace.

Ellie began to scramble eggs in the other frying pan. She put slices of bread in the toaster, then looked out the window again. "He's coming up to the door. Do you know him?"

"Huh? Know who?" Rance didn't give a damn who

was coming to the door. Unless it was Spike reincarnate, it couldn't possibly matter to him.

"He looks sort of familiar," Ellie mused, stirring the eggs. "Get that, will you?" she said when they heard boot steps on the porch, followed by a brisk rap.

Rance shrugged. "Yeah, whatever." He jerked open the door.

"*Dad?*"

Indeed it was. Trey Phillips stood on the porch, a bland, poker player's expression on his face.

"I was in the neighborhood," he said conversationally, one brow lifted, as if he wondered whether Rance would buy his story, "so I reckoned I'd just drop in."

Rance didn't say a word. Couldn't have, if his life depended on it.

It probably did.

Something close to rage was building inside his brain.

Trey was oblivious. He looked past Rance's shoulder and smiled broadly. "Where're your manners, son? Aren't you going to introduce me?"

Rance turned to see Ellie gaping at his father, then at him. Her mouth opened and shut and opened again. Finally she managed. "This is your *father?*"

Hell. Damnation. Rance thought a few more things a whole lot more pithy and off-color than that. But he didn't say any of them because as sure as shootin' his father would smile a polite, despairing smile and make some crack about his manners. Rance did not need a lesson in manners right now.

He nailed his father with a glare that would have killed at fifty paces—if Trey Phillips had been the sort of man that looks could touch.

Of course he wasn't. The glare bounced right off his bulletproof personality. Still smiling, he stepped through the door, not waiting for Rance to offer an invitation. Doffing a black felt cowboy hat, Trey made an almost courtly bow to Ellie.

"For my sins, yes, ma'am, I am his father. John Ransome Phillips III. My friends all call me Trey." He was clearly including her among them as he held out a hand to her.

Ellie blinked. Then, almost mindlessly it seemed, she handed the fork to Rance with a look that said, *Stir your own eggs.* She took his father's hand and said in a whoosh of breath, "I'm Ellie O'Connor, Mr. Phillips. I'm pleased to meet you at long last."

Trey's left brow rose. He looked at her, intrigued. "At long last?"

Rance gnashed his teeth.

Ellie hesitated, as if she'd suddenly realized she might have said too much.

Too late now, Rance could have told her. You didn't give the old man a crumb of information you didn't want him to make a whole loaf out of.

Ellie was trying to ease her hand away, but Trey hung on, still smiling. Waiting. Like a lion waiting for the zebra at the water hole, Rance thought.

"We, um, knew each other years ago," Ellie said in a tone somewhere between vague and nervous. "In... college."

"Did you now?" Trey let go of her hand and rubbed his together. "Imagine that. Friends for all those years. You never brought her home." He turned an accusing gaze on Rance.

"I wasn't coming home in those days," Rance said through his teeth.

"Oh, right. I forgot." Which he hadn't at all, but Trey had always had a selective memory. If he didn't want to discuss the fact that Rance hadn't been home for seven long years, it wasn't that he'd forgotten. It was that it served his purpose not to bring it up. He gave a wave of his hand, as if the memory of Rance's college years' rebellion wasn't worth considering.

"You're not coming home much these days, either," he said pointedly. "Though now that I've met Ellie, I can certainly see why."

The words were pleasant enough. So was the smile. But he was studying Ellie like a scientist with a species of butterfly pinned to a board. He was weighing the attraction—and looking for an explanation at the same time.

One Rance had no intention of giving. His life was complicated enough at the moment without satisfying his meddling father's curiosity.

"What are you doing here?" Rance demanded now.

"I told you, I was in the neighborhood." Once more Trey smiled that bland challenge-me-if-you-dare smile. "Hadn't seen you in a while. Wouldn't think you were running our place, you never bein' there."

"I'm in touch. J.D.'s a good foreman. There's not much he can't handle. Except you."

Trey's teeth set for just a moment. Then he put his genial smile back in place and explained to Ellie, "He thinks I interfere." The implication was that nothing could have been further from the truth.

Rance's hands were making strangling motions.

"Anyway, J.D. tells me nothing," Trey said with some irritation. "Never has. I had to ask Lydia where you were."

Rance made a mental note to throttle Lydia the next time he saw her.

Trey smiled on. "And as I was coming down this way

to check out a bull anyway, I thought I'd drop by…say hello to my son…meet the woman who's so intriguing he can't tear himself away.''

Of course Ellie blushed. Rance wanted to say, *Remember whose side you're on.* ''Well, now you've met her,'' he said, doing his best herd dog imitation as he tried unsuccessfully to maneuver Trey toward the door.

Trey didn't budge. ''My, that coffee smells good.''

Ellie gave Rance a helpless look. ''You're welcome to have a cup, Mr. Phillips,'' she said to his father, ''but we wouldn't want to keep you.''

''Not a problem. I'd appreciate a cup. Been a long drive, and I wouldn't mind a little break. I'm not due at Denison's until early afternoon, anyway.'' He gave Rance a triumphant smile and moved past him toward the kitchen table.

Muttering under his breath, Rance followed.

Of course the coffee wasn't enough.

''Those eggs look mighty good,'' Trey told Ellie as she handed Rance his plate. And while he was at it, the old man decided he wouldn't mind a couple of strips of bacon. ''Not more than two, though,'' he said. ''A feller's gotta watch his diet these days.'' He patted his still-flat stomach. ''Gonna get a paunch on you,'' he told Rance, ''you eat like that every day.''

''He eats oatmeal most mornings,'' Ellie said. ''This is Sunday. It's special.''

''Well, of course it is,'' Trey agreed. He smiled at her, his very own version of the I'm-a-Phillips-and-all-women-fall-at-my-feet smile. Then he dug with gusto into the breakfast she set before him.

Rance hadn't had much appetite before. Now he didn't have any at all.

If Trey noticed, he gave no sign. He set about alternately charming and quizzing Ellie. By the time he'd finished his breakfast and was working on his third cup of coffee, Trey knew her family history for four generations back. He knew about Spike and Spike's parents. He knew Ellie had four children.

"Four? My, my." Both brows arched this time and he looked at Rance with an are-you-sure-you-know-what-you're-doing? look. "Quite a handful. You must find it difficult alone?" Rance heard the question. He understood the subtext, too. It was, Are you trying to snag my son and his money to help you?

"Ellie does quite well on her own," he said.

"Does she." And that wasn't a question at all. Trey turned back to Ellie. "Boys? Girls?" he asked.

"Three boys, aged ten and eight. The younger two are twins," Ellie explained, "and a five-year-old girl."

"Very quiet children," Trey said, looking around as if he might spot them hiding under an afghan or sofa cushion.

Ellie smiled. "Not that quiet. The twins are in town at a friend's for the night. Carrie stayed with my mother-in-law. And Josh is out in the tree house."

"Ah." He sipped his coffee and said no more about them. He started talking about the law firm—a case Rance had passed on to Lydia that Trey had apparently been probing her about. He knew too much as far as Rance was concerned. He'd have to remind Lydia that, for all that his old man was a dear friend of her family, he should not be included in their legal maneuverings.

"You ought to get back and give that girl a hand," Trey said now.

"She doesn't need a hand," Rance said. "She's perfectly capable of doing everything that needs to be done."

"Ain't like you to shirk work."

"I'm not shirking!"

Trey's shoulders lifted in a negligent shrug. He sipped his coffee and shook his head.

Then there were footsteps on the porch, and slowly the back door opened.

"Ah, Josh!" Ellie smiled warmly as the boy came in.

He didn't look like he'd slept much more than Rance had. His uncombed hair stood in ruffled spikes on his head. His eyes were deeper set and smudged looking. His cheeks were still a little red. He looked at his mother and gave her a faint smile. He looked at Rance, his gaze steady and unflinching.

Rance met it, trying to say with his eyes what he wondered if he would ever be able to tell Josh in words. Then finally he looked away. At his father.

The old man sat there, knuckles white against the coffee cup, his mouth open, as he stared at Josh.

"This is my son," Ellie said to Trey. "Josh, this is Rance's father, Mr. Phillips."

Josh's expression grew guarded. He looked at Rance quickly, then back at Trey again. But when the older man didn't say anything, still sat there, unspeaking, Josh looked back at him again, studied him more closely.

All at once, Trey came to life again. He slapped his coffee cup down on the table and stood up. He held out his hand to Josh. "Pleased to meet you, son." And when the boy gravely shook his hand, a smile settled on Trey's face.

Then he turned to Ellie, "That was a mighty fine breakfast, ma'am. Best I've had in years."

Ellie smiled a little warily. "I'm glad you enjoyed it, Mr. Phillips."

"Trey," he corrected. Then he turned to Rance, "Want to talk to you."

And the next thing Rance knew, his father was steering him out the door.

"What in the hell have you been doing?" Trey demanded the moment they were out of earshot of the kitchen.

Rance pulled his arm out of his father's grasp and continued walking toward the corral. "What the hell do you mean, what the hell have I been doing? You know what I've been doing. I'm helping Ellie out."

"You're courting."

"Well, yeah, I guess."

"You been courtin' for weeks! You were courtin' her before you came home."

"Yeah."

"And you been back here three weeks now!"

"Yeah."

"So what the hell are you waitin' for? Marry the damn woman!"

"*What?* Ten minutes ago you were doing your damnedest to get me out of here." Rance raised a hand when Trey would have protested. "Don't tell me you weren't. 'Lydia needs your help.' 'J.D. never hears from you.' What was that?"

"*That,*" Trey spat, "was before I realized she'd had your son!"

Rance stopped dead and stared at him.

Trey stared back. "You're not going to deny it, are you? The boy is the spitting image of you at that age. Right down to that damn cowlick."

"Well, don't tell him that," Rance muttered.

"What? He doesn't know?"

"He knows now," Rance said heavily. "As of last night. I haven't even talked to him about it yet."

"Holy hell, Rance," Trey exploded, "what kind of mess are you making here?"

"I'm not making any mess," Rance said through his teeth. "I'm trying to clean one up. It's—" he raked fingers through his hair "—complicated."

"Don't seem very complicated to me. It'd be complicated if she was married," he reflected, "but she isn't. So it's simple. You get married."

"It isn't simple," Rance said. "I'm not going to pressure her into marrying me!"

"Why not?"

"Because that's not the kind of marriage I want!"

Trey snorted in disgust. "Doesn't mean it's the kind of marriage you'll have forever. It's a starting point."

"Not the right starting point."

Trey paced a furious circle in the dirt. "Well, if you wanted the right starting point, boy, you shouldn't've done things bass-ackwards."

"I didn't know I'd done it!"

Trey stared. "She didn't tell you?"

Rance kicked a fence post. "It's none of your business."

With monumental self-restraint, Trey drew a deep breath, then nodded his head. "I suppose it's not." But then he said, "What's past is past. I'll give you that. But what's going on now, is my business, too."

"Like hell."

"It is," Trey insisted. "He's my grandson."

"Well, he isn't going to be happy to hear it."

Trey scowled. "How do you know?"

"Because he doesn't like me. He doesn't want a father.

He had the best father in the whole damn world, and I come up way short!"

Trey looked at him pityingly. "And you're just going to accept that?"

Rance sighed. He shook his head. "Of course I'm not going to accept it. But I can't push, either. He's a Phillips, remember. When's the last time you pushed a Phillips and got anywhere?"

The two men exchanged a glance that was both rueful and self-aware.

"So what're you going to do?" Trey asked finally.

"Stay put," Rance said. "Help her out. She needs that. She doesn't need me bullying her."

"And the boy?"

"I'll do my best. I can't bully him into accepting me, either."

"Hmph." That was all Trey could say. Then something in him seemed to settle in, take root. He drew himself up and squared his shoulders. "Well, if she needs help, we'll both help."

"*What?*"

"I'm moving in."

Eleven

In her wildest nightmares, Ellie had never imagined something like this: Trey Phillips was living—with his son—in her barn!

Not only that, he was working on her ranch! Eating off her dishes. Playing with her children. Balancing her books.

It was, to put it mildly, making her nervous.

"Can't you stop him?" she asked Rance.

"Last I heard, homicide was illegal in Montana," Rance said grimly. "Not that I'm not tempted, anyway."

"He thinks he's being kind," Ellie said.

"He knows damn well what he's doing," Rance replied. "And kindness has nothing to do with it."

"He's wonderful with the children," Ellie had to admit. "All the children." Though she saw at once that he was aware of just who Josh was, he didn't play favorites. He played catch with Daniel and built playing-card houses with Caleb. He read stories to Carrie. And he talked ranching to Josh. The boy had been a little reticent at first, but somehow Trey had won him over.

Rance hadn't been so lucky.

He had talked to Josh the morning after she did. She didn't know exactly what he'd said. That had been between Josh and him. But whatever it had been, it didn't seem to have smoothed the waters. There was certainly no "happily ever after."

At least not yet.

Though both she and Rance tried to maintain a cheerful demeanor, Josh was distant and sullen. He went out of his way to avoid Rance whenever he could.

She tried to tell herself—and Rance—that things would improve. "He'll come around," she said, and crossed her fingers and dared to hope.

But it wasn't improving fast. And having the old man there, determinedly and obviously succeeding where Rance was not, had to make things worse.

Just this morning, for example, Rance had asked Josh if he wanted to come along to move some cattle. Josh had said no, when she knew that with everything in him, that was exactly what he wanted to be doing.

But then Trey had started talking about going to look for horses. "A fella who's ten and as good a horseman as Josh, ought to start trainin' his own," he said.

And the next thing she knew, he had rounded up all the kids and, commandeering Sandra, too, he had bundled them all into the truck right after breakfast to go look at horses.

"He wouldn't buy Josh a horse, would he?" she asked Rance now. He had sat silently through the whole scene, watching with that hard, knowing look in his eyes.

Now he finished his coffee and put the mug in the sink. "Oh, yeah, he might."

Ellie's eyes widened. "Just like that?" She snapped her fingers, astonished at the extravagance of such a notion.

"He won't buy a bad horse. He's not stupid. The old man is a good judge of horseflesh." Rance's tone was gruff. "And a damn good judge of what makes ten-year-olds tick," he added grimly. "If I had tried that, Josh would have spat in my face. He'd have known I was buying him off.''

"You'd never buy him off.''

Rance shook his head. "I couldn't.''

Ellie finished rinsing the plates, dried her hands and came to put her arms around him. "It's why I love you,'' she said.

His arms came, hard and tight, around her, holding her. And she held him, too. They'd been together, in the same house at least—yet apart—since the night Josh had learned he was Rance's son. Since then their relationship had been on hold.

But her need hadn't been—and neither had his.

"This is hell,'' he muttered.

"And heaven, sometimes,'' she said, resting her head against the curve of his neck and shoulder.

He pulled back a little to look down at her, a wry, disbelieving expression on his face.

She shrugged and smiled a little wryly, too. "At least you're here.''

"I'd be here if we got married.''

Her wry smile twisted a little more. "We can't. Not yet. You know that. Not with Josh feeling the way he does.''

"He'd get used to it,'' Rance argued. His lower body was still pressed against hers. She could feel his need. She had understood. But that wasn't all she understood.

"Would he?'' she asked softly, looking right into his eyes.

She felt a harsh breath shudder through him. His fingers locked behind her, holding her close, but his eyes shut and his head bent so that their foreheads touched.

"Probably not,'' he muttered.

"It isn't just me you're marrying,'' she said, feeling

as if she needed to explain one more time—as if it would help both of them, though she wasn't sure anything would. "You get me, you get us all. And I want us all to be happy about it. I don't want my home to be a battleground."

"I know." His voice was low and resigned. He sighed again. His forehead still rested against hers. And then he straightened. His shoulders went back. His chin came up. "I'm not walking away from this," he told her, his blue eyes glittering with intensity. "I'll wait. I want what's best for all of us—and I think that's me marrying you, regardless of what he thinks. But if we have to wait until Josh gives us his blessing, okay."

Ellie smiled and went up on her toes to press a kiss against his mouth. "Thank you," she whispered with her lips on his. "You won't regret it."

"I already do," he groaned. "I'm just gonna have to work like hell to change the kid's mind."

Easier said than done.

Rance had known it wouldn't be simple.

He'd met with resistance the day immediately after he'd foolishly blurted out Josh's parentage, when he had cornered the boy and tried to explain.

He'd had little idea what to say. Everything that seemed to make sense to an adult, he thought would probably sound stupid to a child of ten.

Josh's reaction didn't change his mind.

The boy hadn't been eager to listen.

When Rance followed him into the tack room and said he wanted to talk to him, Josh had been less than welcoming. "What *else* could you have to say?" he'd said bitterly, his voice was so sharp with pain that Rance had almost looked down to see if he was bleeding.

He shifted from one boot to the other. "I have to say I'm sorry," he began. "I was angry with the way you were acting. That's no excuse, and I acted a whole lot worse. Now I need to explain some things."

Josh turned his back. "Mom already did."

"I know she did. But…it's not enough. I'm your father and—"

"You're *not* my father!" Josh whirled around, eyes flashing. "You're not!"

"Biologically, I am," Rance said. "Maybe not in any other way."

"Definitely not in any other way." Josh glared.

Rance sucked in a breath. "I didn't know about you, Josh."

"Wish you'd never found out."

Me, too, Rance thought wearily. But he took off his hat and raked his fingers through his hair. "I owe you an explanation. Will you listen?"

He shouldn't have put it like that. If Josh said no, was he planning on walking away?

Apparently Josh realized the same thing and came to the same conclusion. His narrow shoulders lifted. "Don't s'pose you'd go away if I said no," he said resignedly.

"No, I wouldn't."

So Josh leaned against the wall, staring off into space, refusing to look at Rance at all, his arms folded across his chest.

It was no invitation to bare his soul, but Rance knew it was the most he could expect. He started to talk.

For a man accustomed to delivering some of the most solid legal arguments in the state of Montana, Rance felt as if he was standing on quicksand then.

Desperately, in a few thousand words or less, he tried to explain to Josh about his life at age twenty-two and his relationship with Ellie that first year he'd been in college. He tried to make Josh understand how demanding his father had been and how determined he'd been to make it on his own.

"Your mother understood that," he said, and he watched the boy's face for a similar glimmer of understanding. He saw none.

Josh's arms remained folded; his face remained impassive. Rance talked on.

He told Josh that he'd loved Ellie. He was honest and said he hadn't wanted to get married. He tried to explain how he'd felt the need to resist being a part of some relentless Phillips machine. "I thought getting married and having kids would make me part of it," he said. "Your mother knew that, too. So she didn't tell me about you."

Josh didn't say anything to that for at least a minute. Then he said, "Did she want to marry you?"

Rance swallowed. "Yes."

Josh nodded almost imperceptibly. He didn't say anything else.

So, desperately, Rance talked on. He let the past go and talked about now, talked about what he was doing now, firm and confident about the man he'd become. He tried to convey that to Josh. Then he told the boy about his love for Ellie and his hopes for the future.

He was blunt and starkly honest. He said, "I love your mother. I would like to make a life with her—and with all of you."

He never claimed to love Josh. He wished he could, but he couldn't lie about it. He owed the boy honesty now at least.

"I want to marry her," he said in the end.

And in the silence that followed, Josh finally looked straight at him. "You had your chance, didn't you?"

Josh seemed determined not to give him another.

Rance was equally determined not to give up.

He wasn't going to bribe the kid, though. His father could make a splash by buying Josh a four-year-old paint gelding and promising the other kids their own horses to train when they got older. Rance would do no such thing.

He felt a faint bitterness that Josh was so thrilled with the horse—and with his father—and still wanted nothing to do with him. But then, the boy didn't know his grandfather like Rance knew him. And warning him that Trey always had his own agenda would do no good at all.

Besides, in this case, the old man's agenda was the same as his. He wanted Ellie to marry Rance.

But no one wanted that more than Rance did.

So he tried. When it was time to move the herd to summer pasture, he thought that he and Josh could work together and develop some rapport. He knew that Josh had done it every year with Spike. He'd missed out last year when Ellie had hired a couple of cowboys to do the work.

"He'll be delighted," Ellie assured him. "Ask. Invite him."

Rance did.

Josh said no.

"But you always went—" Ellie began to argue.

Josh cut her off. "I said no!" He almost shouted the words, then seemed to get a grip on himself. He shook his head. "I got to train Spirit. I can't go."

It was an excuse and they all knew it. Spirit, the new gelding, could wait a few days. Spirit would have waited a few days if Spike had been the one asking Josh to come along.

"Fine." Rance shrugged. "If that's what you want."

He moved the cattle alone.

It rained for three solid days. The wind was so high one night that he had to spend all of it on horseback, moving around the herd, trying to soothe and settle them. It was probably better Josh wasn't with him, he told himself. Be a lot of trouble having a kid along.

But he knew the kind of kid Josh was—the kind of son he'd been to Spike. Josh and Spike would have forged an even deeper bond after a drive like this one.

Would he and Josh ever have that?

He got back to a raft of phone messages from Jodi and Lydia, who had taken to describing herself as, "Remember me, your overworked partner?"

He knew he hadn't been quite fair dumping so much of the workload on her, but he hadn't thought it would be forever. Now he wasn't so sure.

"I need your help," she told him when he called her the night he got back from moving the cattle. He was dog-tired, filthy and ready to sleep the clock around, but Ellie said Lydia had sounded pretty desperate, so he'd made the call.

"Sure," he said, "I'll be there in a couple of days—"

"We don't have a couple of days, Rance. Sweeney's bringing in the big guns. I can't do this alone."

"But—"

"Are you in or are you out? I thought we were partners, Rance. I need you *now*."

Rance shut his eyes and rocked back on his heels. Then his feet hit the floor flat again. "Right," Rance said heavily. "Now."

He hung up to see Ellie standing in the doorway

watching him. He sighed and flexed his shoulders. "I gotta go to Helena. I don't want to, but—"

"I know," Ellie said. She put her arms around him. He pressed his face into her hair and breathed in the sweet scent of her, wanting nothing more than to just stand there holding her.

Then, "Mom!" Josh banged in the door, saw them with their arms around each other and froze.

Carefully, as if she was afraid she would break something, Ellie eased out of Rance's arms and turned to face their son. "What is it, Josh?"

"Nothing." The word was flat and hard, and the resentment in his tone kindled a matching resentment in Rance.

He did his best to squelch it. Then he had an idea. If Josh wouldn't go with him to the summer range because it was something he'd always done with Spike that he didn't want Rance replacing, maybe he should get the boy on his own, away from the ranch and get to know him there.

"Hey, Josh," he said as casually as he could. "How about coming to Helena with me?"

The boy blinked. "Why?"

"Why not? I've got to go to a trial there. I'll be gone a few days." He shrugged. "Just thought maybe you'd like to come."

"No." There was a pause, a look at his mother, then a quick look back at Rance. "No, thanks," Josh said.

Rance went alone.

He worked his butt off. Lydia was right: Sweeney had dragged in the big guns—and Rance wasn't as prepared as he ought to have been.

He hadn't had time, he told himself. He'd been thinking about Ellie, worrying about Josh, working Ellie's ranch, consulting by phone with J.D. about the Phillips's spread.

J.D. could handle most of the decisions, and did. But as he pointed out often enough, he wasn't the "real boss."

"Anything I do, you can contradict," he said.

"Why would I want to do that?" Rance asked.

"You wouldn't," J.D. said. "But the old man would."

Rance didn't even respond to that. It was the truth, and he didn't understand it. And he had enough trouble in his life without tackling that. He would have liked to hand the whole spread over to J.D. at this point.

But when he suggested it, Trey wouldn't hear of it.

"Only a Phillips can run the J Bar R," Trey said flatly.

Well, this particular Phillips was running his tail off. He worked like a dog by day. He burned midnight oil with Lydia every night. He fended off half a dozen willing women whose middle names ought to have been Perseverance. He was less tempted than ever.

Every night he called Ellie to tell her he missed her.

"Miss you, too," she said. "We all miss you."

"Not Josh."

"Well, maybe not Josh," Ellie agreed. "But I think he's coming around, Rance. I really do. He's working so hard. You'd be proud of him. And he's been spending every evening with your dad. They're working hard on Spirit."

"My dad, huh?" Rance wasn't sure whether or not to be glad about that.

"It's a good thing," Ellie assured him. "If he accepts Trey, he'll certainly come around to accepting you."

"Uh-huh." All Rance could do was hope.

* * *

Caleb and Daniel were yakking about *him* again.

"Rance says…"

"Rance knows…"

"Rance can do…"

They did it every day and every night. You'd think the world revolved around stupid Rance Phillips. Well, it didn't. The ranch didn't even revolve around him—and him being gone was giving Josh a chance to prove it. He worked from dawn until dusk every day, determined to show his mom they didn't need Rance at all.

At least his mom didn't say Rance's name twenty times a minute, like some morons he could think of.

"Rance thinks…"

"Rance wants…"

Josh kept his mouth shut, shutting his ears and trying to read his book while they chattered like magpies in the bottom bunks. Then one of them said, "When Rance and Mom get married…"

And then he'd had enough.

"Don't say that!" he yelled at them. He sat up in bed and glowered down at them.

The two of them blinked up at him, like an astonished pair of owls. "Say what?" Caleb asked.

"Say things like them gettin' married! They aren't! It isn't going to happen!"

Both his brothers' eyes got round as the moon. "It's not?" Daniel looked shocked.

"No!"

But then Caleb, ever practical, said, "Then how come Gran'pa Phillips is hangin' around?"

And Daniel added, "And how come he said we should call him Gran'pa if they're not gettin' married? He's not our gran'pa…yet."

Not yours! Josh wanted to yell. But he didn't because he hadn't told them. He'd never said a word about what had happened that night. He'd never told anyone that he was Rance Phillips's son.

"I'll tell them if you want," his mother had offered. "I'm the one who should explain."

But Josh had shaken his head fervently. "No." Nobody was going to tell them, if he could prevent it. If he refused to acknowledge it, maybe—just maybe—Rance would give up and go away.

Josh didn't want him there trying to be nice, trying to be helpful, trying to worm his way in and cut Dad out. If Rance married his mom it would be like his dad had never even existed.

It wasn't fair!

Josh knew that Gran'pa Phillips knew who he was. Neither of them had ever mentioned it. But there was something in the way Gran'pa Phillips looked at him that said he was seeing more in Josh than was really there.

At first Josh hadn't wanted to like him, either. He'd thought Gran'pa was just there to help Rance get what he wanted.

But in fact Gran'pa Phillips seemed to find fault with Rance more than he favored him. He thought Rance was stubborn and hardheaded and had always been determined to get his own way, and he didn't hesitate to say so.

The words were music to Josh's ears. Anything negative about Rance was music to Josh's ears these days.

"Was he really a stubborn kid?" he'd ask Gran'pa.

"Stubborn? Let me tell you," Gran'pa would say and he'd settle back in the rocker or lean on the corral fence and start reminiscing away.

Some of the things Rance had done as a kid Josh didn't

think were so bad. Sometimes he thought he might even have liked Rance...if he wasn't determined to horn in and cut Josh's father out.

The very thought of that hardened Josh's resolve against him again.

Hearing Gran'pa's "Rance stories" started Josh spending time with the older man. But hearing Gran'pa's compliments about Josh's own knowledge and skills kept him there.

They talked ranching, and once he discovered that Gran'pa listened, Josh was eager to tell him everything he knew. He'd listened to his dad enough to know a fair bit about cattle and crops and land. It made him proud to share that knowledge with Gran'pa and hear Gran'pa tell his mother that Josh was "one smart feller."

He couldn't believe it when Gran'pa suggested getting him his own horse. He'd dreamed about it, of course. Training his own horse, the way his dad had done when he was a boy, had always been one of Josh's goals. But he knew they didn't have the money to get a good horse for a boy to work with. Ruckus and the other two his mom had been able to afford were too green for her to let him try training them.

Spirit was the horse of his dreams.

Josh wondered if he'd have been able to resist if Rance had offered him a horse like Spirit. He was glad he hadn't had to find out.

"He wouldn'ta bought you Spirit if he wasn't figurin' on bein' our Gran'pa," Caleb said now.

"He bought him because he says talent ought to be encouraged, and he thinks I'm good enough to train him," Josh replied. Then to bolster that quotation, he added, "He says I'm as good a horseman as his foreman. He says I might even be able to teach J.D. some things."

"Huh," Caleb said.

"I dunno..." Daniel murmured.

"Well, I do," Josh said forcefully. "They are not gettin' married. Gran'pa is just our friend. He is visiting 'cause he doesn't have to work now. But it isn't gonna last. He'll go away and so will Rance. Then I will run the ranch."

They won the case—which had more to do with Lydia's competence and hard work than his own.

Rance worked hard, but there was no denying he was distracted. It seemed like all he was doing was waiting for it to be over so he could get back to what really mattered to him.

And when he finally got there, Trey announced, "Just in time to say goodbye."

Rance blinked. He looked at his father, then at Ellie to see if she knew what he was talking about. But she looked as surprised as Rance did. "Goodbye?" he ventured, hoping against hope.

"Yep," Trey said cheerfully. "I'm goin' home. Leavin' in the morning. 'Bout time, I reckon," he added. "Can't let J.D. think he's runnin' the show."

"I doubt he thinks that, Dad," Rance said drily. "Besides, I was just there."

"You're not runnin' the show yet, either. Not completely. A feller's gotta keep his hand in. So I'm goin'. I got things I need to do and—" he paused "—I figured I'd take Josh with me."

One look told Rance that this was as much of a surprise to Josh as it was to him and Ellie. The boy's eyes widened eagerly one second, and the next his expression turned to a look of wary concern. He gave Rance a quick glance, then shot another at his mother. Rance could see the wheels turning in his head.

"Boy's a natural with horses," Trey went on cheerfully. "I figured J.D. might learn a few things from him."

No one knew more about horses than J.D., and no one knew it better than Trey. Not that he would ever admit it.

He did his best to find fault with most of what J.D. did. If Rance had been J.D.—not a Phillips and not obliged to put up with the old man—he'd have left long ago. The two of them scraped at each other constantly. This was undoubtedly another of the old man's ways of tweaking his foreman—and extending his influence a little more deeply into Josh's life.

"What do you say?" Trey looked at Ellie, not at Rance. "We could take Spirit and let Josh show J.D. what he can do. I can show him around the J Bar R. I been tellin' him so much about it, I figured he oughta see for himself." There was pride and determination in the old man's voice.

Rance knew what he wanted—to let Josh see the extent of the Phillips spread, to impress the boy with the vastness of its land and the number of its cattle, to whet his appetite for the legacy that would one day be his.

"I'd bring him back middle of next week," Trey said. "Not long." He looked hopefully, expectantly at Ellie.

Ellie looked at Rance. He didn't know what to say. In fact he knew if he said anything, chances were that Josh would do the opposite. "Reckon it's up to Josh," he said at last.

"Well, then, no question. You'd like to come, wouldn't you, son?" Trey beamed at his grandson. "And the sooner, the better. There's so much for you to see and to learn. If we start now, by next summer—"

Rance could see it coming—the suggestions that became orders, the expectations that somehow got translated into goals. "Don't push him, Dad."

"He ain't pushing," Josh blurted. He grinned at his grandfather. "Sounds good to me. I'd like to go."

The next few days were like paradise.

As far as Rance was concerned, they were life the way it was meant to be. He and Ellie were together—a couple. Caleb and Daniel and Carrie were their children. The ranch was their ranch. Dealing with it was no more than he could handle. Dealing with the twins and Carrie was a joy. Loving Ellie was the greatest thing on earth.

They were just one big happy family.

He actually felt a little guilty for enjoying it so much.

"Do you reckon I owe the old man one?" he asked Ellie. They had spent the past three days together, day and night. Rance had once thought that such togetherness would slake his desire. It seemed to have the opposite effect.

They were in her bed this time, wrapped in each other's arms. They had loved each other, then slept, and now they were awake again, touching, kissing, beginning to stoke the fires of their passion once more.

"I don't know," Ellie whispered. "Josh sounded happy when I talked to him on the phone tonight. He said he'd been working with J.D. on the horses and driving the truck all over the place. Your dad even let him ride Ranger, which I gather is a great privilege."

"I've never been given it," Rance said drily.

"Well, he's pulling out all the stops for Josh. It sounds like Trey is showing him a wonderful time."

"It's in his best interests," Rance replied. *And for once,* he thought, *it might be in mine.*

Then Ellie moved her hand down his chest and across his abdomen, and her fingers quickened his interest in other things than Josh and Trey. He groaned. "I can't get enough of you."

"Love me," she whispered.

And he whispered back, "I do," and moved to fit his body to hers.

Together they shared five days of paradise.

And then on Wednesday the serpents came back.

Trey was jubilant. "We had a fantastic time." He beamed at his grandson, who was unloading Spirit from the trailer with Caleb and Daniel's help, while Trey started in regaling Ellie and Rance with a report of their five days at the J Bar R. "Didn't we, Josh?"

Josh turned. "Huh? Oh...yeah." He sounded distracted almost, as if he wasn't really there, Rance thought.

"Smartest kid I ever met," Trey went on, once Josh and the twins were out of hearing. "J.D. and I took him out to gather some cattle and do a little doctorin', and I didn't have to tell him a thing. He knew instinctively what to do. Born in him, obviously." Trey's chest seemed to puff out a little. "In the genes. Got a cup of coffee, Ellie?" he asked, already starting toward the kitchen. "I could do with one. Perk me right up. I ain't as young as I used to be."

"Of course," Ellie said. "Supper's almost ready."

"Good enough. I'm starvin'. You put my gear back in the barn," he said over his shoulder to Rance. "Brought me a cot. You can have the straw back."

"I thought you were going home."

"Been home," Trey said. "Now I'm back."

With a vengeance, Rance thought.

For the rest of the evening the old man went on and on about how pleased he was and what a great time they'd had. Josh sat quietly through the whole recitation, then ducked out to the tree house. Probably embarrassed by the fuss the old man was making, Rance thought. He felt a stirring of sympathy for the boy.

Trey barely noticed. He was still talking when Rance thought he'd harangued Ellie long enough and steered him back down to the barn.

"That boy is a peach," Trey said, sitting down on his cot and taking off his boots. "I can't wait till you sell this place and I can have him there full-time."

Rance, who'd been unbuttoning his shirt, stopped dead. "Do what?"

Trey looked up. "Sell this place. You could get pretty good money for it, you know. Like I told Josh, the land's not as good for beef as ours, but it's got some pretty decent recreational potential. Lot of those Californians would give their eyeteeth for a chunk of it. You put it on the market now, and you'll have a damn good nest egg for those children when they go to college." He set his boots beside the cot and wiggled his toes, then looked up at Rance with a smile.

Rance stared at him, poleaxed. "You said that? *To Josh?*"

Trey nodded. "No point in keepin' it, is there? Caleb and Daniel aren't going to ranch. Josh is the only one interested in ranching, and he'll be running our place. Only makes sense to sell it now."

"Like hell."

Trey blinked. "What?"

Rance was suddenly furious. "I said, like hell! We're not selling this ranch. No one is selling this ranch! It's his ranch. His legacy."

"The Phillips Ranch is his legacy," Trey said. "He's a Phillips."

"Only by blood." Rance glared down at his father. "What Josh knows has nothing to do with genes. It has nothing to do with heredity or blood or any crap like that. He knows what he knows not because Phillips blood runs through his veins. He knows it because Spike O'Connor taught him!"

For a moment Trey looked astonished at Rance's outburst. Then he cleared his throat. "I'm sure Spike O'Connor was a fine man," he began.

"A finer man than I'll ever be," Rance cut in. "A better father, that's for certain. Josh might not have had the material advantages as an O'Connor that he would have had as a Phillips, but he had something better. He had a father who believed in him, who cared about him as a person, not as an 'heir,' and who made Josh proud to be his son." Rance shook his head. "And you're not taking that away from him. *I'm* not taking it away from him!"

"Now, Rance—" Trey held out a placating hand.

But Rance didn't stop. "Josh told me when I tried to tell him that I wanted to marry his mother, that I'd had my chance. He was right. I did have my chance. I wasn't ready to make the commitment. Now I am. But just because I'm ready, I don't have the right to push everybody around to get what I want. Josh is right to want to be his father's son—*Spike's son!* I *don't* want to be *my* father's son!"

Twelve

Ellie was hugging her pillow and wishing it was Rance in bed beside her, when she heard the back door open and the sound of soft footsteps come across the kitchen and down the hall.

She sat up abruptly, clutching the pillow to her chest.

She hadn't thought he would come.

Even though he had stayed with her the past five nights, there had been little risk then. Only Caleb, Daniel and Carrie had been home. It was a different story now that Trey and Josh were back.

But perhaps Trey had already fallen asleep. Rance had complained that his father snored like a chainsaw the minute his head hit the straw.

"Much nicer sleepin' with you," he'd murmured against her hair just last night as their bodies spooned together in her bed.

It was much nicer sleeping with Rance than being alone, too, Ellie thought. But she didn't expect he would come tonight.

Still he and Trey had gone down to the barn an hour ago. There would have been time by now, she guessed, for Trey to fall asleep and not notice when Rance left.

There was the little matter of Josh, though. She didn't know how Rance could be sure about that.

Josh was in the tree house. He'd gone there right after dinner. Ellie thought he'd been quiet ever since he'd got home. Then, after dinner, he'd said he was going to spend the night there.

"Us, too!" Caleb and Daniel had chimed.

But Josh had said, "No!" in a harsh voice.

Ellie understood. "Maybe tomorrow," she'd said to the twins. "Let Josh have his night alone." She had seen turmoil in his face from the moment he'd come back. Undoubtedly Josh had things to deal with now that Trey had taken him to the J Bar R. Though Trey had never come right out and said that he expected Josh to take over there someday, she understood that that was his plan. Rance understood it as well.

She imagined that Josh understood it now, too.

It was a burden—and an opportunity. She wished he would let Rance help him deal with it.

But he hadn't wanted anyone. He'd gone off to the tree house to deal with it alone.

Maybe Rance had wandered out below it to see if he could hear Josh's quiet breathing. He must have. Otherwise she didn't think he would risk coming in.

She was glad he had. She wanted to feel his arms around her again, wanted to put her arms around him. When she'd gone to bed tonight, she'd immediately missed the feel of Rance's hard, warm length stretched out alongside hers.

The first time she'd brought him into her bedroom, she'd been apprehensive—worried that because it had been Spike's bedroom, too, she would feel constrained and self-conscious. But it hadn't been like that.

She hadn't been betraying her love for Spike by loving Rance now, any more than she had betrayed her love for Rance by turning to Spike in her need all those years ago. She loved them both. She always would.

She just felt doubly blessed for having shared her love with two such wonderful men.

Now, as Rance stepped into the doorway, silhouetted in the moonlight, she held out her arms to him.

He stopped, and his breath seemed to catch in his throat.

"Rance?"

"I came to say goodbye."

"What?" She scrambled out of bed. "What are you talking about? What's wrong?" She almost tripped over the covers as she flung them aside and hurried to him.

"I have to go. Dad and I both have to go."

"Why? What's going on?" She gripped his arms and looked up into his face. It was too dark to read his expression, but she didn't need to see his face to feel the tension throbbing through him.

"Because I can't let happen to Josh what happened to me." He raked his fingers through his hair. A harsh breath shuddered through him and he seemed almost to force himself to be calm. "My dad told Josh we were selling the ranch."

Ellie frowned. "The J Bar R?"

"No. *This one.*"

"What? He can't do that!"

"I know he can't do that. But you could do it. *I* could do it," he added, "if we got married—which he thinks is a foregone conclusion."

"But we won't," Ellie said practically. "Will we?" she added, a sudden fear catching her off guard.

"No. No, of course not. It's Josh's legacy. I told Dad that. Which he doesn't understand. But that's not the point." His voice was ragged.

Ellie tried to follow what he was saying, but he didn't seem to be making sense. "Trey can't run his life,

Rance,'' she said with all the calm she could muster, ''if we don't let him.''

''Trey can't. But I can! I am! Don't you see, El? I'm doing to him exactly what my old man has done to me all my life! My dad has had his agenda ever since I was born. He was bound and determined to get his way—and I was just supposed to go along for the ride. I've fought with him for years to make him quit ordering my life to suit his goals. *And now I'm doing the same damn thing to Josh!*''

''You're not making him give up the ranch.''

''No, I'm not doing that. But I am in love with his mother, and I'm trying to make him accept me in his life.''

''That's not the same thing.''

''Not to you. Not to me. But it is to Josh. If I stay— if I push him—I'm doing to him exactly what my dad did to me. And that's wrong.''

Ellie knew what he was going to say. She wanted to cover her ears, wanted to shake her head and deny it. But she couldn't. So she just stood there as he slid his arms around her and rested his chin on her bent head, and she listened as he said the words.

''I'm going to leave.''

She didn't respond right away. Not in words. Her heart responded. It twisted in anguish deep inside her, the pain so sharp it seemed to wring the breath from her. She started to tremble and, with everything she had, she willed herself to stop.

Tears threatened, and she blinked them back. She didn't want to cry. Wouldn't *let* herself cry! Crying would hurt him more than he was hurting now. And she couldn't do anything that would make this harder.

Still her fingers dug fiercely into his back, holding him, refusing to let him go. *Not now. Not yet!*

And she felt him tremble, too. "I love you, El." His voice cracked. He cleared his throat. "You know that, don't you?"

She choked on her answer, and had to wait a second to get a breath to form the words. "I know."

"I would marry you in an instant, if this was just about us. But it's not. You knew it wasn't just about you and me anymore, the minute you found out you were pregnant. You knew it wasn't about you and me when I wanted to marry you this time."

"I wasn't telling you no forever," Ellie said desperately. "I only wanted to wait until he was comfortable with the idea."

"But he's not going to get comfortable with the idea. I thought I could change his mind. I thought I could be enough, do enough—*push* enough—to make him go along with it. And maybe I could," he added grimly, "but it wouldn't be right. You've been acting like a grown-up for eleven years now. It's about time I started."

She lifted her eyes then and looked at him. The moonlight cut harsh shadows in his face. She uncurled her fingers, loosened her grip on his shirt and touched his cheek.

It was wet.

"Oh, Rance."

He shook his head, then pressed his face into her hair. His arms tightened around her, and she felt his lips move against her ear. "I wish I could stay. I wish I could marry you and be here for you—and for the kids. I love them. Even Josh. Hell—" his voice broke "—especially Josh. That's why—" He stopped, couldn't finish.

He didn't need to. "I know," she whispered. "I know."

They stood there. They held each other, clung together. And Ellie knew that Rance was hanging on to the moments just as she was, savoring them, memorizing them. They would need them to remember through a long, lonely future.

And then he pulled back just enough to kiss her. The passion they'd shared was still there, but banked, contained, surpassed by something greater. This kiss was tender. It ached with longing.

"I love you, El. I'll always love you."

And then he was gone.

It seemed like a bad dream.

It was her life.

She tried to tell herself, as the days passed, that things weren't that much different. On the surface, perhaps, they weren't. They were "back to normal," she told Sandra with contrived cheer. "Just us again."

Sandra raised her brows, but fortunately didn't ask any questions.

Daniel and Caleb and Carrie did. So did Josh, surprisingly. The morning after Rance and Trey had left in the middle of the night, he'd said, "Where's Rance? I want to talk to him."

Ellie had shaken her head. "He's gone," she'd said. Just that. No more.

Josh had looked straight at her. "Gone?" As if he didn't believe it.

She'd nodded. She'd made herself smile. "Looks like you're going to have to start doing more than your share again."

Josh *had* done more than his share. He'd worked long

hours every day. He'd never complained once. The other kids talked about Rance and Trey. Josh never said a word. He looked at her, though, whenever Rance's name came up.

Ellie thought she was a very good actress. She managed to smile every time.

Financially things were better, too. Every week Rance sent a check. No message, just a check. It was more than enough to cover any support she might be expected to need for Josh. It was more than enough to take care of all of them. She blinked back tears.

In material ways then, life was better than after Spike had died and before Rance had come.

But it was empty.

Ellie was empty.

She missed Rance day and night. She loved him. She wanted him. She needed him. Yet she couldn't deny he was right.

It wasn't what either of them wanted—but still she knew he was right.

If they had married without Josh's blessing they would have been as selfish as they'd been when they conceived him. Then they'd been young and self-centered—thinking only of their own needs and their own pleasure. The world had been simple in those days. It had revolved around them.

The day Ellie had learned she was pregnant, the scope of the world suddenly changed. It wasn't just about her anymore. It wasn't just about the moment. It was a bigger world with long-term consequences for other people—for Rance, who didn't want to be a father.

For the embryonic Josh, who was already her son.

She'd made her decisions back then based on what she thought was best for all of them. For Rance, for Josh, for

Spike, for herself. Not just on what she wanted—not on what would have made her gloriously happy—but on what was best. She had, at last, acted like an adult.

Rance, faced with the same realization, had just done the same thing.

It didn't make him happy. It didn't make her happy.

But the world, as they both knew now, wasn't about just the two of them.

No, Ellie couldn't argue with what he'd done. He was right.

But somehow it didn't make her hurt any less.

Someday, Rance told himself, it would hurt less.

Some morning he would wake up, and the first thought in his head wouldn't be that Ellie wasn't there. Some night when he went to sleep, the last thought he had before sleeping wouldn't be how badly he wanted to be holding Ellie in his arms.

Some night he would actually sleep again for more than an hour or two at a time without waking up and reaching for her. And someday he would go fifteen minutes or maybe even longer without seeing her face smiling at him in his mind.

Someday.

Not now.

Now he had Ellie on the brain. He asked himself a hundred times a day if he'd done the right thing, and when the honest answer always came back yes, he asked himself why it mattered so much to do the right thing if it made him miserable.

And the answer was, he didn't know. But it did.

"Are you all right?" Lydia asked him—once a day at least.

"Sure. Fine. Just...thinking." He didn't want to talk

about it. He knew Lydia would listen. Lydia would comfort. But he didn't love Lydia—and Lydia didn't love him.

"This is the damnedest fool thing you've ever pulled," Trey told him over and over. "What the hell good is leavin' going to do?"

"It's going to give Josh what I never had," Rance told him. "His own life—without anybody else tryin' to run it for him"

"We won't sell the damn ranch, then," Trey said.

"No," Rance agreed. "We won't."

Trey was furious with him. He didn't care.

Trey said, "I'll go back. There's nothing stopping me from going back!"

"There's me," Rance said, curling his fingers into fists. "And there's your conscience—if you have one."

It was, perhaps, an overreaction. He knew in his heart that Trey wasn't a bad man. He wasn't even a bad father, most of the time. He was just determined that the world be run according to his wishes.

And even more than in his own life, when it came to Josh, Rance wasn't putting up with it. Not from his father.

Not from himself.

What he needed, he decided, was a really demanding case. Something so compelling that he wouldn't sit around, daydreaming about Ellie, when he was supposed to be doing research instead.

Water rights were compelling. They meant the survival of any given ranch at any given time. Rance understood that. That was why, he told himself as he tried once more to focus on the casebook he'd been staring at for the past hour, he should be able to put Ellie and the kids right out of his mind. The battle between *Thomas v. Richards* which he was due to start fighting in court this coming Monday, was important. It should be able to hold his attention.

Besides, it had been almost three weeks since he'd seen Ellie and the kids. Soon it would be a month. They probably didn't even remember him. He didn't need to be staring off into space thinking about them.

There was a knock on his door and it opened partway. Jodi had a strange expression on her face.

"What's up?" Rance asked.

"There's someone here to see you."

He frowned. "I don't have any appointments this afternoon."

"No. He...doesn't have an appointment."

"Who is it? What does he want?"

"He didn't say what he wants," Jodi answered. "But he says he is your son."

He should have been home hours ago.

One hour ago, Ellie's rational mind corrected her. It wasn't that late. Only just six. Josh had ridden off on Spirit to check on the cattle above the ridge shortly after breakfast this morning. He'd taken a lunch, but Ellie had vetoed him camping out up there and coming home tomorrow.

"I'd worry," she told him. "I want you back tonight."

"But, Mom, it's a long ways."

"You can do it," she'd insisted. "If you leave now, you can be back by five."

"Well, don't worry if I'm not," he'd said. "It all depends on what I find, you know."

It was exactly the sort of thing Spike would have said. And it was a perfectly sensible thing to say—if you were thirty, not ten.

But Josh *was* ten—a child, for all that he refused to act like one—and she wanted him home!

"I shouldn't have let him go," she said to Sandra as she paced the kitchen. "We should have waited until Wattie could do it. Or I should have gone with him."

Sandra listened to her mutterings and didn't argue. Her mother-in-law understood her worrying. "He told you not to worry, Ellie. He's probably just late because there was a lot to do."

"Probably. I wish Rance was here." The words came out unbidden, almost as if they had escaped from her, as if they had a mind of their own. *I wish Rance was here.* She hadn't said his name in days. A week. She'd made herself think about something else—talk about something else—and yet the second she let her guard down, there he was. Again.

She stopped and stared out the window, as if she could conjure Josh up if she just stared long enough in the direction from which she expected him to come. Then Sandra's work-roughened hand covered Ellie's own. "It stays light late at this time of year. He's a boy. He's probably lost track of time."

But since Spike had died, Ellie had made sure her children knew not to lose track of time. Wondering what had become of them, worrying that they were hurt or lost or...worse was something she couldn't tolerate.

"I should have got a cell phone," Ellie fretted. She began pacing again.

"He'll come," Sandra said. "Come on. The others are starving. We've got to feed them dinner."

They all ate dinner. Or rather Sandra, Caleb, Daniel and Carrie ate dinner. Ellie kept jumping up every time she heard a sound.

"Oh, there he is!" She must have said it ten times,

leaping up each time to run to the door and look, only to come back more worried than ever when it always turned out she was wrong.

"I'll go look for him," Daniel offered.

"We both can," Caleb said.

Ellie shook her head. "No. No, that's all right. I'm sure...I'm sure he's fine."

But when six became seven and seven became eight, she wasn't sure at all. "You don't suppose he's just staying up there, anyway, do you?" she asked Sandra. She could almost make herself angry, thinking about it. Anger was better than being worried sick.

She fed the horses, folded the laundry, paced the house and then the yard. Sandra was doing the dishes. Ellie picked up a towel and began to dry.

She wouldn't have thought Josh would do something like that—deliberately defy her order to come home. But Josh had not been himself for quite some time.

At first she'd put it down to Rance having been here. She'd recognized early on that Josh had seen him as a threat to Spike's memory. Then, when he'd learned he was Rance's son, he'd been even harder to deal with. All the efforts Rance had made had gone to naught. Josh had been determined to fight him.

So, Ellie had thought, he would be happy again when Rance was gone.

But Rance had been gone almost three weeks now—and while Josh had been different since Rance's departure—the change had not gone the way she'd expected. He wasn't more cheerful. He was simply more determined. He threw himself into the ranch work. As if he could do it all himself. As if he was already the rancher they all knew he would be someday.

And he didn't talk—not about Rance, not about the

ranch—not even about Spike. He was driven. Determined. And so far from the child she'd known for ten years that Ellie had to admit she really didn't know what to expect from him anymore.

So maybe he had defied her. Maybe he was up there now, cooking over a campfire, settling in under the stars, oblivious to the worry he was causing his mother.

She threw down her dish towel. "I'm going after him myself."

"Ellie, you won't get there before dark!"

"I will. I'll take Ruckus. He's the fastest."

"Ellie! If something happened to you—"

"Nothing will happen to me. I promise. But I need to know nothing has happened to Josh!"

It was like the night she'd looked for Spike. She'd never wanted to relive that experience, could happily have gone to her death never having felt this grip of terror again. *It can't happen twice,* she told herself. *Please God, it can't happen twice.*

But in a just world, she knew, it shouldn't have even happened once.

"Oh, God," she muttered. "Please."

She wanted Rance. She wanted him to go with her. She wanted his warm, solid body hard against hers, holding her and telling her it was all in her mind. Josh was fine. Of course Josh was fine.

Her mind was her worst enemy, Ellie knew that. How could it not be? Her mind remembered seeing Spike's horse at the edge of the woods, saddled, riderless. Engraved on her memory was the sight of Spike's lifeless body—

No! She couldn't think of that!

Tears blinded her. She dug her heels into Ruckus's side, urging him on. All the while she kept her eyes peeled for any sign of Spirit. For Josh. Either. Hopefully both.

It was going dusk when she finally reached the area above the ridge where Josh would have been—if he'd been there.

She called his name. She took the flashlight she'd brought along and flashed it in high wide arcs, hoping to get a response from Josh who carried one, too. But there was no reply. There was no Josh.

She turned, fear gripping her heart, and rode Ruckus home.

Rance had done a good job on Ruckus. He was quick but surefooted as he picked his way back down the mountain in the growing darkness. Ellie shined the flashlight now and then, but mostly she trusted him to pick his way. She hung on—and prayed.

Maybe he was home already.

Maybe he'd come some other way.

Maybe she'd just missed him.

Maybe...

"Oh, Josh." His name was a prayer on her lips. And then, unbidden again, came another name. "Rance!" She cried his name. She couldn't help it.

If he'd been here!

If he'd stayed!

Trying to do right, had they been wrong, after all?

Ellie swiped at tears that touched her cheeks. She swallowed hard at the lump choking her throat. "Come on, Ruckus. Come on."

She needed to get home. Needed to find Josh. Needed to know.

The lights in the house were all on when she rode in. She didn't stop at the barn, but rode straight into the yard. They must have heard her coming, for at once the door opened, and Sandra stepped onto the porch. She looked at Ellie as desperately as Ellie looked at her.

"No?" They said the word at the same time, hoping against hope. The children crowded around Sandra—Caleb, Daniel, Carrie.

But not Josh.

"No," Ellie whispered. "No."

She slid out of the saddle and simply stood there, her face pressed against Ruckus's neck, trying to hang on, to gather strength, to do…to do whatever had to be done.

The headlights coming over the hill caught her from behind. She spun around into the glare, then as they curved down the road and out of her direct gaze, she tried to see who it was. A neighbor, she hoped, bringing Josh home. Or Rance.

She needed Rance.

If something had happened to Josh, how on earth could she ever tell Rance?

"Rance!" It was Daniel who shouted his name.

And then Caleb and Carrie did, too, and Sandra said, "It is," and Ellie blinked back tears to get a better look through the darkness at the truck that had almost reached them.

Oh, God, it was!

How had he known?

The kids were running, but she was faster. She ran right in front of the truck, and he slammed on the brakes and jumped out almost before he'd stopped.

"El!"

"Oh, Rance! Oh, Rance. It's Josh!" And she flung herself into his arms. "I can't find him! He went up the ridge to check the cattle! And he's never come back! I've looked! I can't find him! Oh, God, Rance. I can't do this without you. I don't care how right we were. I can't do it alone anymore!''

His arms were around her, hard and tight and he was kissing her—her cheeks, her mouth, her hair. And he was saying, ''You don't have to do it alone, El. He doesn't want you to do it alone. He's here. *I'm here.*''

The words barely penetrated. But his calmness did. ''He's here. I've got him. He's here.'' Rance kept saying it over and over while his hands rubbed her back and chafed her arms. ''I've brought him home. Josh is here.''

And finally she understood. She swallowed her tears and shuddered. She couldn't seem to stop shaking. But she understood. She pulled back, looked at him, into his eyes, saw them smile at her.

''H-he's with y-you?''

Rance turned her in his arms. He didn't let go, though, just steered her around the side of the truck and let her look in the cab. There, slumped against the passenger door, sound asleep, was Josh.

Ellie shook her head. ''Where did you get him?'' Her voice barely worked.

''He came to my office.''

Her eyes widened. ''Your office? Where? Not in *Helena?*''

''In Helena.'' Rance pulled her back hard against him and wrapped his arms around her, then let them slip down to add Caleb and Daniel and Carrie to his embrace. They all stood there looking at Josh.

''That's a long way,'' Caleb said.

''A real long way,'' said Daniel.

''Gosh,'' Carrie said.

''H-how?'' Ellie asked.

''He had somebody's older brother buy him a bus ticket. When he got to Helena, he had to find my office.

It isn't very close to the bus station. He had a hike, but he made it.'' Rance's tone held a hint of admiration. "He's a damn resourceful kid."

"He terrified me," Ellie said shakily. "I thought—I remembered—" But she just shook her head again, unable to even say the words.

Rance's arms tightened around her. "I know. I should have made him call. I was going to, but he said he'd left you a letter on your bed."

"My bed?" Ellie sighed, and one last tremor rippled through her. "I never even noticed." She looked again at her sleeping son. How could he ever have thought she'd just go to bed without knowing where he was?

"He's just a boy, El," Rance said gently. "He doesn't know how parents worry."

She could tell from his tone that he was including himself in that remark. And somehow it didn't seem so surprising that, even if he hadn't brought Josh with him, Rance would have turned up to worry with her.

"Come on," he said now. "Let's get him inside." Then he turned to the other kids. "It's late. All you guys need to go to bed."

Taking charge. Just like that. Ellie looked at him. There was tenderness in his eyes. And warmth. And banked passion. Most of all there was love.

She wanted the words, but she couldn't ask for them. The children had no such compunctions.

"Are you stayin'?" Daniel asked him.

Rance smiled. "Yep."

"Will you be here in the morning?" Caleb pressed.

"You bet."

Carrie tugged at the leg of his jeans. "Can you tell me an' Clarissa an' Lone Bear a story?"

Rance's smile widened and he touched her hair. "I think that can be arranged."

He gave Ellie one more squeeze, his eyes saying things her heart was dying to hear. But she was willing now to wait.

Rance went around to the other side of the truck and opened the door, catching Josh's limp body against his. The movement jarred the boy. He started, blinked and looked around sleepily. "We home?" he murmured to Rance, still leaning into his embrace, not pulling away at all.

Rance scooped him into his arms. "We're home," he said.

Ellie felt a sob catch in her throat.

The sound made Josh turn his head. He smiled at his mother. "I brought 'im back for you," he said.

Tears blurred Ellie's vision. "Oh, Josh!" She shook her head and reached for him, hugging him between her body and Rance's. "There are telephones. Why did you go? I was scared to death. You could have called him if you needed to talk!"

But Josh shook his head. "No, I couldn't. It's like Dad said, 'some things gotta be done man-to-man.'" He shifted a little, and Rance let him down so that the boy stood on the ground between them. He looked at his mother. "I did it," he said quietly. Then he tipped his head and looked up at Rance. "Didja ask her?"

Rance shook his head.

Josh's brows drew down. "Why not? What're you waitin' for?" he asked impatiently.

Rance grinned. "Nothin'. Nothin' at all." He tousled Josh's hair roughly and the boy caught his hand and held it there.

Then Rance looked at Ellie. "Will you marry me?" he said.

She said yes.

He'd thought she would. He'd told himself, of course she would.

But even so, he'd had the terrible fear that somehow, even with Josh's blessing, it wouldn't happen. Something else would come along, someone new would step in, some other obstacle would rise up and shatter his hopes, his dreams—dare he say, his expectations?

But she said yes.

And then she kissed him. Right then. Right there—with Josh still standing between them. Though, bless him, he slipped out of the way, to look up at them. And out of the corner of his eye, Rance could see him smiling.

Then he felt a hand come out and tighten around his. Not Ellie's hand. A smaller, callused, boy's hand. A young man's hand. Because Josh had behaved like a man today.

And as Rance kissed Josh's mother, he whispered. "He's quite a man, our son."

Later, when the kids were all in bed and Sandra, having given him a hug and a warm welcome to the family, had gone home with the promise that she would see to Spirit, whom Josh said he'd left in her small barn, Rance finally had Ellie alone.

They were on the couch, their arms around each other. and he could feel her heart beat against the wall of his chest. There had been a time, not so many hours ago, when he'd despaired of ever holding her like this again.

"Tell me what happened, " Ellie said softly. "Why did you— Why did he...?" She stopped, wonderingly. and just waited.

Rance's mouth tipped up in an equally wondering smile. "He told me it was because he had to do the right thing."

Ellie shifted her weight, easing her body alongside his. "What do you mean?"

"The night Dad brought him back, the night I told the old man there was no way I was going to do to Josh what he'd done to me, Josh was right outside the barn." Rance gave a wry shrug. "He'd come to tell his grandfather that he was never going to give up the ranch, that he was never going to be a Phillips. And he heard me telling the old man the same thing *for* him."

It was one of those miracles that Rance didn't want to look at too closely.

"Did you mean it?" Josh had asked him this afternoon. It was the first thing the boy had said to him, when Jodi had shown him in and left the two of them alone.

"Mean what?" Rance had been so astonished to see Josh standing in front of him that he hadn't had a clue what the boy was asking. *What are you doing here?* he wondered. *Why did you tell Jodi you're my son?*

My son.

It was the first time he'd let himself really think the words, the first time since he'd left them that he'd dared.

Did he dare?

And then Josh was answering him. "Mean what you said about my...my dad? My...other dad." He looked at the floor, then back up at Rance. "And that I don't have to be a Phillips?"

My other dad.

Was he going to get a share, then? For an instant Rance's eyes closed and he sent a small prayer winging heavenward. *Thank you, Spike, for loving him, for raising him, for being a father to him. And, most of all, thank you for sharing.*

Then he opened his eyes again and looked at Josh squarely. The boy was standing painfully straight, his fingers knotted into fists at his sides. "You don't have to be a Phillips, Josh," Rance said softly. "Ever. Not unless you want to be—and only as much as you want to be. It doesn't matter to me. I will always be proud to call Josh O'Connor my son."

And then Josh breathed again. He grinned a little. And so did Rance. And then he stood up and shoved his casebook back on the shelf and said, "You want to go get a Coke?"

Josh nodded wordlessly.

They walked out of the office together, Rance with his hand on Josh's shoulder while Jodi and Lydia looked on openmouthed.

"Rance?" Lydia said. "Where are you going?"

And he'd said, "Home."

That's where he was now. Home. Home at the O'Connor ranch. Home where his family was. Home in Ellie's arms.

"We talked a lot, El," he said now, still marveling at how once they'd got past the first bit, it hadn't been so hard at all. "He told me he'd looked for me the next morning but Dad and I had already left. And then he told me he'd decided it was just as well, that things were back to normal, the way he'd wanted them, and he was determined to make them work."

"He worked," Ellie said. "Every day. All day. Like he was possessed."

"Yes." Josh had said something like that, but not in those words. Then he'd shaken his head and told Rance that it wasn't the same anymore. "Everybody was lonelier, sadder. Especially his mom."

Ellie nodded. "I was miserable. I tried not to be."

He kissed her slowly, savoring the taste of her, wanting her now, but wanting more to tell her what had happened. "Whichever it was, he decided to do something about it. He told me he'd made a mistake about me. He said he was sorry." Rance marveled at the kid's guts. "He said Spike told him it wasn't bad to be wrong, but it was bad not to admit it if you knew. And then—" Rance smiled "—he asked me if I'd come home and marry you."

They looked at each other, then. Their eyes locked, sharing a joy so pure and so perfect that tears brimmed and spilled over.

"I love you," Ellie whispered against his lips.

And Rance whispered back, "I love you. All of you."

The tour bus was back.

"I am *not* goin' on a honeymoon in any damn neon pink tour bus!" Rance was nearly apoplectic, pacing a rut in Ellie's big, braided rug, glowering out the windows at the offensive vehicle, which was idling and fouling the pure mountain air with diesel fumes.

"It's not for you." Trey came down the stairs two at a time, looking brisk and cheerful and not at all like a man who had agreed to watch four children for two weeks while Rance and Ellie got away.

Rance hadn't wanted to "get away," at all.

"I just got here," he complained. They'd only waited a week before tying the knot. Just long enough to assemble his friends and hers, for Ellie to make Carrie and Clarissa bridesmaids' dresses and for a scab on Daniel's forehead to heal.

"We can't go anywhere," he'd told his pushy father.

"We might not be an old married couple, but we've got four kids."

"I'll watch them," Trey had volunteered.

Rance had agreed, only because he didn't think even his old man would be fool enough to do that.

"Never underestimate a Phillips," Trey said now, smiling beatifically at Ellie and Rance. Then he turned and hollered upstairs, "Come on, kids."

And the next thing Rance knew, Josh and Caleb and Daniel and Carrie—with Lone Bear and Clarissa snug in her arms—came down the stairs wearing backpacks and looking, for all the world, like a production number from *The Sound of Music*.

"Here comes Sandra now. So we're all set," Trey said, glancing toward the door. "We've made plans, the six of us. Do you know these children have never seen the ocean? They've never been to the redwoods? They've never ridden on a trolley car or crossed the Golden Gate Bridge?" He was almost rubbing his hands together in anticipation. "Say goodbye now," he told the kids. "Then go hop on the bus with Grandma."

Rance barely managed to get his mouth closed before Carrie planted a smacking goodbye kiss on his lips.

Over her head he stared at his father. "You and Sandra are taking the kids to California in a neon pink tour bus?"

Trey just grinned. Caleb and Daniel ran to get on the bus. Josh stopped long enough to roll his eyes and grin. Then he looked at Ellie and at Rance and nodded with satisfaction and gave them a thumbs-up.

"I don't believe it." Rance was still shaking his head when the bus pulled out. Four little heads appeared in the back window. Four hands waved madly. From the front Sandra and Trey waved, too.

"I believe it," Ellie said. "Your father always has a plan."

"He does?" Rance felt a stab of apprehension. "What plan?"

Ellie waved one last time and then, as the bus disappeared over the rise, she slipped her arms around him and lifted up to kiss his lips.

"What plan?" Rance insisted.

She took his hand and, smiling, drew him after her toward the bedroom. "Come along now and I'll show you."

"Oh." Rance grinned. "Well, even I'll go along with that."

*   *   *   *   *

Life has never been easy for ranch foreman,
J.D. Holt. But it gets a whole lot more
complicated when Rance's partner, Lydia, decides
she's waited long enough for the man she's
always loved. Watch the fireworks in

A COWBOY'S SECRET

and other Code of the West titles,
coming soon from Silhouette Desire.

SPECIAL EDITION

Stories of love and life, these powerful novels are tales that you can identify with— romances with "something special" added in!

Fall in love with the stories of authors such as **Nora Roberts, Diana Palmer, Ginna Gray** and many more of your special favorites—as well as wonderful new voices!

Special Edition brings you entertainment for the heart!

SILHOUETTE® Desire®

Do you want...

Dangerously handsome heroes

Evocative, everlasting love stories

Sizzling and tantalizing sensuality

Incredibly sexy miniseries like **MAN OF THE MONTH**

Red-hot romance

Enticing entertainment that can't be beat!

You'll find all of this, and much *more* each and every month in **SILHOUETTE DESIRE**. Don't miss these unforgettable love stories by some of romance's hottest authors. Silhouette Desire—where your fantasies will always come true....

If you've got the time...
We've got the
INTIMATE MOMENTS

Passion. Suspense. Desire. Drama. Enter a world that's larger than life, where men and women overcome life's greatest odds for the ultimate prize: love. Nonstop excitement is closer than you think...in Silhouette Intimate Moments!

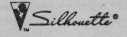

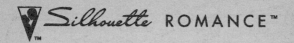

Silhouette ROMANCE™

What's a single dad to do when he needs a wife by next Thursday?

Who's a confirmed bachelor to call when he finds a baby on his doorstep?

How does a plain Jane in love with her gorgeous boss get him to notice her?

From classic love stories to romantic comedies to emotional heart tuggers, **Silhouette Romance** offers six irresistible novels every month by some of your favorite authors! Such as…beloved bestsellers **Diana Palmer, Annette Broadrick, Suzanne Carey, Elizabeth August** and **Marie Ferrarella,** to name just a few—and some sure to become favorites!

Fabulous Fathers…Bundles of Joy…Miniseries… Months of blushing brides and convenient weddings… Holiday celebrations… You'll find all this and much more in **Silhouette Romance**—always emotional, always enjoyable, always about love!

WAYS TO *UNEXPECTEDLY* MEET MR. RIGHT:

♡ *Go out with the sexy-sounding stranger your daughter secretly set you up with through a personal ad.*

♡ *RSVP yes to a wedding invitation—soon it might be your turn to say "I do!"*

♡ *Receive a marriage proposal by mail— from a man you've never met.....*

These are just a few of the unexpected ways that written communication leads to love in Silhouette Yours Truly.

Each month, look for two fast-paced, fun and flirtatious Yours Truly *novels (with entertaining treats and sneak previews in the back pages) by some of your favorite authors—and some who are sure to become favorites.*

YOURS TRULY™:
Love—when you least expect it!

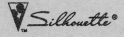

YT-GEN